About the author

Martin Morton lives mostly in the Adriatic on a boat.

Visit Martin Morton at www.martinmorton.co.uk

Trust Only
Book 7 of The Claudia Series

Martin Morton

Trust Only

Chimera

CHIMERA PAPERBACK

© Copyright 2021
Martin Morton

The right of Martin Morton to be identified as author of
this work has been asserted by him in accordance with the
Copyright, Designs and Patents Act 1988.

A CIP catalogue record for this title is
available from the British Library.

ISBN 978-1-90313-679-9

Chimera is an imprint of
Pegasus Elliot MacKenzie Publishers Ltd.
www.pegasuspublishers.com

First Published in 2021

Chimera
Sheraton House Castle Park
Cambridge England

Printed & Bound in Great Britain

Trust Only
The Claudia Series Book 7

Other titles in the series:
The Water's Edge
The Water's Depth
Careless Hours
The Mist in the Valleys
Catch Me
Lion and Giant

Introduction

Hi, and welcome.

I very much hope you will enjoy the unfolding story.

Trust Only is about a particular phase in our characters' lives, yet is a complete story in itself.

For any new readers to the Claudia Series, however, I thought an introduction might be helpful.

Isobel Allen, now our principal narrator, is an interior designer with a colourful past. Her business was solely London-based until two years ago when, having completed a very successful project on luxury resorts, Peter Dickinson helped her open a Hong Kong-based Asia business.

In *Trust Only*, the story tells of the development of relationships between the Dickinson clan — centring on Alphonse Newman, the head of Property and Resorts — and the Shen family, their business partners in Asia — centring on Meitang, the illegitimate daughter of Shen Wengwei, the head of the Senlin Group.

Interwoven with Isobel's dealings with the developments in Asia is the pull of old associations back in London, into which history draws her.

I hope you find the story absorbing and entertaining,

Martin

Trust Only
1

I like to spend a fortnight every two months in London, but I had a bad feeling about the call just now. I wasn't due there for four weeks and I was planning to spend next week at Psamathe Phuroc in Vietnam; it's the first big opening of the new resorts, the first one I reconnoitred out here, the first with all my genuine designs — not the copies they put into Psamathe Morkuda. But now — even allowing for Merle's penchant for hysteria — I wouldn't feel comfortable about not getting back there.

Until that last call, she'd surprised me by how well she's run the London end since I've been out here. I had my misgivings; she's not really a businesswoman, but I can stay close to it all electronically, and she's always been very professional — apart from that Will phase a few years ago. But she wasn't making a lot of sense on the phone. I know the relationship with Gerry Calvert is difficult — he is the most unmitigated bastard — but he is also, currently, my most important London customer. After Alphonse, of course, but that's more of a partnership.

Alphonse appeared sympathetic — but I know him too well now — he was hiding some annoyance. I said to him, 'I'm only the designer' — but we both know I've developed some special relationships with his key clients — and next week was not going to be a holiday. Although I would have had some fun.

It doesn't sound as though London will be like that. Not if the head of my business has told my key client to fuck off.

I think I owe you some background: it's more than a year since I opened the Hong Kong business — Allen Chou Li — and I was staggered by how quickly we got busy. Daiyu, the architect, and Harry, the salesman — that's the Chou and the Li — are so well-connected that lots of business came our way immediately. I was amazed. I shouldn't have been; the Shen family wanted us to be successful, so they helped a great deal with both contracts and contacts, but it meant I had to find a London solution quickly. I love my Asian adventure but, ultimately, London will be home. I need to stay well-rooted there. Merle had been doing more work for me and, although I have some good young people there, she was the only one I felt I could trust to run the operation.

Michael, her husband, manages Gerry's finances. They're still not divorced, although they've been apart more than five years. There was a time when I would have known about all the details of her relationships but, after Will, it seemed better to let her grow up on her own. I thought that was working well. I'm no longer so sure.

The whole Gerry and Michael thing is very unhealthy — and I don't play with Michael so much, so I'm feeling quite detached from all that. Maybe that was a mistake.

2

Alphonse wouldn't have called Isobel mercurial, although he was aware that she seemed so to many of the people they met; she had such a vibrant personality that, out here, she seemed, to most, a fabulous alien creature. But he'd been conscious from early on of how professional she was, so, for her to take off for London at a day's notice, the week before the Phuroc opening, was… He settled ultimately for 'surprising,' aware that his initial response had been harsher.

He looked across to the Kowloon waterfront, still all lights and bustle, still almost enthralling, but he was distracted by his irritation that they should have been having an evening together. Everything else was stress — and next week would be particularly so without her. He slowly admitted that he was being unfair. She had her own business to run, throughout the region here and still in the UK. His was even more widespread, so they could meet only rarely. Next week would have been a wonderful opportunity to get more time with her, although the business benefit for her was, in her opinion, less obvious — 'limited,' she'd called it, 'and Daiyu's there, anyway.' He knew, however, that many of his VIP invitees had, either subtly or brazenly, asked if Isobel would be attending. That would have meant that her project pipeline could have expanded even more; well, Daiyu could do that too. She impressed in different ways.

Isobel had found a way, with Daiyu, of fusing elements of Western design into modern Asian projects that had attracted a lot of attention — and generated a lot of business. They needed resources quickly and they'd found a poorly led design company that they'd been able to buy out and take over; it had given them a team of young designers who blossomed the instant the old owner had been disposed of. Daiyu, no longer kowtowing to a male boss, was proving to be splendidly ruthless. The man had attempted to contact Alphonse to complain of his degrading treatment — 'instant ejection — by a woman!' had been the message relayed through Harry. Alphonse had funded the purchase through the Dickinson office. The man had assumed that Daiyu was his assistant, only to find that she was in before him on the fateful Monday, requiring him to vacate his office immediately.

Daiyu would be at the resort to share the load, but he finally had to admit, he'd simply wanted Isobel's company.

3

I love my little house. Coming back in, I realise instantly that this is home. There's an other-worldliness about looking out on Kowloon from a picture window on the thirty-second floor of a Hong Kong tower that I find captivating — but I'm always conscious that it's time-bounded somehow, although I have no deadline there, no planned year of exit. But there's nothing apart from this crisis that pulls me back here at the moment, there's just business — and the sense of being at home.

But the Hong Kong apartment's not mine anyway. The lease belongs to Peter Dickinson, the rent goes through my books. My neighbour — Alphonse is three floors below me — laughs when I complain about the cost. He assures me I have a very good deal: 'I have people below you paying fifty percent more,' is what he tells me. 'I'm lucky I'm not pulled in for money-laundering.' I assume he's joking. Well, I'm sure he is, he's one of the straightest men I know, apart from him being gay.

Back here, I close my front door, and this is all mine. Freehold.

And, because it's home, the jet lag's never so bad — I feel OK. I'm not looking forward to the evening, though.

Merle will be here in an hour. Time to unpack and shower.

***

She looked calm when she arrived. And elegant. And beautiful (I try to kid myself that she's looking older, but she isn't). The chestnut hair still cascades in waves to the shoulders; I experiment with hair, she doesn't need to — just puts it up for big nights out. We hug lightly. We're both tense. I usher her in.

She starts before she even sits down, "I feel terrible. You shouldn't have come…"

I hold up my hand. She stops. "Just sit down. I'm opening white wine…" She nods. "have you eaten?"

"I can't."

I shrug. I've eaten too many meals on the plane and it's the middle of the night for my stomach. I don't actually need white wine, but I do need her to relax. "Have you seen Sandra? Where is she?"

"Gerry's put her in The Argosy, I think."

"Have you seen her?" I repeated, but obviously she hadn't if she wasn't sure where Sandra was. She was always a snob about her. I was surprised she'd got involved, but I do need to find out exactly what happened. I'll go there in the morning. It's a very discreet private hospital in Chelsea. Both my spoken and unspoken questions were going unanswered. I wasn't surprised. "You know I need a less garbled

account before I go to see Sandra or talk to Gerry, don't you?"

"You're going to see her?" She looked startled.

Her question didn't surprise me. It did disgust me a little. But these aren't feelings you can give way to.

"It's not the first time for her anyway, apparently. I didn't know that before I flew at Gerry and then rang you."

"Merle, you'd better stop. Nothing you're saying is making this any better," I said it sharply. I must have looked stern. She crumpled.

"I'm sorry, it was awful, and I felt a bit guilty. Well, a lot guilty…"

I held up my hand again. "Don't! Let me piece this together. And I'm almost certain I'm going to be blaming Gerry, not you. Where were you? Conrad's?" She nodded. "Was he there?"

"No, he was in Saudi, but he's come back straight away."

"How did he find out? I suppose Boris called him."

"Is that the big man who lets us in?" I nodded. Merle doesn't seem to live in this world sometimes; she ghosts blindly through it. "I suppose he must have done. Do you think he knows what goes on all the time?"

"Oh, Merle!" My exasperation is obvious. "Of course he does. Conrad wouldn't let people use the place otherwise. Were there many of you there?"

She looked puzzled. *"It was pretty full. There were even some at it in the kitchen — I always wondered why he put such a sturdy table in there. Why do you ask?"*

"Merle, I need the full picture. You've told my biggest client to fuck off…"

"I thought your Alphonse was your biggest client…" She stopped there; she was getting one of my stares, I suppose. She will either deny or attempt to minimise her culpability for anything. It's not so obvious at work, but I have to watch out even there — although I made it very plain right from the start that I would regard her as responsible for everything, and she's responded well. Until she spoke to my biggest client like that. *"I'm sorry,"* she mumbled.

"Was Gerry directly involved?"

"Oh, definitely, but there were others, especially those two very big black men that Gerry likes to bring along and look at. They were sticking their things in her in between Gerry and others doing the caning. I've never seen him so vicious. I left the room."

"Were you playing?"

"No. I don't in big groups…" Here she began knotting her fingers and looking down into her lap. *"I let Gerry play sometimes, but only in little gatherings — and he's never like that. Well, not since that last time in Wiltshire, that's years ago now."*

"So, what brought this on, do you think?"

"I don't know what they were on. Well, lots of booze, of course, but there was other stuff going round. Your

friend was on some stuff too, and she never seems to know when to stop anyway..."

I know it's a danger with Sandra; her tastes are extreme, and she hates to give in and stop anybody. I've intervened quite often for her at parties in the old days, but it was never so serious a danger. We used to exclude the tops with extreme tastes. In fact, it's wrong to call them tops at all. At that level they're just bullies or sadists. A top, for me, is someone who's looking after their bottom. I admit, it's a rare top who can give Sandra a satisfying evening. I can, but I need one or, ideally, two good men to help me. But ending up in The Argosy is not the culmination of a satisfying evening.

"Anyway, there was a huge kerfuffle and all of a sudden that big man, Boris, you called him, was guiding two paramedics downstairs. Everybody was squeezing into the other rooms, pretending to have had nothing to do with it. Gerry found me — he was completely off his face — and told me that if I played properly, these things wouldn't happen. That's when I told him, 'You want me in an ambulance too, you can fuck off.' Told? Well, maybe I was screaming. I just thought he was disgusting. I can't have anything to do with him again."

She's talking about a major client — but I do take her point — and I've had my own problems with Gerry over the years. But Sandra is a sort of friend, and I'm more worried about her than the business.

Sort of friend? That sounds terrible, doesn't it? What do I mean by that? We're friends on our playtime party circuit, or were, I should say; it's a few years since I did much of that. We'd always found each other genial company, and she liked me to look out for her. She was aware of the dangers of her enthusiasms.

I don't suppose I'll get anything more useful out of Merle now. I'll see how Sandra is in the morning.

There were no other big issues with work. It's barely two weeks since I was here but there was a little to catch up with. She's managing to build a pipeline of prospects. But my curiosity about her private life has diminished. I know she has her diversions and entertainments. She is a beautiful woman, so it's easy for her, too easy. But I think the closeness to Gerry is unhealthy, and she's never really got over the one true love thing from the Will time.

She doesn't stay long. We work well together but the other spaces in our mutual life are filling with dirty pools of awkwardness. I still play with Michael on the odd, rare occasion when he makes contact, but I can't ask either of them why they're not divorcing. Can't? It's probably won't. I lack the interest and I wouldn't get an honest assessment. But maybe I have to delve into that too now.

And there's a message to call Claudia. She's in New York. I'm pleased she'd texted. We have these once monthly conversations, but it's been me ringing her lately. I don't think she's happy that I'm so close to Alphonse.

4

"Thank you so much for calling. Where are you?" So many phone calls started that way now, thought Claudia; Isobel should be in Hong Kong, she was convinced, but she'd grown sensitive to the times of day in voices. This was an evening voice.

"I'm at home in London. Is this a good time for you?"

"It's perfect. We've just wrapped up for the day. I've an hour before I have to get ready for dinner. But what are you doing there? Aren't you in Vietnam next week?"

"Well, Mr Newman thinks I should be, but something's blown up here."

"Oh, dear. Serious? I suppose it must be, or you wouldn't have flown back." Claudia was aware that her knowledge of even her outer circle's whereabouts was unnerving, not least to herself, but it was pointless to hide it.

"Well, it's a long and complicated story — and not a little sordid. I'm happy to talk about it, but it's not one of our priorities, I don't think."

It sounded like it was weighing on her mind, however. A year ago, they would have spilled into random conversations like that. Isobel had become a friend, but Claudia had to admit, her closeness to Alphonse created tensions. And her calling him Mr Newman, conscious subterfuge or not, only made that worse. But Claudia was in her 'get over it' mode — and she did have a project to discuss. And that had its complexities — and maybe also a slightly sordid dimension — she would be exorcising a ghost.

"I do have a priority, actually, but I'm sorry it takes a priority to make me leave a message. I'm apologising for not picking up the phone as often as I used to."

"I'm glad you've said that. I was getting worried. I appreciated all the help getting started out there, but the continuing chats mean a lot to me. I was worried you were going off them."

"No, no, not at all, it's just been…" And she hesitated.

"No, it hasn't been, I don't think. We know who makes it awkward — and he shouldn't do — although I don't think we should be blaming him, we're big girls." This was pure Isobel, deadly accurate, deadly frank. "He loves you very much. You know that. But, on very rare occasions — we live in the same building but hardly ever see each other — we can relax together, and he talks. But I do get tired of hearing how wonderful you are, to be honest."

And it was easy to laugh with her — without quite being able to banish those irritating little weeds of jealousy, sprouting in her mind's garden.

"Have I said too much?"

Claudia laughed again. "No, but shall we say you've said quite enough? I know, if I felt sufficiently curious, I could have a blow-by-blow account of your encounters."

"You're right, of course, but you have to tell me there was nothing Freudian in the way you put that."

They laughed again. But there probably had been, and now she needed to get that image out of her mind. "I'm on the phone to talk renovation."

"Ah, are you finally going to let me do the Barnes house? Wow, yes please, but can't I deal with Peter? I loved his approach to budgeting for you. I suspect you'd be a tyrant."

"Well, you're right on at least one count, it is Barnes I want to talk about, but I don't think I'd be that bad running the project."

"Has he ever told you what he spent on that bedroom? It's still in my show presentation, by the way."

"No, he hasn't, and I don't want to know. Look, I was hoping to sit down in the place with you and talk it through, but I'd imagined your people would do the project."

"Oh, no, no, no, it's mine, I tell you, it's mine! I've been dreaming of doing that ever since I did the bedroom. I love the house, it's a perfect size — well, it's very grand, but it's the size of canvas I love to paint on, if you see what I mean. Anyway, when are you back? I've rather cleared my diary with this trip."

"I'm back Saturday morning. How about coming for lunch on Sunday? Peter will be off again by then."

"Claudia Brodie, you are a minx, that sounds like you've just halved my budget. But Sunday lunch would be wonderful, thank you. Wow, are we really going to have a girlie afternoon? I haven't had one of them for ages."

Neither had Claudia, when she thought about it. She'd had a very good time in New York with Tania, but the business demands were intense and the new acquisition they'd reviewed left almost no time for chat. So, now she was getting excited about Sunday — more for catching up with Isobel. The project itself needed doing — and Peter was too sensitive not to notice her perennial hesitation. The fact that he'd stopped asking about it was evidence enough of that. And Yvonne still lingered; banishing her spirit would help Claudia relax, but changing the house to her own tastes implied a commitment that she wasn't certain she was ready to give, even after all this time.

5

Sandra looked like shit. She was very pale and drowsy. They were monitoring her heart rate and a cannula was flopping in the crook of her elbow, waiting for the next cocktail.

There were flowers. I looked. One vase from Gerry — that was a PA's size, I could imagine the briefing: 'Just a friend of mine, nothing too ostentatious' — and a larger, definitely ostentatious one from Conrad. That didn't surprise me. I'll meet him for dinner. I'll find out how much this has unnerved him. Not much, probably.

"You're in London now," said Sandra, dopily.

"I flit in between, it's fun. How are you feeling?"

"Same as I look. Shit. And I don't want a lecture."

I smiled. That wasn't really fair. I don't lecture, I don't think. "How long are you going to be here for?"

"A couple more days. I don't know what's wrong with me."

"They wouldn't tell me anything. I'm not family. That occurs to me... Does your brother know you're here?"

Suddenly she was animated. "Of course not, and you're not to go fucking telling him."

26

I laughed — not at all appropriate — "I'd have no idea how to find him. And I'd probably get an earful for leading you astray."

"Of course." She was relaxing now she'd confirmed I would say nothing. "I'm still his innocent little sister."

OK, she was smiling a little; she wasn't playing tragic victim, then. Gerry would get away with it — again.

"Can you remember what happened?"

"Not really. Look, I've said, I don't want a lecture, OK? I know I'd had too much stuff, and you know I'm a bit extreme, but I was a bit out of it by then. I passed out, I think, well, I must have done. Now I'm all aches and pains, inside and out. They just tell me it's probably only bruising, and they're checking for infections."

We've had conversations before during unwelcome aftermaths, but she still goes back for more. I don't normally take positions on how people enjoy themselves, unless someone in the group isn't actually enjoying it. From the shape she seems to be in — they wouldn't keep her this long unless they were worried — even Sandra must have gone way beyond the point of enjoying herself, but if they'd got her that doped at the party, they weren't thinking of her enjoyment. Gerry never does, not for anyone else anyway, only himself. I went to his parties mostly to look after other people. Only parties he was hosting — he doesn't get invited anywhere else.

Only mostly, I said, not only — did you notice? — because I usually had a little fun myself — once I was sure people were safe.

Sandra will no doubt have fun again, sometime. If she hadn't been so doped, maybe she'd have had a chance to learn. But I doubt it. You have to be a bit pathological to take her past her boundaries and, generally, we don't let that sort in.

***

Conrad picked me up! Well, his car did. It took me to the Dorchester. I think friends of his own it. Please don't misunderstand me, I was delighted, but after a week like we'd had, a pub snack and a chat would have been more appropriate. Well, that would never be appropriate for Conrad. I met him first more than a dozen years ago. I hope, even then, that I didn't let people surprise or shock me, but the reputation that had preceded him hadn't let me expect the person I finally met. He just looks so normal. Yes, that's a euphemism for boring and undistinguished. And quiet.

We talked. OK, I talked, I do babble on, I know, so it's not a great burden for me, but I do prefer the great conversationalists. Peter Dickinson is one. And even Gerry, on a good day, can be amusing company.

But Conrad, who, I've come to appreciate, is wealthy, worldly and wise, is not a member of that charmed circle. But he does seem to know everything about everything and everyone. So, whatever I dive into, he knows the background. I mean, it's ages since we've had time together — before I got involved in the Far East, in fact. But he knows the Senlin Group, he's heard of the Shen family, and he understands exactly how they go about business.

Most of his business is Middle East, though. I think it's energy, but it spills over into other areas. When he hosts his partners, he makes sure they're well entertained. Mostly he gets girls in hotels organised for them, but the guests with more exotic tastes are taken to his cellar. They don't mix with his friends, though. Sandra's been a few times, she's often a star, but he's always on hand then to make sure she's not abused.

This is why he seems so upset this evening — it's not that he cares exactly, it's more that their relationship is one of mutual benefit and he has a commitment to secure her well-being. He'd been to see her this afternoon. "I should have checked," he's saying. "Boris would know to blacklist Gerry Calvert, but the booking came through the McKenzies. He thought you might be involved."

This is a difficult topic in an open restaurant, but Conrad is so quietly spoken our words aren't going to spill on to nearby tables. Well, mine would normally, but these are special circumstances. He's a smallish man, too, unobtrusive, his greying hair always perfectly trimmed; his rimless glasses nevertheless bring your attention to his eyes, which are grey, but do have some laughter lines. You look at his mostly serious face and think any smile is going to seem incongruous, but, when it comes (it's rare) it's charming — and he has a relaxed laugh, too; he just doesn't let it escape often. It certainly isn't escaping this evening yet.

"Anyway, it sounds like she'll recover OK. How do we keep an eye on her?"

"Conrad," I put my hand on his, "she's nearly forty." He nods quietly. "And I'm afraid trying out dangerous play partners is part of her kink. You should know that." He nods, unsmiling. He likes to take his own risks. He didn't know me the first time we played. But we were at a party; others were watching.

"Boris is very upset. He got worried when he saw Gerry, but he arrived with the McKenzie party and he knew I'd approved them; he could hardly turn their guests away. Why does she... they're not together now, are they?"

He was asking about Merle and Michael. "No, they're not, and I don't really understand how they do it, but it's a long time since I involved myself in Merle's non-professional life."

"Beautiful woman..."

"Fuck off, Conrad, you're with me this evening." And, now it finally comes, that lovely laugh, as warm and comforting as a treacle sponge.

"And I'm enchanted to be so." He takes my hand and kisses my fingers. "You know, I sometimes wonder why we never..."

"We still do, Conrad, OK, it's more than a year but..."

"Oh, I know that, but we're so perfect, yet..."

"You know, I've never thought you guilty of charm — and that still hasn't changed," I get another helping of laughter, "but I know what you mean. You should be perfect for me. I'm certainly perfect for you," he's smiling, "but apart from the excitement of the moments themselves — and that's considerable, I'll grant you — we've never struck that magic match to light the fire, have we?"

"I suppose not." And, bless him, he's looking glum as he's shaking his head.

"I made the mistake early on once of thinking I'd sparked your interest." He raises his eyebrows and looks surprised. "But you turned up with two fat sheiks who wanted to be spanked together."

Laughter again. I'd been worrying needlessly about this evening. "I remember them. One of them died, you know, not long afterwards, quite mysteriously. It simplified my business arrangements, but I became quite paranoid about dealing with the other one after that."

I was a little shocked. "You think he was involved in the death?"

He shrugged. "I certainly wasn't going to follow that up too closely. I keep arm's length from my business partners when they want to get involved in other areas. I just make introductions. Gerry does it differently, I think. When his Russians want to get into other things, he gets a piece of the action. I'm only telling you to be careful. But you weren't wrong about the other thing, by the way."

"Weren't wrong about what?"

"I was getting interested, wondering about how we might be together, but that business at the time shook me a little and made me focus elsewhere. I felt quite threatened." I was looking at him — and shaking my head. "No, I suppose you're right."

"I know I am. But you tried it once — marriage, I mean. Not that I'm suggesting that your thoughts about me went that far."

"They did, actually. But you're right to bring up my marriage. That should have taught me. Did you ever? You didn't, did you? At least, that's what I'd always assumed."

"You're right, I didn't. I'd had a few lukewarm proposals, about as enthusiastic as yours just then, but I'd never been tempted to accept one until now."

He looked momentarily shocked, until I laughed loudly. We were relaxed together by now. We'd missed each other and we suddenly had disrupted diaries with blank spaces. It was easy to organise a playdate for Saturday. I would need it after dinner with Gerry tomorrow.

6

Alphonse was expecting no surprises. He worked with a lot of good people but no one was as meticulous as Daiyu. They met seldom, but there was seldom a need. Most of the developments were on time and the occasional issues were always flagged early — always with options for resolution.

They would fly to Vietnam tomorrow, but he wanted a briefing on everyone who would be there. The launch party would be lavish, and it was important to make the most of that investment — and the clients of Allen Chou Li would be among the prime future customers of Psamathe resorts.

He knew how much the project meant to her. In her time with Yang Lijun she'd directed most of the architectural work on the development and, since joining Isobel, she'd been able to follow that through into the designs. Psamathe Phuroc was almost more hers than his. That its ultimate owners were Peter Dickinson and Shen Wengwei seemed an even more distant thought for her than it was for him.

For him, today would be a rare office day. Arriving there was always a thrill; it was, after all, a showcase for Allen Chou Li, and Isobel and Daiyu had put all of themselves into it. The effort — and the money, as Peter

33

would playfully remind them on his rare visits — had paid off, but Peter made the comment, with an inevitable warm smile, only after the awards had come in and their business was flooded with interest.

Alphonse shared a corner office with Mei. Their office days were infrequent, and he would have been content with something smaller and further back. The view, while still spectacular, was not his favourite, that was from the Kowloon side, and was anyway almost identical to the view from his apartment. But Mei had commandeered the corner office. Daiyu's revenge came in the rent she charged them for their space.

The other feature that intrigued him — every time he walked through the underground passage between the buildings — was that he travelled further to work vertically than he did horizontally: down twenty-nine floors and then up twenty-seven. And there was Daiyu, waiting in the large meeting room with the harbour panorama.

Daiyu was thirty-seven — it would have been very hard to guess accurately; he'd been intrigued enough to check her file when they were setting up the business. She was apparently happily single. It seemed she had easily let her relationship with Yang Lijun lapse when she'd left his business. He could imagine her doing that calmly and matter-of-factly. It was hard to think of her in the grip of passion. It was actually hard to think of anyone like that, unless you had direct experience with them, but the thought came into his head about her in a way that he thought about no one else.

She was a similar height to Isobel, but slimmer, and he was aware of a frisson of competition in the way they dressed — and that infected Mei too, on her office days, when she abandoned the black suit that served her for all the property meetings they travelled to. It meant that any day in the office was, visually, a delight. The standards didn't apply if you turned right out of the lift shaft and went through the double doors into the design room — Alphonse called it 'economy' — where jeans, tee shirts and trainers were almost a uniform.

She stood when he entered. He took both her hands and kissed each cheek. "You look enchanting," he said.

She tilted her head and gave him a sceptical look, but said, "Thank you, kind sir, and you, of course, are impeccable as always."

Of course, he thought, but it was easy when you had to dress only for air-conditioning. Even the underpass between the buildings allowed little of the day's usually steamy weather to intrude.

"Is your allocation all taken?" he asked when they sat down. The woman from reception came in and, unbidden, poured coffee for them.

"Yes, of course," she said, with a sly smile, "and with the people we want." That puzzled him. It showed. "We've had to be very firm with some of them. We don't want them sending friends and relatives in their places."

"Is that a big problem?"

"Not really. This is a big deal — and we've booked refundable deposits from everyone. If they send a substitute, we bill them. We'll be billing some of them anyway, we've offered two nights free, but some have booked for longer."

"You get away with all that?" Alphonse was surprised.

"We work through the PAs. They don't want their bosses missing out on a major launch — and they know there'll be bonus discounts for them later when they make the trip themselves. Don't worry. I think we may be more blunt with each other than you Christians can be."

He smiled. He'd told her once of how Peter had been stunned to be unflatteringly categorised as just that by a countryman of Daiyu's, and she sometimes used it to tease him if she felt he was being overly soft or sensitive. She had little time for the inefficiencies of tact, as she referred to his style of working. That's what made her and Isobel such perfect partners, although Isobel's devotion to the truth was also matched, in her case, by a devotion to the provocative.

He could see that commitment to openness in Mei, too. She sometimes made him shudder in some of their property meetings, but he couldn't think of one deal that had gone badly because of her approach. But that would be the afternoon meeting. This morning was about Daiyu's clients — and future Psamathe guests.

She'd impressed him from the very first meeting when Yang Lijun had come to present their ideas on the Psamathe developments. She'd given the presentations. At first, he'd wondered if that was because her English was so much better, but when he and Raymond posed questions, it was usually Daiyu who answered — always accurately, always succinctly — and he quickly came to appreciate that the bulk of the work and the ideas were hers.

Later, in the bar with Raymond, he'd confessed that his first thought had been that she was simply a professional concubine for Yang — she was an impressively attractive woman — but that unworthy thought hadn't lingered beyond the introductions; she was very calm, and very confident. 'Don't feel bad, boss,' Raymond had said. 'There is something going on between them'. And he'd assumed straight away that the relationship must have been of Daiyu's choosing. Nothing in the two years since had made him doubt that assumption.

But what was interesting him this morning, as they went through the invitees, was how perceptive this cool technocrat was into the personalities and foibles of her clients. "I'm impressed with these insights," he'd said at one point.

She smiled. "It's not really me, it's Isobel." She paused. "Well, it is me on the pure Chinese ones, I suppose, but it's something Isobel has forced me to think about. We're designing spaces for people, not for businesses, that's her mantra." He laughed lightly. She looked puzzled. "What is it?"

"It should no longer surprise me, but… Mantra — your English is so perfect — and it even sounds English." She smiled. "I mean, Mei's is extremely good, but that West Coast accent always seems a little out of place."

"I studied in London; she was in San Francisco."

"I know, I know. It's my attitude that's unhealthy." And it was, but that was only a venial sin, he thought. "My mother never lost her French accent, of course; she knew it made her ridiculously charming; she's never really tired of flirting."

Daiyu smiled and nodded. "That, Monsieur Alphonse, explains a great deal."

He laughed. "I think I've been trapped into displaying vanity."
"Oh, no," she said, "that's always on display. What you showed there, unusually, was conceit." And they both laughed, but he somehow felt their relationship was changing. It was uncomfortable, but also closer and, well, pleasant. "But we must get back to these equally conceited friends of ours," she said, pointing to her screen.

***

The afternoon was more difficult. He and Mei had struggled to pick a list. Some of their major leaseholders wanted to send their managers and Alphonse wasn't sure Mei had dealt with that quite as sure-footedly as Daiyu had. He'd been quite blunt in his directive: 'I don't want them using these trips to replace their incentive bonuses. I want to invite the customers of the future — not their minions who won't be able to afford it.' He suspected she'd been too literal in the way she conveyed the message.

He knew she'd invited no one who'd ever queried a lease condition. But she always stayed cool and consistent with the conditions she imposed. She was going to be good.

She'd come to feel like a younger sister he'd never had. Their last night in Morkuda, that weird, unique threesome of eighteen months ago, was never mentioned again, not even by Isobel. But it had kick-started what had become a very successful business partnership. She stayed very eager, and very quick, to learn. She worked immensely hard to be well-informed about all their property options in the region. It reminded him of his approach in the early years. Her ideas were always well thought through and she brought an edge to negotiation that he felt he sometimes lacked. It meant that the recent deals were driven by her with him only in the background. He'd come to realise that buyers or vendors wanting to talk with him directly were not necessarily insisting on seniority or gender; they were looking for a softer deal. He'd told her that recently and been rewarded with a huge hug and a kiss and even, almost unique for Mei in his experience, a small tear in the corner of her eye.

Her guest list for the Phuroc opening had contained a few surprises but that made it a useful review of her business pipeline. But he'd smiled when he'd seen Lily's name on the list. It wasn't a name they discussed, but it made sense because the Thai opening was only three months away and Lily, as the architect's assistant on the next project, would effectively be filling Daiyu's role in that. It occurred to him that her room wouldn't be used; she'd probably be with Mei, but, when he reflected briefly, it made sense to keep a professional distance even with your lovers — especially with your lovers. Let them have their own room for when times get tense.

The next name surprised him. "Shen Liqiang? Lee is coming? Was that your idea, or his?" Listing Lily and Liqiang together was probably more than happenstance; this would be where personal relationships would be discussed, if necessary.

Mei, with the Lily issue out of the way, was untroubled by the question. "I sent the invitation. It's a big project for the family."

"Did you invite Shen Wengwei? It's not in Lee's area now." Alphonse knew that must have sounded tetchy.

"Of course, but he's not coming."

Alphonse thought back to a strange meeting he'd been invited to in Shanghai two months before.

Wengwei's PA had made it plain that Alphonse was to come alone and 'be discreet.' It had been, inevitably he thought, a bizarre meeting but, since his affair with Liqiang was over, Alphonse felt no great discomfort at the prospect — although he realised that, having been asked, effectively, to travel without Mei, the meeting must be for more than a simple property review. Wengwei wouldn't know that Alphonse knew of Mei's paternity — yet that had been the first surprise of the meeting. 'How's my daughter doing?' had been his opening question. The interpreter had been asked to stay outside until required, so Alphonse guessed that some shock was coming — but he'd expected an inquisition on his relationship with Lee — although, for him, that would be only a post-mortem.

'She's doing extremely well,' he'd said, remaining, he thought, very calm. The two men had stared at each other for what must have been several seconds until Wengwei's face began to crease into a grin. 'I thought you knew,' he'd said. 'I can't keep secrets from the Giant, he has spies, I know.' And he'd laughed — almost approvingly, Alphonse thought. He'd called Peter 'the Giant' since the Morkuda meeting. It meant he could refer to himself as the Lion — it had been part of a joke he'd made at the time. Alphonse talked about her fierce work ethic, which had been expected, but also about his admiration for her negotiating skills. He'd described her as firm, but imaginative — and Wengwei struggled with the word, but 'clever' seemed to satisfy him, and bring a smile out of him.

It was a useful opportunity to mention that they made less and less contact with Mei's official father, still nominal head of the Senlin property division. The dismissive wave of the right hand told him all he needed.

'About Meitang, I happy,' he'd said, concluding that part of the meeting, then something had switched in his face. He was looking very stern. 'About Liqiang, I also happy.' He'd looked anything but. 'Happy you no see each other any more.'

Alphonse stayed calm again. This was actually easier. It had been an affair, he'd had feelings of love — just not as intense as Lee's, and he'd been less willing to compromise on the way he lived. In principle he could have based himself in Shanghai for business in the region but his evasiveness on that suggestion of Lee's had made them both realise they were having an affair, and not heading for a partnership. Lee had been more reluctant than Alphonse to accept the end but, as he'd found increasingly often, geography helped in effecting disentanglements. That's what, ultimately, the longer separations had become. But Lee was a beautiful man — and Alphonse finally had the flicker of an insight that even his father appreciated some of his virtues — 'He's doing better job now.'

There had been a long pause at that point, but Alphonse had guessed that Wengwei was about to say more. 'Much better than brother.' Another pause, but this sentence was not finished. 'Not so good, maybe, as sister.'

That was it! That's what he wanted to know. 'They are both extremely capable people' — careful with your English, he'd told himself — 'very clever, very hard-working, they can see a long way ahead…' Wengwei was nodding.

'But sister more ruthless, yes?'

Alphonse had laughed, and worried instantly about how appropriate that was, but he found himself nodding to Wengwei's smiling face.

The meeting had been brief, as he thought it might be, but it gave him the time to look at some properties in the city — just cursory, superficial views, but he needed the city to speak to him more. The half dozen trips he'd had in his Lee year had not allowed him the right business perspective on the place.

And now Lee was coming to Phuroc — and he realised that he had no idea how much Mei knew — of his relationship with Lee, or if she even suspected her own true paternity. She'd certainly been happily avoiding any contact with her official father. That would have embarrassed Alphonse, since Shanghai was still, nominally, their main office, but everyone they dealt with seemed to appreciate how their group was run.

7

Gerry had asked me to dinner. That told me he was nervous, although that's the sort of thing his brazenness usually conceals. He'd also be aware that, commercially, he had the upper hand. I'd completed his and Ellen's apartments, but the Wiltshire house is a big project — and he has other properties, of his own and his Russian friends, that Merle has quoted for. Wiltshire is more Ellen's project than his, which means it's more extravagant than he'd like it to be, but that's the price he pays for preserving the fiction of a harmonious relationship.

Well, maybe it's not so much a fiction. They still host occasional parties together but it's a long time since they paid each other any attention at those — not that I've been to any recent ones; Ellen's seen to that. It's strange how pleasant and amenable she is on the projects but how dismissive of me she is socially. I think she'd like to cut off Merle too, but that wouldn't fly with Gerry — or Michael, for that matter. Maybe I'll be clearer about how that works after this evening.

We're meeting in his apartment first. That suits me. If I don't like how the conversation goes, I can simply head home. He's good business for me, him and his contacts, but I don't like what's happened to Sandra and

I want to know who else might be at risk. Things never used to get so out of control but, socially, I've been away eighteen months.

"Thank you so much for coming." He kisses my hand. It's a silly affectation of his that I've always been happy to indulge. I knew I'd get Dr Jekyll to start with this evening; Gerry is mostly charming and, to be honest, I don't think I've seen the demented Mr Hyde more than twice. But that's why he gets invited nowhere these days, from what I hear, so there's a more common professional element to his fun these days — yes, I do mean he pays!

Sandra doesn't take money, but I know lavish presents are accepted — and then often sold. It helps her avoid seeing what she does as prostitution, but it's up to you to have a view on that one. I could understand you moralising, but I'm comfortable with it.

And Merle? I told you, I have no idea how that works. But it's not like me to be so incurious. I suppose I think of what she could have had — but she was always too self-centred. Anyway, regrets are silly things — even though she still suffers from them. Will's happier now than he would have been. We talk occasionally. He even looks at my accounts — we started in Hong Kong with Dickinson money, so he has to check. I think he gives everything to a junior, but he did say they were in good shape.

Gerry isn't Will. Apart from being very successful men, they're opposites.

Gerry is short and, frankly, a little ugly but that's not what you notice. He radiates self-assuredness. It's quite imposing. He dresses well, if a little ostentatiously, and keeps himself well-tanned. His hair is neat but has been infiltrated with new growth occasionally over the years and is also kept a colour no longer appropriate for his age. But who am I to comment on that!

We sit in the study. I'm proud of the apartment but it was an odd commission. I'd known him and Ellen for years; we'd met at parties where they had, of course, even early on, little to do with each other, so when he approached me about wanting an apartment redesigned just for himself, it hadn't surprised me. What surprised me was the follow-up call from Ellen. She wanted the original apartment renovated and she made it clear it was her project and Gerry would have no say. I insisted on knowing if they were going to live separately — if I don't ensure I meet all the needs of cohabiting couples, projects always turn out badly. But they were both quite firm. They weren't separating, merely living separately.

I'd seen Gerry watching her being fucked quite often in the old days; she likes it rough and he used to like watching that. But I've never seen her watching him. Their tastes aren't really compatible, except insofar as they give each other freedom.

So, this is quite a male apartment in terms of colours and styles. The subtlety of it, and I would defy you to spot this on a simple tour, is that most of the furniture can be adapted for parties. Gerry has a dungeon in the Wiltshire place, but the fun tends to spread through all the rooms unless people have very specific kinks. Here, most of the furniture can be very quickly adapted for all manner of uses, the various metal loops and hooks are all concealed, if I may say so, with elegant artifice...

We did have a small party, when the commission was finished, with a number of Gerry's usual play partners — Sandra was there — and I had to demonstrate how each piece worked. It was a peculiar atmosphere. It had more to do with curiosity than lust initially but, by the time sufficient bubbles and powders had been dispensed, the ambience had become joyously boisterous. That was the first time I'd noticed Sandra getting really wasted. It wasn't dangerous, I was there, and most of the tops were good people — thinking about and giving what the bottoms wanted. Gerry was the only baddie, but I'd heard his 'my champagne, my party,' too often to be anything other than seriously unimpressed. I had some fun, though. There was one guy with a magnificent tongue. I had met him before. I even let him tie me — now that is a cleverly designed chair, I must modestly admit — I needed to check it out in practice. Wow, it worked even better than I'd expected. I was completely open for him. He made me come three times before he even stuck his cock in me.

That was my last London party, come to think of it. But I'm here on serious business and, fortunately, the memories of what I've seen happening on the two chairs we're now sitting in haven't lingered.

"You've seen her again, I assume."

He doesn't seem troubled, and I'm not going to play games. "Yes, she'll be out tomorrow." I stare at him. I'll make him ask. I know where this is going.

"Any ill effects?"

"Physically or emotionally?" I'm staying calm, no tone of accusation in my voice — well, I'm trying not to reveal any.

"For fuck's sake, Sadie! We all understand the games we play."

"That's true for most of us but, being frank, Gerry, you play a different game." He's just staring back hard at me. I have to work out what I want out of this. It should be simple, really: it's a recovery for Sandra; proper treatment of her in the future; and, if he can respond positively, maybe we'll keep the contracts. I like most of my clients, I've been successful enough to be choosy, but Gerry's always been in a twilight zone for me: good business; interesting parties; and he's generally very good at understanding the designs; but I'm not having my friends hurt. "The top's role is to attend to the bottom's desires."

"I'm a different sort of top." He's quite defiant.

"What you do isn't topping, Gerry. Yours is a different sort of kink. I don't like saying anything's bad, people are as they are — but I only believe in the consensual. If people don't come back again, or it takes

money or drugs — and that's the impression I have nowadays — you're playing a different scene. And I suspect you've been doing that for a while."

He's at least thinking about what I've said. "Merle comes back."

This is true. "I think you have a little routine there, don't you — and she's probably the only woman you're a little bit in love with." I know how they play. I have seen them at the early parties.

"What's she said?"

"Just that you and she still play sometimes, but that was a very brief part of our conversation. I doubt whether her tastes have changed; they were surprisingly unvarying. How many people do you invite for her?"

"Four, at most."

"Including Michael?"

"Not including Michael."

"But he's always there."

"Yes, he's always there."

"At his insistence, or hers?"

He purses his lips and shakes his head. "It's never come up."

"Have you asked her on her own?"

He's slow responding, so when he says 'no,' I don't believe him. He's probably the one who touches her when they've all come on her — and she's quite robust about what she can take — and she has a very pretty arse, dammit, but she much prefers male tops — it's them coming all over her so visibly that excites her. I think she'd rather go off and make herself come, so Gerry is honoured in a way. But there's never any penetration. Not at parties. I assume she's had other relationships where there has been; well, she's told me she has, but we don't really talk about them and, like most bottoms, she has a great capacity for deceit. Particularly for self-deceit, is what I'm thinking. Don't get me wrong, I do care about her, but it just can't ever be like it was when I was helping Will to learn to please her. But I was deceiving even myself then: I'd fallen in love with him too. But at least I knew he and I weren't suited, so we had a wonderful arrangement until he met that woman — yes, Martha, his wife. Sandra still talks about him — but she met him only two or three times.

And I'm here to talk about Sandra, not Merle. "We can talk about Merle over dinner, Gerry. You're obviously more concerned about Sandra." That's bollocks, of course. Gerry, as ever, is concerned almost exclusively about himself.

"Yes, and I know you're close to her."

"I suspect you've seen her more than I have over the last two years."

"Yes, maybe, but not in conversation situations."

No, never in conversation situations. "It's not her first time in the Argosy, is it? They won't have a very flattering patient record of her: drugs, extreme masochism — way beyond an abusive relationship — although she's had enough of those. If I could stop you being quite such a sadistic cunt, her life might not be that bad. I presume the costs are going through the books of some offshore company?"

He's nodding. We're in a comfort zone for him — tax and information avoidance. At least she's being taken care of — and so is he: The Argosy is watertight discreet.

It's not the first time I've called him a cunt, by the way, and I still get a dinner invitation.

"She's an asset to you, Gerry. Let's face it, you have to organise your own parties, and I suspect that's better for you anyway. You don't want gossip slipping out. And for your kinkier friends, she has a lot to offer." He's thinking and nodding. "I just think your own personal tastes are too destructive. You may have her hooked on the lifestyle and the presents and, God knows, she won't settle down, but you're not making best use of her."

How am I doing this for Sandra? Wait a moment and listen.

"What you do is dangerous to her physically and mentally. Her hands were shaking when I was with her — that's probably drink deprivation after four days in there — but she's in denial about what happened the other night. So, the thing you most wanted to know is that you're safe."

He doesn't react in any way. That tells me I'm right.

"I don't know what you do about your outlandish tastes. I'm going to make the hopeful assumption that you'd been on a bad mix and lost control."

I get a small nod now. I want to be this generous, or maybe naïve, otherwise I have to say he's psychopathic, and there's no easy way back from that. But he's not my problem.

"Look after Sandra, Gerry, or this will get out. I know you have some odd business partners but I'm guessing they all share a distaste for publicity."

I'm trying not to make this appear like a threat — that would never be effective with Gerry — but I'm worried about my friend — and what I've introduced her to. Now I'm waiting for a reaction.

It's slow in coming, but eventually, he says, "You're right, of course. I rather lost it — too much stuff, I'm afraid. And she never seems to want people to stop."

"You know that's no excuse, don't you? It's a lovely room she's in at The Argosy, but it wasn't what she was looking for. Are you going to look after her?"

Again, he's slower than he should be but, "I'll do what I can," is the nearest I'm going to get to a commitment tonight. I think he can see the dangers — to his business, of course — he's never going to worry about Sandra herself.

Now he can tell me about Merle over dinner.

And about Michael, although I suspect he'll say less there.

Michael was a fun play partner for quite a time. I introduced Merle to him — only on a project for him, I never thought they'd get together. They're both bottoms, but each fell in love with the image the other was projecting and then managed to put their disappointment behind them when reality dawned. Why they're still together, I don't know — it can only be something financial, I assume. But Michael and finance is a mystery to me.

He'd got fired from the office he was heading a few years ago — he'd been running some off-book stuff through Gerry and he got caught. Gerry took him on, and Michael's been evasive ever since about what he does. I don't pry anyway, but he often used to talk to me in the quiet periods after playtime. I used to like that — I hate the 'guilt and shame runaways,' nobody does that to me twice; I spank and play for fun, yours and mine, and guilt has absolutely no place in that scene.

8

Alphonse had made two trips as the Phuroc site was evolving. He was sure there must have been problems but Yang Lijun, who'd accompanied him each time, constantly reassured him that all was proceeding exactly to plan.

Raymond, Alphonse's head of resorts, who'd timed his visits differently, kept an alternative perspective, so was more truly reassuring. Teddy, the resort manager, who was staying on site during the rebuild, was observing many problems, but seeing them all being promptly overcome.

Alphonse was finding himself unusually tense now. He was arriving, with Daiyu and Mei, the day before the first guests would arrive. He'd been aware, on the journey, of some friction between the ladies over who would occupy the seat next to him. He had the aisle seat on the plane, so Daiyu had been able to lean across when Mei was not monopolising him, but she'd swiftly occupied the rear seat of the car, leaving Mei standing disgruntled as the driver dealt with the luggage before she reluctantly occupied the front seat. Most of his business was with Mei, but Daiyu, having effectively designed the resort, had more to tell him about how things would work over the next week. She confirmed what Raymond and Teddy had said, there had been the usual number of problems — but Yang Lijun had solved them all with the developer.

There was still lots of activity in the gardens as the car moved smoothly through the main archway, but it seemed to be only final mowing and adding small, bright plants to the borders.

The entrance, now he could see it for the first time without contractors' lorries and suppliers' delivery vans, looked utterly splendid. Yang had contrived a wonderful canopy that looked no different from his, or Daiyu's, sketches, in spite of having had the budget for it eliminated in their last Morkuda week discussion.

He gestured up to it as they got out of the car and got only a shrug and an enigmatic look from Daiyu. They were within the overall budget. He would certainly have heard from Mei — and Raymond — had that been threatened.

Teddy and Raymond were waiting. He'd expected that — but Yang Lijun emerging from the doors was a surprise although, since he was smiling, it was a pleasant one. There were obviously no last-minute disasters — and there were the new contracts to be awarded for the next phase of developments, as well as some property projects he and Mei were working on; Lijun was securing his pipeline, no doubt.

He wouldn't have described his greeting as only perfunctory; for a cool, dry man like Lijun it was effusive enough, but he went on to devote a lot more attention to the ladies. Alphonse was speaking with, or rather listening to Raymond, but he was still watching the Chinese trio, who intrigued him. There was still something obvious between Lijun and Daiyu, however coolly she was reacting. With Mei, he displayed a fawning deference that made Alphonse think he already knew who Mei's real father was.

But he was keen to check the programme with Raymond: the VIP confirmations; the press arrangements; and the countless other worries that were all so new to him. Morkuda had been big, but Phuroc was the first of a now-planned dozen so the roll-out from here was many times more important. Here was also the closest resort they would have to China: just over two hours flight time from Hong Kong, four from Shanghai. This had to be the resort that would draw his new devotees — that is what he was aiming for — further into the Pacific.

Raymond's breezy confidence soon had him relaxing. "We'll start with a tour, boss. Come on, Teddy." He nodded to the manager and they walked to reception while the staff dealt with bags.

"Did you want to do a tour now?" Alphonse called to the ladies but, of course, nothing would get done before a shower and a change — and that would normally have been his own way but he knew, as did Raymond, that he couldn't relax until he'd seen that all was in order.

Which, of course, it was. And that gave him time to himself before dinner. He'd chosen a villa, rather than a suite, since he saw himself entertaining a lot. He smiled to himself in the mirror of the enormous bathroom, aware that the entirely commercial justification for choosing the presidential villa — who better to show it off than he — had an element of self-indulgence. He could imagine Isobel delighting in pandering to the vanity of people who demanded this level of sybaritic opulence. He would not spoil himself like this again — but then came another smile — until the next big opening.

It was fortunate that neither Peter nor Shen Wengwei were coming. He would naturally have had to offer them the grandest villa. Peter would simply have enjoyed his discomfort — 'No, my dear man, you must show it off, of course, it's your business, you'll have the guests,' and would then have teased him frequently later. Shen Wengwei, he was sure, would simply have taken the villa.

The bell, he thought, must be room service — he'd wanted the first day to himself. The butler would be useful after the guests had arrived. But it was Daiyu. He must have looked surprised. "Am I disturbing you?" she asked, but she was already stepping in.

"No, of course not. Have you looked around?"

"Of course, and it's always the most bizarre and thrilling moment; in your head are all the early sketches, the chosen images from more than two years ago, the evolving plans, and finally…" She was turning around, taking everything in. "It exists, it all becomes suddenly real and — if you're very good and you're very lucky — it comes together like this."

"You're happy with it?"

"I'm thrilled. Are you? You're the customer."

"I'm absolutely delighted," he said but suddenly her arms were around him, her head on his chest.

"I wanted it so much to come off for you…" She was hugging him tighter. He was overwhelmed. There had never been more than a handshake before. Slowly she eased back and took his hands. She was looking up at him, her eyes shining. She looked entirely happy — and comfortable, which was more than he felt. Now she laughed. "I'm making you nervous."

"No," he said, with no conviction.

"You're a big boy, my darling Alphonse, you can handle my thank you." She went on tiptoes and kissed his lips.

He could have given himself to the kiss, it was more than friendly, but she hadn't forced herself and he found himself feeling strangely ungallant as she leaned back, still smiling at him. "I know we'll have a very abstemious week — I've always admired your self-control — but I think one glass of bubbles is entirely justified."

"Oh, I agree." He was recovering his poise, and relieved to be able to retreat from physical engagement. "But perhaps we should invite Mei to join us?"

Now he got a sly grin from her. "Did you want Lily to come too?"

"She's here already?"

Now the smile was cheeky. "Mei works very hard, as you know better than anyone, and making relationships work in those circumstances hasn't been easy for her. Lily is the only affair she keeps going — but Lily, of course, is quite a free spirit, and that puts Mei on edge. Anyway, I'm sure Mei's head will be back in the game when your property people arrive — but let's not begrudge her a happy hour or two before then. Am I getting that drink?"

Alphonse had stalled briefly. "Yes, of course, come through, talk to me more." Then he laughed. She looked puzzled. "I think I know where I'm going, there's a wonderful kitchen here with champagne in the fridge, but you must know the layout better than I do. Or do they blur with so many projects?"

Now he got, for a moment, the serious Daiyu face. She looked almost indignant. "No, they none of them blur, and especially not this. It's a very special project."

It felt almost awkward to touch anything so obviously new. He took a Bollinger from the wine fridge. Daiyu took the flutes from a glazed cupboard. He popped and poured, thinking about how to regain control of a situation that had completely surprised him. "Let's try the view," he said, ushering her towards the veranda. "Don't you have an old relationship to consider this week?" he asked when they'd sat across from each other on the wide sofas.

If he'd been trying to unnerve her, he'd failed. She was still relaxed and smiling — but, when he reflected, he was more curious than anything, Yang had clearly been very happy to see her. "Lijun, you mean?"

"Yes, I understood…"

"Cheers," she said, and they clinked glasses. She was running this conversation. "And congratulations on a magnificent project." They drank, she wasn't avoiding the topic, she was just giving it its appropriate, not very elevated, priority. "But, yes, we had a relationship for a while." She paused, staring levelly at him. "It was not exclusive, on either side. Funnily, that gave him more problems than it gave me. It's one of the dreary features of married men. They seem to need fidelity from you when they, by definition, offer none." She paused, then chuckled. "Of course, it wasn't just his wife he was also having sex with." She drank, looking thoughtful. "He never understood, but I minded that less than the deceits." Now she chuckled. "I was always open about my arrangements. There were actually very few." Her eyes narrowed. "I was extraordinarily busy professionally, but the principle of my freedom was important to me — so I always told him about the odd encounter I enjoyed, even though I knew how it would provoke him. That's not why I did it, though. But I'm not going to claim either that I was trying to make him feel better about all his arrangements. I just wanted us to be open, but he never could be."

"He has regrets, doesn't he? I could see it in the way he greeted you today."

She smiled. "Yes, of course he has regrets." Alphonse realised he was dealing with a confident, even slightly vain, woman. "But I just don't want the bullshit. I knew what it was, we were having an affair. I was tired of him pretending it might be different, especially as I didn't want it to be different."

"What was worse, his deceits, or his reactions to your other interests?"

"Well," and she sipped again, "the former, were certainly more numerous, but the latter were more unpleasant. Anyway, what are you doing this week. How will things be between you and Liqiang?"

"I was enjoying the distraction of your affairs. He's a worry I don't need. I didn't know he was coming until yesterday — he hadn't told me — and I don't know why he's coming. It's not really his business any more."

"No, it's his sister's."

That… was completely unexpected. He tried not to react — to her comment — or to the sense of betrayal that unaccountably welled up inside him. Did she know this, or was she fishing? Had she been offering these confidences to get him to relax and speak freely. He'd felt their relationship slowly melting into a friendship but now… was she a spy, an infiltrator… what did she want? But her brow was furrowed, maybe she'd expected him to acknowledge what she thought was common knowledge between them. No, that would be crediting her with too much.

"I've obviously said something I shouldn't have. I'm sorry."

It was hard to react in a way that wouldn't affirm. "No, not at all. Are you saying that Mei's father is Shen Wengwei?"

She was staying calm, but not contrite. "I'm not just guessing, Alphonse, but it was a clumsy way of telling you that I'm looking after you this week." She moved from her sofa to his, sitting close to him and taking his hand in both of hers. "I don't know how you stay as calm as you do with all this going on around you — and I'm not helping by broaching that particular topic in that clumsy way. I heard the rumour initially from Yang Lijun, but I put it down to pillow-gossip, you know, trying to impress by divulging secrets. I didn't think it was any more than speculation; he'd been talking about who Wengwei had been having affairs with, and putting that incompetent, Mei's mother's husband, in charge of property, seemed to at least make the story plausible. But when Isobel told me, that seemed to confirm it."

"Isobel told you?" He knew he sounded cross, even though he tried to avoid it.

She gripped his hand a little harder. "Don't be cross with her. I know what you're thinking: if she tells me, then I'm allowed to tell anyone," he nodded, "but she told me for a reason. She's looking after you — and so am I, so I know more about you than you want me to know but, my dear, dear man, I have only your best interests at heart. But I am going to admit to you now, that when you're cuddling my warm body tonight and talking pillow-gossip with me, that I'm also going to be there for my own pleasure. Understood?"

He found himself laughing lightly.

"You think it's funny?" She tried to sound offended, but he could tell she was teasing him.

"No, and forgive my lack of gallantry, but I've only ever been propositioned as boldly as that by gay men."

"I think women appearing in your cabin on a boat is quite bold. I liked that story."

"Isobel, I hope."

She nodded. "She was just reassuring me you were more than gay, you know, in case there was to be more than cuddles and gossip tonight."

"But if it's just cuddles and gossip?"

She leaned towards him and kissed his cheek. "Then I shall be perfectly content. Actually, I'll sleep in the other bedroom if you'd prefer. It will help me avoid Lijun knocking at my door tonight."

"No, I know I'll want cuddles and gossip." He leaned towards her now and kissed her gently on the lips. Whatever happened now, their relationship had changed. But a worrying thought came to him. "Mei doesn't know, does she? About her father, I mean."

She seemed to consider for a moment. "You know her much better than I do now. I think you'll notice first if she finds out." And he didn't think she had, but he still had Shen Wengwei's conversation in his mind.

Dinner was important. This was his first taste of the resort's cuisine, its move beyond 'Vietnamese International' as it had unselfconsciously described itself. It had been bland and passable, and entirely misaligned with their new aspirations. Teddy had fired the chef. Alphonse had to trust in Raymond, who'd backed Teddy. The old cuisine was the fault of either Teddy or the chef. Not recognising the problem would have been grounds anyway for firing Teddy, but it was by no means certain that the chef had been the sole cause.

But the new man certainly impressed. When Teddy ushered them through from the bar, the man was standing, in his kitchen whites, in the empty eighth space at the round table laid for seven. Raymond guided Alphonse to the chair opposite the chef. Mei sat unselfconsciously next to Lily. Daiyu sat next to the chef, enabling Lijun to sit beside her. For the first time Alphonse was seeing him without an assistant and, even at the bar, where he'd stood next to Daiyu, it was obvious that his feelings had been enhanced by his missing her, but Alphonse knew how jealousy could deceive. He was strangely aware that he could have felt it himself, but for the occasional sidelong smiles she sent him.

It meant he was between Raymond and Teddy which, for the purpose of the evening, was ideal.

Teddy introduced the chef, Pham Van Duc, telling them how proud he was to have plucked the man from a Michelin restaurant in HCM — Alphonse had grown used to the Ho Chi Minh abbreviation. Duc, small, smiley and appearing initially self-effacing, seemed to grow when Teddy's introduction was complete and gave a brief but compelling introduction to Vietnamese cuisine and his philosophy of fusing it with the French influences from the colonial past. His French-tinged accent lent authenticity to his story, but he knew not to talk for too long, and with a 'mais, c'est à l'ouevre qu'on voit l'artisan,' he clapped his hands and waiters appeared with their first dishes.

He returned to introduce each course briefly and Alphonse, whose worries had quickly melted, became enchanted by the sequence of dishes, each mercifully small, and their extraordinary mix of flavours, textures and colours and by the ninth, and final course, he was glowing. He turned to Teddy. "Could you please ask him to join us for a moment?" Teddy looked strangely nervous, which was odd, thought Alphonse, since he'd been making only positive comments all evening. Alphonse turned to Raymond. "Is he still worried?"

Raymond laughed. "Of course he's still worried, boss, but I know you better. You're happy."

Now Teddy was back with Pham Van Duc, who returned to what had begun to seem like his pulpit.

"Duc, I'm going to say I'm speaking for everyone, because I've been watching them and listening to them.

I came here hoping that you would produce cuisine that would at least match what the resort's accommodation aims to offer, but what you've just given us was heavenly, c'était absolument merveilleux. I can see you making this a destination for gourmets and foodies. You seem to have found a perfect balance between the Vietnamese and the French. I can't think of a meal I have ever enjoyed more." The hyperbole wouldn't harm, he thought, recognising that the sauce of intense relief had made every dish delightful.

Duc bowed deeply and smiled. "But may I thank Nguyen Van Tad," he nodded to Teddy, now smiling and looking entirely relieved, "for the wonderful opportunity he has given me, and the faith he has shown in me."

"Yes, yes, guys," this was Raymond now, "but we want this with eighty covers in the room, not all of whom will always be blessed with my boss's generous spirit. Although he is French, really, so you must have done well to please him." He seemed to have found the right tone, Alphonse thought, to let the compliments still radiate while the warning echoed. But these guys were obviously good, and Alphonse remained relieved. He stayed chatting for a while over tea with Raymond and Teddy. Lijun had plainly failed to entice Daiyu to the bar, and Mei had quickly disappeared with Lily. Alphonse found himself fighting the urge to return to his villa, wondering how long he would have to wait for Daiyu.

Not at all, he found. She was stretched on the sofa with the Bolly in an ice bucket.

"Were you really that pleased?" she asked with a teasing smile.

He poured for them both. "I can't deny that my relief was intense, but I really did think it was wonderful." Suddenly he felt nervous. "Didn't you?"

Now her smile was genuine as she took her glass from him. "I thought it was stunning. I've already texted Isobel, we've both been worrying for you — well, and for ourselves. We're building our reputations on your resorts."

He felt his phone buzz. It was a text message from Isobel: 'I gather dinner went wonderfully. Enjoy the rest of your evening!'

He looked to Daiyu. Now there was a third, different smile on her face. "Isobel," he said. She nodded. "She knows you're here, doesn't she?"

The smile continued. "Of course."

Alphonse was feeling disorientated. He had relationships that mattered, the least complicated of which was with Isobel. It felt so unencumbered — no obligations, no expectations — someone to relax with. He called Claudia infrequently because of the tensions he knew it caused with Peter. Raymond, here, and Hayley, running the London office, were, it was true, working relationships, but he had utter faith in them both and it was possible to be completely open with them — he knew they were aware of his 'secrets,' even without him discussing them, and it meant they could help him through any crises. But it now felt as though Isobel were injecting another confidante into his life and, much as he liked and admired Daiyu, he didn't think he was ready — and he had no idea what her needs and desires were.

At some unidentifiable point during the evening, the male body had taken over from the mind. There was a strange anonymity about the dark head of hair resting on his shoulder, the fingers languidly stroking his chest — he must have dozed a moment.

"She said you were very good." He was instantly back with Daiyu, and not some sensual object.

"And your view now?"

"You want to know?"

He chuckled. "I don't know whether I do, really. If you tell me you're happy, and you enjoyed fucking me, that would be good."

She looked up into his eyes and her hand slid down to his slumbering cock. "You did a wonderful job of pleasing me, thank you."

"Is there a message in that? Something you're saying by not saying?"

Now she chuckled. "She did say you were too sensitive. We put it down to you being gay — not gay as gay, as such — but worrying too much about a woman's reactions, rather than your own needs. You were doing that to make me happy — and you did. I don't know how much I pleased you."

"I had a wonderful time — correction, I am having a wonderful time." He hugged her to him. "And I don't think of myself as anything in particular — gay or bi or anything. I just occasionally get into certain people."

"Including me?"

It sounded like a question prompted by curiosity, rather than insecurity. This was a more profoundly confident woman than Mei, say. More confident than Claudia — and he had a momentary flash of guilt. Would he tell her of this? No, he wouldn't — ergo: guilty! Would Isobel tell her? They spoke quite often. This was unfair, his kissed Daiyu's forehead.

"Certainly, including you. I've found you enigmatic and intriguing."

"I could handle beautiful and enchanting, you know." She laughed at him. "You don't have to restrict your sensitivity to the purely physical."

"Enchanting? You've been a very subtle sorceress, then. Today has been a very big surprise to me. I've known you for two years and I never saw us like this."

"Like this, you mean?" Her hand was getting his cock to respond again.

"Exactly." He laughed. "And I'm not going to believe you've been harbouring carnal desires for me."

"I've found you enigmatic and intriguing." Now she laughed at him. "No, I picked up the gay thing straight away, you're too effortlessly stylish, and I don't go looking for things anyway. I was happy enough with Lijun, it filled a need, but it brought too many irritations."

"That sounds a little colder than I think you really are. Have you been in love?"

She looked up at him, kissed him and stroked his cock a little more firmly. "A few times, but don't worry, you're in no danger. I think we're friends now, though, is that OK?"

"One of the enchanting things about you is how you can pose a superfluous question so charmingly artlessly. Yes, friends definitely, of course we are — and it's definitely OK."

"And friends don't worry about what other friends their friends have."

"Are you telling me this won't interfere with my relationship with Isobel?"

"That's part of it. But you also have relationships with Liqiang, with Mei, and with Claudia to worry about. I'm just trying to offer some simplicity."

He laughed. "You've made it sound ridiculously complicated, but what's in that for you? — before I let you distract me with other concerns." She looked into his eyes, and her hand waved his cock — and they both laughed. He was stiff now. "It's not that simple, is it?"

"Actually, it is, almost. I love working with you; I like being with you; you have a lovely body — him included," and she waved his cock again, "and, if we stay grown-up about it, I don't have to worry about all the love crap."

"Well, as romantic propositions go…" They were both smiling as their lips moved together. His hand, resting on her hip, now slid down across her belly.

"Yes, she's still ready," she said, as his fingers moved into the small, well-tended tuft. "So we will again… but later, please. Talking when naked should be one of life's great joys — I'm not really into the fuck and snore routine. I thought we might do better than that."

"What had you envisaged?" But he let his fingers move to her clit — she was too much in control otherwise, he wanted to feel that coming together was at least a little driven by desire. And she moaned gently and opened her thighs a little, gripping his cock further now.

"Stop that, please," she said suddenly, closing her legs, but smiling at him. "I know you can be patient."

"I've been told that — and the funny thing is, it's often said as a criticism, not a compliment."

"Oh, my poor man." Her hand moved from his cock to his face and she pulled his lips onto hers again. "Aren't women terrible? We want to be overwhelmed by animals driven mad by desire, yet we want to discuss dreams with poets for hours. Is it easier with men?"

Now he laughed loud. "Yes, it is, I suppose. We're coming from the same place." She sneezed with laughter as his unintended pun caught her an instant before it occurred to him. "I didn't mean it that way." She was still giggling and the moment for serious reflection had, thankfully, passed. They settled into silence for a while. He was reflecting. He knew he was a cool lover of women; even Claudia, who didn't like speaking openly about those things, had commented on how tender he was; Isobel, invariably frank, had said, 'I'd like a really rough fuck occasionally, Alphonse' more than once — but it wasn't his way.

"So, you want to be ravaged by a wild beast, is that it?"

She looked up and kissed him again. "At the moment, I'm thrilled to be here — and more of this would be wonderful, if it's what you want. We might have little preferences we want to explore later but the most important thing for me is to be able to lie naked beside you and talk." She cuddled in closer to him, then slowly slid her hand back to his cock. "The next most important thing, though, is that you give me a good fucking occasionally, OK?"

He laughed. "Very OK!"

9

I have no idea who Conrad has invited. He usually finds an interesting mix — and we've even had the odd evening on our own. They're some way in the past now, probably when he was wondering whether our relationship should have been more than it ever became. But evenings like this, are some way in the past for me now. I get few party opportunities, so I'm curiously excited about it — and I have a large bag of carefully selected goodies with me in the taxi. And I'm carefully plucked and preened and cleaned (an explanation? Really? This is a story, not a manual) — and ready for anything. Since Alphonse has been my principal (and infrequent, it must be said) partner this last eighteen months, I'm ready for more adventurous adventures again.

Boris lets me in. Before I let him guide me to the stairs down to the basement, I ask how he's doing after last week. He seems surprised to be asked, and a little touched. "It wasn't good," he says in that thick accent of his — don't ask me, it's something central European, it sounds like bullfrogs burping. But he's a lovely, gentle man. "You see her, she better now?"

"Yes, she's home now."

"I should have done something when I see that man."

I touch his arm — I'll admit, I love to squeeze his bicep, it's astonishing, it's rock-like and my hand goes nowhere near halfway around it. "It's absolutely not your fault. There are a few people I could blame, but not you at all — and Conrad doesn't like you going down there anyway, does he?"

"No, not till party over — or when he call because guest difficult." I've seen that once or twice. You have to watch carefully: Boris is amazingly discreet, even the most boisterously out of control seem to move out very quietly. He's brought me to the door, I can hear voices from below, but only voices. Sometimes there are slaps and shrieks, but I prefer to find my way into an evening like this, so I like to arrive before the real action starts.

There are a couple in the front room — doors are always open here, of course, because Conrad had them removed, even the bathroom — and she's going down on him. They're youngish and I don't recognise them — I've been away a long time, it occurs to me again. I head for the kitchen at the back. The other rooms are empty. I see Conrad, who looks pleased to see me, detaches himself from a blonde and gives me a huge hug. "And how's my guest of honour?"

I'm slightly taken aback. I'm comfortable being prominent, but this is a surprise. Does this mean a number of different delights are available to me?

Conrad, amongst other things, is a voyeur, so he'll want to watch me playing with people — and I'm enough of a show-off to be comfortable with that. Not an exhibitionist, you notice; I think that's a rather specific kink. Just a show-off.

Suddenly Ellen comes up to me. "I thought I'd find you here," she says, and looks almost friendly — that doesn't fool me, I've been on her banned list for their events for years. Conrad has a smirk on his face. I don't know if he has a plan for her. I don't think Gerry will care enough for anything she does — or is done to her — to upset him, but it surprises me he stays so indifferent. She gets more embarrassing as time passes. They used to party together, but less and less lately — and Gerry will certainly not be here tonight. There aren't that many I recognise. In the old days it would be at least half but Conrad, bless him, has refreshed his crowd with younger people. Ellen looks more out of place than ever. She moves on quickly anyway; we share no interests. "This is Suzanne, by the way." Conrad is referring to the tall, languorous blonde who hasn't strayed far from him. He turns to her and addresses her as one might an old person or a foreigner. "This is Sadie, I've been telling you about her."

"Ah!" She nods her head with her mouth open — but then she smiles, and I'm being too harsh. "I am very happy to meet you. I think I learn from you, yes?" I'm not good at identifying accents. I can only tell you that she comes from a different place from Boris.

"What has Conrad been telling you?"

"He say you know how to treat him. I must be better."

"He's telling you to be better, or you want to be better?"

"Oh, I want to be better. I like make him happy."

Conrad is smiling benignly. This makes sense. Another reason why he and I wouldn't have worked is that, while I understand his kinks better than anyone, I think, he does seem to default to tall blondes. But it's hard for someone new to take him as far as he likes to go. That won't be until late in the evening, though; mein host will usually want to see everyone else happy first, even Ellen, I suppose — but I've no idea if he's planned anything for her, although there is a small group of brutish looking men in the corner. One of them detaches and comes over to me. "Hello, Sadie," he says. It's the man with the tongue.

"Seb!" I am very pleased to see him. "You've had more tattoos, I didn't recognise you." That has the benefit of being true, one now extends to his forehead — so I can avoid telling him that he has more forehead these days, and the adorning thatch is now more silver than bronze. "Show me the stud!" He pokes that long, fat tongue out at me. The stud tonight is a large skull. "I shall look forward to that very much."

"Me too." He smiles again at me. It's plainly his party piece; it's interfering with his speech, but I'm not going to be worrying about that. Ellen has made her way over to his friends. They are borderline ambiguous.

The leather, studs and tattoos project a gay aura, but they're not dressed for style and they look genuinely hard — and that certainly describes Seb, so it may be that Conrad has choreographed something for Ellen with them. I can't guess at what his motivation is. It's somewhere in my mind that there's a revenge plot somewhere, but I'm probably overthinking it.

An aside here: I'm bound to step in if anything non-consensual happens — yes, yes, I can be bossy like that — the difficulty comes with people like Ellen who enjoy rough trade and the violation element is part of the thrill for her. So, I let scenes play out for a while, and my burden is not usually too onerous. I wouldn't say I was a voyeur, like Conrad, but I do like to watch people enjoying themselves — and I'll join in if I think they want me, that's the difference.

Conrad observes me watching Ellen trying to break into the group of Seb's friends. "Have you organised a treat for her?" I ask. He shrugs and smiles.

There will be more stimulating sights than Ellen being rough-fucked by that quartet later — but I'll watch when the time comes.

Suzanne is addressing me. She's handed me a drink. "You like what Conrad likes?" Conrad takes the magnum with him and tells us he'll see us later. I get a grin from him — he's set me up for this, but that's OK. He'd also left me with a lingering thought at dinner — not the marriage thing, no — it was something about how he stays arms-length from his Arabs' other interests, but Gerry works with his Russians. But it's a party night. That will have to wait — and it's time to educate Suzanne.

"I like doing what he likes having done." I'm quite pleased with how I've put that, but I've puzzled her. So, to start gently, I ask, "Do you spank him?"

That was easy to understand. She nods vigorously. "Yes, yes, he like that."

"Do you like it?"

"No, no, I no like spank, I like fuck."

I'm wondering what her pimp has taught her. If Conrad's taken her under his wing, she's probably had a lucky escape. He will get bored with her quite soon, but he will also make sure she's met a few people by then and, with a little bit of enterprise, will be able to set herself up independently later. "No, I mean do you like spanking him?"

"Oh, sure, I like spank him."

"Have you always spanked men?"

"No, just Conrad, but I enjoy it."

She hasn't convinced me, so I don't need to ask the more complex questions about Conrad's enjoyment of anal play — spanking for him is no more than an hors d'oeuvre — I'll simply remain a sceptic until she shows me otherwise. These kinks need to be embedded even before your sexuality dawns, in my view. She's plainly had no curiosity — about spanking, anyway. Still, I will delve a little. "What else do you enjoy?"

"I like to suck cock — and I like lots of men. Conrad likes to watch me."

"But you enjoy it."

She is smiling. This seems genuine. "Yes. I like three at once, then I have more." I'm still suspicious there's a script being followed here, but she's a beautiful woman and some of them like to exercise control that way.

"Do you come a lot when they're fucking you?"

She giggles. "A little bit, sometimes, but I like it best when Seb lick me later."

I laugh loudly here. She looks more hurt than puzzled. I give her a hug. "Please don't be offended. I think he's spectacular too. I came three times the last time he licked me." That helps her relax, she smiles and hugs me back. I'm still worried about her, though. Typical of me; I come here for fun but I'm already Auntie Sadie, concerned for Conrad, concerned for Suzanne.

More people come in, mostly attractive, mostly younger — and most look like they're here out of conviction and not for commerce. Conrad's good like that — he's aware that some of his older friends come with professional company, but he doesn't get sniffy about it. More of them just find people to bring who are intrigued by what goes on. The majority, though, are the devotees, who've been before, and I'm seeing a few faces I recognise now, including a tall man with a very high pain threshold who makes a beeline for me.

"Dominic!" I cry joyously, hoping like fuck that I've remembered his name right.

"Sadie," he says, kissing me. "How utterly delightful. I was thrilled when Conrad said you would be here." His name was easy of course — the irony of him being called Dom when he's such a bottom, how could I have doubted my memory?

"This is Suzanne. Suzanne, this is Conrad's friend Dominic, or have you two met before?"

"Oh, no," he says, taking her hand to kiss it. "I should most certainly have remembered." His eyes lock on hers as he raises his head. She looks impressed. She should be. He's fiftyish, silver-haired, tall, slim, and stylishly dressed. But her infatuation will probably be brief when she sees her new hero writhing under my cane.

Don't get me wrong. He's attractive and charming and I will be doing exactly what he enjoys me doing. His failing, if I may call it that, is his lack of engagement with the female body. His subsequent attention to the clitoris is, at best, dutiful, more usually only perfunctory. I had a private date with him once. It was a wonderful dinner, but I only managed to come (after him, naturally) by playing with myself and thinking about somebody else. This is a frequent failing of bottoms; they're often self-obsessed and manipulative, and callous of the top's pleasures, believing we should fend for ourselves.

Even Conrad to a degree, but his voyeurism will ensure that Suzanne will have her fun — although, if he *saves his own fun until later, there may well be only the three of us left. But that's planted an evil little thought in my head. She's engaged with Dominic, all sparkly-eyed and breathy — probably already thinking of a future relationship with emotional and material benefits. I'm thinking that her cunt might be very nice to eat later, as long as she makes Conrad happy first.*

Or maybe she'll have the rough boys first — after Ellen, of course, who'll latch on to them while they're treating her with a contempt that she's actually enjoying. It's strange, she'll be domineering and dictatorial with Gerry, but likes being a whimpering slut with men who just abuse her. But kinks are kinks — and I've enjoyed rough in the past. I've just grown toppier and more controlling as I've grown older — I'll have to work out how much potential Suzanne has in that way. You need to be sensitive and empathetic to be a good top. Oh, dear, I've thought of it, so it has to get written — but you need to get to the bottom of what your partner wants.

I may be wrong, but it feels to me like she's just been following Conrad's instructions. I think that's a view Dominic is coming to as well; he's now turning to me, allowing her to escape — I think she'll do a speed date review of other people here. Conrad won't mind. He may just have auditioned her to make sure she can make a contribution to his parties. His reputation relies on these being freely playful. That's why the ambulance event the previous week will have so offended him.

But Dominic distracts me. "Will you have a space on your card for me later?" he asks, as if he's asking for a waltz.

I switch quickly to the Mistress Pain he wants to hear. "I shall expect you at the table at eleven. You were a bad boy last time and failed to attend to me correctly. You shall receive thirty — and your hands will be tied. You will not come before I finish!"

He attempts to look crestfallen but we both know this is the way he wants it. If he can persuade someone to join us, she will be told, by me, on no account to let him come before the appointed time. If he finds no one, he will expect me to wank him; I'm good with that, I'm a top, I give pleasure. And he knows he's in luck tonight, he knows my clit will have other sources of entertainment. I'll even be saving some energy for Conrad; he's no Seb with the tongue, but he is skilled and almost romantically attentive.

Now Dominic has his appointment, we're happy to separate; we neither of us wants this atmosphere of friendliness between us to persist — Mistress Pain does not cane friends. I'm briefly distracted by a small scene at the kitchen table: the hard boys, and the name is doubly appropriate, have a young woman pinned with her dress pushed to her waist and they're taking turns. She looks happy enough, even though they're handling her roughly. I think she'd like them all to come but they're not going to spoil their enjoyment. But she can tick four in the box and move on — I know, I know, are you getting used to these dreadful puns?

I tell Conrad that the women who play a numbers game don't add a lot, but he just says they're like rolls of bread at dinner. They stop the greedy feeling hungry between courses.

I find, increasingly, that I need to bring focus to evenings like this. In my younger days I could play quite indiscriminately but now I want more refined experiences. I will enjoy Dominic — I do like a tough bottom; and I've promised myself Seb, but I may draw the line at two — I want to save energy and enthusiasm for Conrad later. So, that's three encounters. It would be wrong to plan any more. I'll see what's available by way of spontaneous stimulation.

But Seb's arm is around my waist. "It's been too long," he's saying.

"I'm sure you're very much in demand," I tell him — that's true, probably; there are marginally more sensitive lickers, but his tongue is large and its ironmongery is always arousing. I don't really know if I'm ready, but I should get into the swing of this, and it's easy to let him kiss me — although the skull on his tongue, that I will soon enjoy lower down, is disconcerting in a French kiss. But it's sweet that he engages me like that. I can feel his cock thickening on my hip as his hand slides my skirt up. Yes. it's pleasant, I'm catching the mood — and he wants to make sure I am. The party's filling up, it's not obvious how we get

comfortable, but that's a lot of the fun. We don't do dignified so I'm only amused when I'm guided to the big chair and bent over the arm. It crosses my mind momentarily that I've not been bent over bare-arsed for quite a while but I open up to make sure he can access everything and I'm quickly lost in the moment. I'm soon at the edge — but this is where he's very good; the skull comes off my clit, and he lets that fat tongue slide inside me. I remember now. It was three times that once, but they were very slow and well-spaced. But I was on my special chair then, he was mostly in front of me. Never mind, I'm comfortable, I can push my arse up and he can lick everywhere. He leans back occasionally to admire me but keeps stroking: my back, my cheeks, my thighs — only occasionally brushing my clit, he's judging from my moves and sighs that I'm staying exactly on the edge. Then I feel his chest rubbing against my thighs and bum; I love it, it's very sensual, and he knows. Then his hands spread my cheeks and his tongue-tip is tingling me. He flicks the skull around the rim; oh, it's gorgeous. I've always loved it, I'll tell you more later, but right now I'm groaning, it's just delightful. I'm treasuring the moment and I'm surprised, after a while, to feel him manoeuvring and, quite quickly, his cock is in my cunt but, as he presses down on me, he whispers reassuringly, "Sweet little pussy deserves a treat. Nobody's coming yet but Mr Dick wants to let you know he loves you too."

I smile; I believe him, he's keeping a good rhythm, pushing quite deep, and he's right, I think, she does appreciate a little in-depth attention. She's very wet anyway but not unhappy when he slides out and kneels down again behind me. The tongue, and the stud in particular, slide on to my clit. I shiver, and I feel him chuckle, he knows I would quickly explode, so I'm relieved when he returns to my arse — that is the thrill where I stay best on the edge; the tingling with the thrill of more stretching, more nerve ends singing to me, my body shuddering, just controllably. There's an intense focus down there but the feelings are radiating all through me. I find myself gasping and shuddering. "I'm going to come. Do what you want. Come with me!"

My orgasm has reached inevitability. I would like him with me — but I'm still slightly surprised to feel him rise and begin to push into me. First my cunt, then I feel a quick squirt of lube and he's in my arse, pushing hard. I'm away anyway, but it's an additional thrill to feel him thrusting. There's no stopping him, he's deep and rough now, and I'm loving it. Wow, oh, wow.

He slides out slowly, then he's on his knees beside me, trying to kiss me. Very sweet, but uncomfortable. I ease myself up and we embrace. I push him into the chair, sit on his lap and wrap my arms around his neck. No conversation, it's always banal or ludicrous and he has the taste and sense to know that — then I find it's me who says, "That was a lovely fuck!" I feel ridiculous but he just hugs me. He's good, very good. Good enough not to pursue me when we disentangle a little while later.

I think about him when I'm back in the kitchen, pouring myself a drink. He's a party stalwart, is Seb, I feel quite honoured that he's let himself come. I'm sure, at his age — too much grey — that recovery times are not what they were. I don't know when he'll be able to join his mates.

I'll be fine soon, I'm pleased to say, but it's nearing eleven and my next activity won't take so much out of me. I'll wait a few minutes, of course. I need to pique Dominic's anticipation. Suzanne sidles up. She looks a little flushed, she's obviously been active — but she's taken time to repair makeup — as have I, of course. "You're seeing Dominic soon, aren't you?"

"Yes, has he asked you to help?" She nods. This is good. I'll want her to help me with Conrad too later and he'll get more out of it if we're a trained team. Yes, I'm good to him, but he deserves it. "The important thing with Dominic tonight is that I've promised him thirty so, whatever you do, whether you're sucking or wanking him, don't let him come until I give you the signal, OK?"

She nods emphatically. I'm sure she's understood and I'm glad she'll be helping. I'd like to keep that a low-pressure activity. My God! I suddenly think, has Seb taken that much out of me? Or am I getting old? Oh, for heaven's sake, Sadie, don't start doing things for reassurance, only do them for fun. But a younger couple comes up as Suzanne goes in search of Dominic. They look almost shy, that's rare in here. "Do you mind talking about the fun you were having in there?"

I smile. I almost laugh, but they want my help, obviously. It's easy to guess what he's trying to get her to do — and she looks more curious than reluctant. So, I address her. "What are you intrigued by?" She looks nervously at him. "Don't mind him, we can get him to enjoy everything, I should think." They both chuckle. "But what boundaries are you trying to push?"

He looks to her to respond. I'm not impressed but I won't jump to conclusions. "I like how it tingles when he plays with my arse, but it hurts a lot when he tries to push that thing in, so we never get that far."

I look at him. "Are you big?" Good, I have him on the defensive. "Show me!"

He hesitates. "I think he's big," she says, and hers is the only opinion that counts of course. "Show her!"

He has two women asking to look at his cock. There may be a man who could refuse that request, but I've never yet met him. He unzips and manages to wank himself quickly into a passable erection. "Oh, you are a big boy," I say. That's not the first time I've used that very serviceable lie — but it is a decent cock anyway. "I can see why there's a problem." I turn to her, "But have you played with him that way? What's your name, by the way?"

"I'm Pamela, Pam, and this is Paul — and no, I haven't."

"Because you don't want to? And I'm Sadie."

"I've just never thought of it," she says, but Paul is looking nervous.

"I'm only asking because it's best if both parties understand what's involved. He should understand how it feels and how you need to take your time getting ready. Did you watch all of Seb and me?"

They hug each other a little. "We did, we wanted to see what you were doing and how you managed."

"Well, you'll have seen how Seb spent a long time on me, making sure I was relaxed — and he has a divine tongue, it's long and thick, so he knew I could take him. And you two are right to persevere, by the way, it's thrilling if it doesn't hurt, but you, young man, need to understand the limitations. We should play with you first." There's a wicked glint in her smile, yes, this might work.

"I've never done anything like that before," he stammers. Men bring all sorts of baggage to anal play, but most enjoy it when they lose their inhibitions. Our Paul, I would guess, is going to be reluctant to lose the anal cherry quite so openly here — yes, I do have a strap-on in my bag-of-tricks.

"I'd like to help, but I think you'd like things a little quieter than the party, wouldn't you?"

He looks relieved, but she's obviously game — and disappointed.

She is more adventurous than he is.

"Look, I've promised to have fun with a friend in a minute." I look at my watch. "In fact, he's waiting now.

But I could take you upstairs later, Conrad won't mind, and we can have a little party to ourselves. How does that sound?"

Now they're both looking enthusiastic and nodding. Good. I'll enjoy that. I might even ask Seb to join us. I think our Pamela might get even more out of the adventurous agenda than her timid consort. "I'll look out for you when I've finished with Dom."

That was unnecessary. I caught sight of them watching when I was dealing with him. He was getting a little noisy, but I know what he likes, and Suzanne, bless her, seemed to be judging it perfectly, sucking once or twice but mostly gently wanking. When number thirty came down, and I did make that hard, he was ready to explode. Pushing two fingers in his arse at that point was unnecessary, but instructional, I thought, to our observing lovebirds. They both looked rapt. I studied them while feeling him pulse. Suzanne, bless her, was a trouper, she clamped her mouth on him after the first blob shot out. I think she'll have made a firm new friend this evening — as long as she doesn't take too many expectations of her own satisfaction to those encounters. I give Dom a kiss and stroke his back gently, then tell him I'll leave him with Suzanne to untie him. He nods and mouths 'thank you.' She's up beside him now and gets the message. I think that's best for everyone — you see how good tops think!

I usher Pam and Paul to the kitchen. Spanking is thirsty work and I need a drink. And I would like to tell

Conrad what I'm doing. His view, normally, is that parties are parties and people should come expecting to participate, not to hide. He purses his lips disapprovingly, when I corner him, but I remind him that he, Suzanne and I will be alone together upstairs later. Then I get that indulgent smirk of his. I don't suppose I'm the only one who elicits it, but it usually feels special. And I'll treat him well later.

I manage to catch Seb before I re-join the couple and I whisper 'front room upstairs in fifteen minutes.' I get the merest of nods. I'd see him more often if I were in London more.

"Come along, dear ones," I say, picking up my bag. She smiles at this, he looks alarmed. He'll have to do better if he's going to impress me. I really think she will be having some fun — but let's not jump to conclusions, that's the wrong approach. We're embarking on a voyage of discovery.

We passed Ellen being attended to in the main playroom, I paused briefly. I doubt whether she truly expected the double anal they had subjected her to, and I know she's never been a fan of being whipped but I discovered, in passing, that my commitment to consensuality is not absolute. Her screams were not her normal orgasmic cries — but she wasn't yelling yellow, I think she'd gone beyond that — I just, unusually, chose not to interfere. My troubled conscience will doubtless remind me of that tomorrow; for the moment, I seem to be quite disturbingly indifferent. I'm otherwise occupied anyway. I guide my young couple up the stairs and into the front room.

Conrad's front room is a huge drawing room which should be far more elegant than it is, but there are large, well-stuffed armchairs in there which will suit our purposes admirably. Paul attempts to close the door behind us. "I promise you'd regret that," I say, pulling it a little ajar again. "It's bad party etiquette and the four rough boys would certainly regard it as a provocation — and not everyone shares my commitment to the consensual." I suppose I should cross my fingers as I utter that piece of hypocrisy — but I'm focused on Pam and Paul, my new dear ones.

We stand by the big chairs. "I think it's time to shed clothing." She's quicker than he is — just as I thought. He's even quite limp. I kneel down in front of him and signal her to join me. She's perfectly relaxed about sharing his cock with me. I'm speculating that he'll be more hesitant about sharing her body with Seb later. Heh, heh, but I won't be breaching consensuality there — she'll be wanting Seb by then!

It doesn't take long, taking turns, to raise him and, with the attention of our mouths, I can appreciate why patience and lube will be necessary for what they want to do; he's not huge, but impressive, nonetheless. Still, I'm not feeling any engagement about wanting to fuck him myself — this is for them initially, I'll think about my fun later.

He's having his now. He's standing, eyes closed, and groaning. I let her suck him while I retrieve a tube from my bag, which I've dropped beside us. I think it's a smile I get from her when I squirt a large dollop on my fingers — but her mouth is rather full. "You may have to ease off," I say, "he's quite close already and finger play can push them over."

She takes her mouth off him and says, "I know it does me."

He's starting to protest but half of my finger is already inside his arse and he's caught dangling on the precipice of pleasure from which he would only very reluctantly retreat. She's wanking him, feeling how stiff he is — it's quite visible to me — and I push a second finger in while retrieving a toy with my other hand. It's a useful device, a plug with graded beads. I hold it beside his cock. "Look, Paul, you'll try this first, just to appreciate what you're expecting from Pam later. We'll want to see you take the whole thing before we set you free on her with that huge cock of yours."

The interesting thing for me here is how much interest she shows in playing with him. She's a pretty woman and clearly adventurous but she may be a little bottomy to apply herself properly to his pleasures. We could be more than doubling their pleasure in each other if they can open themselves up.

I'm beginning to get hopeful about him. He's pushing back on to my fingers, clearly enjoying the sensation — as most of them do, of course.

"I want you over the arm of the chair now, Paul."

"You're not going to cane me as well, are you?" He tries to sound jovial, but I could tell, when he was watching me with Dominic, that there was more consternation than intrigue. She, on the other hand... well, maybe we'll come back to that. For the moment it feels like it's time for Auntie Sadie's consensuality talk. I stand up and motion her to do the same and we're having a very pleasant group hug. I slide my fingers out but she continues to keep him hard with her hand. "We'll be doing nothing that you two don't want to do, but I feel quite encouraged that you'll open yourselves up to some new pleasures." I look to her. "Does he spank you?"

She smiles. "He slaps my bum sometimes when I'm sat on him. I like it, but I also like the way he plays with his fingers."

"Well, I think he liked me playing with my fingers."

He twitches, but then relaxes. "You're right, of course."

"That's all we're doing next, fingers and the toy. Are you ready to lie on the arm?"

He's still hovering, looking at each of us in turn before muttering, "Let's try."

We take turns with fingers — I keep refreshing the lube — and the other one holds his cock in turn. He's relaxing and I can tell from his movements and his stiffness how turned on he is. "We'll have to go easy on him, he's close."

She smiles and nods. "I know."

"You should try the toy now." I hand it to her. "Just go slowly. He should manage it all, but he can say 'yellow' if it starts to get too much."

"Do we give up then?" he asks, his head still buried in the seat of the chair.

"Of course not," I say — they both want this to work, I think. "We just go a little more slowly. You're in good hands."

He's squeaking in a little pain before she has the last bulb in, so I take over. In most cases it's just about patience — patience and lube. It takes me a while, but he's very clearly thrilled when he's not screeching. I tell her to leave his cock — there's still a danger he might come on his own from just the plug.

But he reaches for his own cock when we leave him. "I wouldn't do that," I say quite sharply. "It's not going to help you with Pam if you come on your own now." He pulls his hand away quickly. "Good man," I tell him and ease the plug out, wiping it carefully. "You've done very well, but remember, you're hoping she'll take a lot more than that. I'm here to make sure you go gently — or I'll make you take the strap-on I have with me, just to show you what the real thing's like. Ah, Seb, glad you could make it." Seb has stepped in quietly. For a moment Paul looks horrified and stands up rapidly covering his stiff cock with his hands. Pam looks puzzled, but pleased.

"Seb, my dear man, Pam and Paul here were intrigued by what we got up to and I'm trying to help them. I'm trying to teach Paul how to get her ready, to help her relax, and I just thought you could give the best demonstration of how he should do that."

"You want him to…" splutters Paul.

"Did you mind me sucking your cock just now?" I'm teasing him, but I'm right, of course. "Should we ask Pam how she feels — and Seb too?"

I appreciate there's an element of coercion here, but Paul could always say no. Pam isn't going to. She's seen how I was reacting to Seb's ministrations earlier. And Seb, I can tell from the smile and the bulge, is very keen to help.

"You sit on the chair, Paul, if you're lucky she might suck your cock while Seb's licking her. Don't come though, or Seb might have to do your job later." Oh, the poor man, he's so torn, but this could be the making of him as a lover. I think that's the least she deserves. You're right, I'm more impressed by her than him — but we'll help them both.

And she's already smiling at Seb and bending over the chair arm. He tries to stay cool but he's kneeling between her legs pretty quickly. She's quite tall and, as she pushes her arse up high, she gives every access to him. I catch a glimpse of how wet she is just before his face docks on to her cunt and she's soon sighing very deeply. I'm guessing the young lady will be able to come quite often, so I'm not going to worry about her.

Paul is looking a little piqued but, distracted as she is, she does take hold of him and stiffen him up again. I lend a hand. He'll learn later to enjoy all this, but we'll pander to him until he does. Meantime she's obviously finding Seb's attentions heavenly. He's a pro, though, I think he'll keep her calm enough to let her make a decent job of sucking Paul while she's enjoying his tongue — and they do seem to work a rhythm out. I can slowly withdraw and just watch.

Sometimes now Seb leans back a little to enjoy the view — thank you, Seb, now I can see too. It's very pretty: perfect, flawless cheeks and very neat labia and a beautiful, tightly puckered little pink arsehole. It opens a little as he stretches her cheeks and starts to rim her with his tongue. I slide a finger up on to her clit while his hands stretch her. In a while his tongue, pushing further in, will give her all the stimulation she needs — she does seem delightfully excitable and I withdraw quickly. Seb now has to pull back just to stop her coming. She's alternately gasping and taking Paul deeper. I don't think he'll last long. It's often the way, when men get over their inhibition about watching their woman being fucked, they get very excited by it. Of course, in the aftermath, it can have disastrous consequences but that's up to them. Seb looks to me for guidance, bless him. I nod. He moves his tongue back to her clit and she's obviously getting ready. This is where he goes very carefully, he kneels up and dribbles lots of saliva into her gaping bumhole and begins to push that fat tongue in — his bearded chin will be tickling her cunt — that's gorgeous, it's what I was getting earlier. She's making extraordinary noises with Paul's cock deep in her throat and he's very close to coming - and then there they are, coming together in noisy ecstasy before spending ages on the down-slope of their pinnacle.

Paul eventually slumps, but she still has her arse pushed high and is moaning. This really is where we girls have a better time. I get a wicked smile from Seb and I hand him some lube. Paul's head has lolled back and his eyes are closed. I get a surprised sidelong glance from her when she feels the cold lube on her bum. I nod and she gives me a huge smile.

Seb is not huge, this should be OK, but he's enjoying some finger playtime with her anyway, slowly pushing more fingers in while his pinkie keeps her clit amused. She is unquestionably ready again and pushing up to get more of him.

She's still stroking Paul's softening cock, but I think this is just a distraction mechanism. I stretch her cheeks apart as Seb, condom now in place, pushes slowly into her arse having first, politely, pushed his cock briefly into her cunt — he's such a gentleman! As he breaches her arse, we get some gasps but they're only from apprehension. She's not pulling away at all, she's pushing back even.

This is a first for her then, if what they told me was true, and I don't want her too sore for when Paul does recover — and nothing is more certain than that he'll want her arse later — so I slide a finger onto her clit and manage to tickle Seb's balls — or he'll take too long — why wouldn't he, he's obviously having a wonderful time now, pushing deeper and deeper as her gasps are becoming more guttural. That makes Paul's eyes open and he's suddenly aware of what's happening but the two of them are already coming. I try to give him a soothing look, but the others are now completely indifferent to him and shuddering violently. I move and take hold of Paul's cock. His spasms of jealousy are being deflected by new spasms of lust, his cock is rising again: 'well done, young man,' I think.

"You're a big boy, Paul," and I really am not lying, "you needed her relaxed — and now you'll be able to go very slowly." She's gasping more slowly and is kissing Paul's chest tenderly. I think she knows what's going to happen — but I also think she wants more — ah, those were the days.

Seb is still kissing and stroking her cheeks and lower back but he looks up. "Do you need me — and I do mean just you."

"You lovely man," I say, "I'll catch you later." He understands I need to be left with these two.

"Come on, Paul, that was just a small cock in a condom, she needs the real thing big time now." I hear Seb chuckle and I get the bird from him as he leaves the room. "Come round here!"

She wriggles, adjusting herself, offering him that gorgeous view of her little pink hole, glistening with lube and completely closed again. I squirt more lube on and push two fingers in, enjoying her sighing as she welcomes me. I'm reassuring myself she can take all of him, but I am enjoying the playtime enormously — maybe I'll top her sometime, but that's not tonight's priority. More lube and I have four fingers in her. She's going to be fine — if she doesn't come on my hand first — and Paul is thrilled by watching this. He's very ready. "Go slowly now." I look up at him, smiling. I get a nod of thanks, (he doesn't fool me, I know they'll have a difficult, emotional day tomorrow, but they'll have much more enjoyable lives if they get through this. Well, he will. She will, anyway, I think).

This time her gasps are a little different. She's not pushing back. "Careful, careful," she gasps. I swear I can see his cock grow when he hears that — at any event there's a little wicked smile at the edge of the serious, pre-orgasmic look.

I squirt more lube on his cock on the out-stroke. This is his second coming, it could be quite slow, she could be a sore lady tomorrow — but I'm sure she'll wake with a smile. But I don't want it to be too difficult for her. "You're a very lucky man tonight, Paul." I let him see me squirting lube on my black beaded plug. "Luckier than the mad Marquis."

He only nods and pushes deeper. It's probably the best fuck of his life so far. And her noises reassure me that it's also hers. I slide the plug into him — not deep, but I get a sigh from him and a screech from her as he thrusts himself deeper. "Easy, easy," she gasps, but she's sighing deeply.

I let them move a while and find their rhythm. This is lovely, maybe they will be good together — and even I begin to wonder if I'm becoming more of a voyeur, watching this decent cock pushing deeper into this beautiful arse. But I remember my responsibilities. They're going to want to do this by themselves tomorrow. I don't want her too sore to enjoy that, so I slide my fingers to her clit again and push the plug more firmly into him until I'm sure the train is coming. If I get this right, I'll have them both coming together. Gosh, there's a lot of him and he is pushing harder — and she's obviously on the edge of discomfort, but now she's pushing back at him. That's perfect! They're going to get there at the same time and they're screaming. It's wonderful. Out of the corner of my eye I see Conrad poke his head round the door. I get a big smile from him and he retreats immediately. These two go on for ages, him pumping and pumping, her gasping and wanting more. Wow, this is becoming improbable but even they reach a point where they begin to subside, and I can ease myself out from between them. He slumps on her, kissing her back and shoulders. I throw my stuff into my bag, pull my dress on quickly, kiss each of them on the available shoulders and whisper, "Cuddle in the chair for a while, no one will disturb you."

I know where the real bathrooms are. It's time for a shower and a reboot!

I feel very refreshed when I come down later. I pass a distraught-looking Ellen heading for the front door. She's walking awkwardly. I say nothing — even if I were genuinely solicitous (and obviously I'm not), anything I said would be regarded as sarcastic — but I do get a hateful glare anyway. I attempt to have no feelings. Certainly, regret at her going would not be one of them.

I look in on my lovebirds. They have stirred from their armchair embrace and are dressing slowly, touching and kissing all the time. Pam motions me towards them. "We want to say thank you." She's smiling. His expression is more ambiguous, but he is hugging her.

"You have a wonderful woman there, Paul, but if she'll let you play, I'm interested." He looks a little reassured. "Although, if I'm honest, I'd be more interested in a threesome." That's caught them both out. "You and I are both tops, really, and she's a bottom, she's wonderful for either of us/" I turn to her. "Unless the gay thing freaks you out." She shakes her head and smiles.

"Gay freaks me out," he says, gruffly. I thought so — he's too straight to fully enjoy her.

"I don't think you'd mind me kissing her while I'm sat on your cock and she's sat on your face." I'm saying it friendly, but I know he's feeling awkward. She isn't. Now I'm feeling a little sorry — for her, not him. There's a pause, she's waiting to gauge where his mind is. "I'm hoping tonight opens up a richer sex life for you," I say.

"You came to me, remember. I know you'll feel a little awkward when you talk it all through tonight, but you can give me a call if you want." I pull out a card and put it in his pocket. That will help him feel in control, but it's really only her I would have any long-term interest in. I can leave them now — we hug, perfunctory from him, eager from her — and I say 'bye' and make my exit. I have other things to attend to, my own pleasure included.

I'm a top for Conrad; I get an enormous amount of fun out of that. We'll wait, though, until everything is quiet. There's still a lot of activity — and people are having fun. On the big bed I see Suzanne keeping at least three people happy — she has a lithe and flexible body, and an eager mouth, apparently. That girl will do well.

I find Seb in the kitchen with one of his mates. I get a big grin. "This is Alfie." I shake hands. Alfie looks big and hard, but he has a lovely smile and a soft voice.

"Didn't I see you pleasuring the older lady earlier?" I think I can single Ellen out with that rather catty description. He knows who I mean, of course.

"Tell me about it," he says, but he's still smiling. "He was supposed to be in on it," he jerks his thumb at Seb, "but I think you gave him the goodies."

"But you were attracted to that beautiful older woman?"

"I'd rather have been in the queue behind him, but we'd been a bit set up and the old..." then he remembers

he's a gentleman, "but Conrad had asked us to keep Ellen happy." Just as I thought. "He said she was wild and we like to please. Mind you, I'm not that keen on double-entry. I think she found out that she wasn't either. We'd been warned she screamed, so we didn't think too much of it. She could have said 'yellow', " he mumbled. "It's hard to judge when women want rough." I try to look sympathetic, but you know my views; tops have to read situations. But it was only Ellen. "Anyway, Freddie's good with things like that, he checked her out and patched her up. He has charm and a soft touch — he has to have that, he's the one that loves whipping. I'm not sure she was as keen as Conrad made out she was"

"Was he the one with you? Or the one in her mouth?"

"He was with me. He's a big boy too. It was very tight. Arthur was in her mouth. He's not happy. It was only when she bit him that we knew we had a problem."

I'm keeping a straight face — but it is hard, especially with Seb smirking.

Just then Conrad sidles up to us. He's tut-tutting — but no one's taking him seriously. "Thank you, boys, anyway. I'm sorry she left you up in the air." I'm getting one of his long stares. "You may find though that Sadie's a more fun proposition." And yes, I'm instantly attracted to the idea. OK, I had fun with Seb earlier but with Pam and Paul — and with Conrad later — I've been organising other people's fun. And these boys appeal, well, the two I've got to know do.

I look up at them — these are big men — and it's a long time since I had a really good gangbang. Yes, thank you, Conrad. That will do nicely. I take Alfie's hand and tell Seb to round up the others and to meet us on the big bed. I'm ready for this.

10

Claudia and Peter were having a quiet morning. They'd caught up on each of their weeks over dinner the evening before, and he was using the excuse of leaving at lunchtime to organise his luggage. It was a task that took only minutes but, just as she'd gone downstairs to get breakfast, it was an excuse to avoid two bodies becoming entangled and feeling that an attempt at passion was an obligation. Claudia loved him, but it had been months since anything physical had happened — she didn't think he felt desire — and she knew she didn't.

"I'm surprised you're not calling in on the Vietnam launch while you're out there." She was pouring his tea at the breakfast table.

He grimaced. "It would be two days added to the itinerary, I can't cut the Chinese leg short, and I'd rather get back home for the weekend."

"I'm glad you'll do that." And she meant it. There was warmth between them that hardly varied, he was a lovely man, still very attractive — just not in the old physical way for her — and even at their best they'd been more playful than passionate.

"What time is Isobel coming? Will I see her?"

"You might; we've just said lunch, not a specific time."

He tried to look annoyed. "Yes, and my driver is your chef. Why does Hannes choose you as his Sunday duty?"

"Because he'd rather cook for two appreciative ladies than take a grumpy old man to Heathrow. When's your car coming?"

"One."

"She'll probably come early to catch you and prompt you into being as lavish on the whole house as you were with the bedroom. She thinks I'll drastically curtail her budget. She knows she could charm the ingots from your vault."

"I don't want to skimp…"

"Oh, listen to you." She stood up, leaned towards him and kissed him. His hand slowly stroked her bottom. She moved closer to him, her hands on his shoulders. "We can go back to bed, you know."

He lowered his hand and looked uncomfortably away. "It would feel like a rush." He hesitated. "I thought, maybe next weekend…" He still wasn't looking at her.

She sat down and took his hand. "I love you, you know, but the house is full of yoof next weekend, or had you forgotten?" He groaned, but good-naturedly. "Are you rethinking Vietnam now?"

He laughed. "No, I like it when their friends are around. Although we'll keep the cellar locked this time."

They were lucky Andreas had had the forethought to stow all the old kinky equipment away when the children began to stay over more often. Abbi had been worldly enough at twenty to guess that the cellar had darker purposes than a mere storage space, but had seemed content with Claudia's explanation that the previous owner had lived an interesting life. Her sly 'so Peter left it untouched for twelve years before you moved in,' had prompted only a complicit sly smile from her mother. If anything, it seemed to make Abbi more relaxed with Peter, now she'd discovered he had a colourful, even dark, side. She asked no more about the place. At least she was fair enough to grant the oldies the same freedom that she now demanded for her own affairs.

Isobel arrived at twelve, saying, "Ah, I hoped I might just catch you," quite brazenly to Peter as he embraced her in the hall.

"Oh, no, you don't, madam," he said jovially. "I know your game, and I'm putty for you. It's the boss's project." He nodded towards Claudia.

"Actually, I can't accept that," Isobel said seriously, which had Peter looking as startled as Claudia felt. "Don't worry, my little frightened rabbits, but could we have ten minutes together now, while you're both here?" She was cheery again now, but still seemed earnest, so they both nodded.

"Library?" said Claudia. "Hannes is busy out in the kitchen and he's laying the table in the garden room for us. We'll enjoy the spring sunshine with lunch."

They sat down on the opposing library chesterfields, with Claudia remembering her fateful conversation with Peter all those years ago on the sofa they now, once again, occupied together. "I'm sorry to come over all formal about this," Isobel said, "but this is a project for you both, or it's not a project at all. Now, after our time in the bedroom, Mr D, I have a good appreciation of your tastes, so I'm quite happy drawing up schemes with Claudia as long as I have your commitment that we three review them together before any physical work is commissioned. Are you both OK with that?" They looked at each other. It seemed so obviously sensible to Claudia, and Peter seemed happy that the point had been stressed. He was nodding. Isobel looked at her watch. "Twelve-twenty on April the fourteenth, we have committed to a tripartite sign-off when plans have been drawn up." She slapped her hand theatrically on the gavel of the sofa arm, saying, "Done!"

And Claudia was glad; it felt like an important, and belated, step forward. It would help spending time together here easier if Yvonne's ghost were no longer resident. Probably.

"Another point we don't have to fix now, but I would like a guide figure, is budget. My health warning is that you will get what you say. I won't come back with a scheme that needs twice what you nominate. So, if you say one million, I won't come back with a scheme that costs twice that."

Claudia was startled. She knew the question was out there but had somehow assumed they would come at it more gently. And not arrive at a figure like that.

Peter wasn't looking startled, merely reflective. "I'm going to ask you to review the paintings we own as part of the project. Andreas has the catalogue. You should think about what would integrate well here in your new scheme."

"The Georgia O'Keeffe will be staying, I can promise you that, and," now she was smiling slyly at Peter, "it would be wrong to locate such prestigious masterpieces into some low-budget makeover, wouldn't it?" Claudia found herself shaking her head at Isobel, but smiling nonetheless.

"Agreed. I'm also very happy with the layout of the house," said Peter, "but all the bathrooms, except ours, need renovating. Is that fair?"

"Yes, but will you let me look at the kitchen, utility, and breakfast space? I think that's always going to be the hub, the beating heart of the home, and it needs to work for you all, including Hannes. But, apart from that, I love the proportions of this place."

"Good, then I'm happy looking at the higher number you were just discussing."

Claudia was speechless. Even Isobel was briefly silent, but only briefly, "So, we're saying schemes with new bathrooms up to two million, plus structural changes around the kitchen."

Peter's laugh bellowed around the quiet space. "I meant two including any structural changes, but let's say you've negotiated me up."

Isobel had an irritatingly satisfied grin on her face. The bitch has just doubled her budget anyway, thought Claudia with wry amusement — and a little admiration. Then she herself moved her mind quickly on from it being their money being spent to being her project for a transformation.

"It's not too early for a celebratory drink, I think," said Peter. "Shall we go and disturb Hannes's preparations?" He stood to guide them through to the garden room, which felt fresh as the spring air wafted in from the sunny blossoming greenery through the open doors.

Isobel stood in the doorway and turned around to get all perspectives. "I try to soak in as much as possible before I let any ideas form, but I am so excited by this already. Oh, I will be involving Merle McKenzie, by the way. Will that cause any problems? I just think you should have someone in the time zone for whenever anything concerns you."

Peter looked blankly at her. "That's Will's Merle, darling," said Claudia, "before he met Martha."

"Oh," said Peter, nodding without apparently comprehending, until another idea plainly caught him, and he looked to Isobel. "But weren't you and he close for a time?"

Isobel laughed ruefully. "Well, we were, and I think we still are, as you saw at Morkuda, but we're completely respectable now. And the bastard doesn't even make his phone calls monthly — and when he does call, it's only to tell me that my Far East accounts are in order."

Peter smiled. "Yes, I do see those. You're doing very well, aren't you? I'm surprised you've got time for jaunts back here."

"It's not really a jaunt," said Isobel, as her face clouded. "I've had a little crisis blow up here."

"Forgive me," said Peter, "I put that clumsily." But Claudia knew that trick of his, a provocative question concealed as bumbling. "If you're missing the Phoruc launch, it must be important. I know Alphonse wanted you there."

"Oh, I think Allen Chou Li has his needs covered." Isobel was smiling again, recovered from what she'd taken as a jibe, thought Claudia.

"So, what blew up here? Am I allowed to ask? I'm guessing there's a personal element to it. I'm only doing China and Japan this week because there are people issues. Anything else can be managed with phone calls and emails, but the people aspects need face-to-face communication. Am I prying too much? These are the things that bring colour to our business lives, we should relish these painful inconveniences, they remind us we're human. Cheers!"

Hannes had brought champagne to them. Isobel still looked uncomfortable — and Claudia felt that way too. She'd never quite got used to Peter's tactics for getting people to talk, but was usually surprised, nevertheless, at how effective they were.

"You're right, of course. It affected my biggest UK client, but there were people aspects to it."

"And your biggest client?"

"I do mean just here. Globally, it's Alphonse, of course, which means it's you." Peter waved a polite but dismissive hand. "But here it's a man called Gerry Calvert. Have you heard of him?"

Peter nodded slowly. "I've crossed swords with him in the past, but the businesses don't overlap any more." He turned to Claudia. "He's been to one or two parties here in the old days."

"I assume you're talking cellar parties."

Peter had a serious face. "Yes, but I stopped inviting him." He turned back to Isobel. "If you need help with your problem, don't hesitate to ask. I would guess it has some unpleasant elements to it."

Isobel seemed to relax. "I think it's under control, but thank you for the offer. And you are in the right area."

"Are you going to enlighten me?" Claudia directed her question to Peter.

"Me?"

"Yes, you. What have you got to tell us? I have you for five more minutes. I have Isobel, the rest of the champagne, and all afternoon."

He chuckled briefly, but then looked serious again, looking at Isobel. "Gerry likes to think he's a player, but he's just a sadist. Only his own fun is important to him." And the two of them were nodding knowingly to each other.

But Isobel brightened quickly. "No need for an instant decision, but I'm assuming the cellar won't be returning to its original purpose…" She looked to each of them. Claudia felt embarrassed, but it was a valid question.

"No, that was a different phase of life," said Peter, untroubled.

Isobel smiled wickedly. "Don't worry. I've developed a real talent for designing furniture with a subtle second purpose."

Peter looked intrigued. Claudia's embarrassment rose further but now Isobel was laughing at her — and then cuddling her. "Look, I don't think he knows anything about it, but the chaise in your bedroom will give you some opportunities for adventure. I made the outrageous assumption that your life together was not all vanilla. Anyway, cellar to a funky games and party room to make this place a draw for your kids' friends?" She waited for them both to nod. Claudia looked to Peter, hoping he would like the idea.

"Fantastic, exactly what it needs."

"And, when you've investigated the chaise together, you can let me know if you would like similar pieces elsewhere." She was chortling, Peter was smiling — and

Claudia knew that her embarrassment was finally colouring her face, which turned Isobel's response into an earthy chuckle.

Peter didn't help. "You've now made it even harder to leave, but leave I must." He hugged Isobel warmly, but his kiss for Claudia was almost passionate — long enough anyway for her to overcome her surprise and respond.

Now she was a little more sorry to see him leave. Perhaps next weekend, after all… in the privacy of their bedroom.

Hannes came back in as soon as Peter had disappeared and topped up their glasses. "I can be ready soon," he said, "but it's designed to let you be leisurely."

"Leisurely is good…" said Claudia, looking for Isobel to nod, which she did emphatically, and they settled in the big chairs by the doorway.

"I want to find out more about you," said Isobel, before Claudia had even settled. "I'll come back in the week, if I may, and I'll bring Merle with me. I can take pictures and measurements then. I'll make contact with Andreas?" She looked for confirmation. "He's the man I liaised with on the bedroom project, isn't that his name?"

"Yes, Andreas," said Claudia, wondering how much Andreas knew about the secrets of the chaise — still, if even Peter hadn't been told…

"I'll get building plans from him. But I want to get to understand what you have a taste for — what sort of environment you want to live in — where you sit on the cool minimalist to sumptuous traditionalist spectrum, for example. So, I'm going to make you do something very uncomfortable this afternoon." And there was Isobel's wicked grin. "I'm going to make you talk about yourself. All of it… and I shall know when you're cheating." She paused. "But you don't do that very much, do you?"

"No, I don't," said Claudia, and that was mostly true.

"I'll be straightforward with you, too. I do listen to a lot about you, but you can't possibly be as good as he thinks you are."

"Good? Are we talking about Alphonse?"

"Yes, and I used that hopelessly ambiguous word 'good' deliberately. But he adores you, that was one of the first things he ever said to me."

"How is he?" she asked — but regretted it immediately. She was asking a woman who shared his bed occasionally.

"He's fine, but he misses you. I think you're both a bit too honourable to make your lives more complicated — but that's part of what you love about each other. Anyway, there's much more to Claudia Brodie than a frustrated love for a gay man in Hong Kong. Tell me where you grew up, and how."

And that story took them though the meal and on to coffee. There were several hesitations, Claudia was very uncomfortable talking about herself, but Isobel's good-natured promptings kept her going.

And they were back in the easy chairs again, enjoying the air and the birdsong from the garden, by the time she got to her 'meeting Peter' story. Hannes had cleared everything away and was discreetly absent, having put two tulip glasses of grappa beside their coffee. "I don't know about this on top of champagne and red wine," she said, but Claudia was feeling pleasantly relaxed.

"I thought we were just getting to the interesting bit." Isobel raised the small glass. "You were just arriving at your first naughty party. I'd assumed you must have seen the cellar in action. How active were you?" Now she got Isobel's gimlet glare — and then her laugh. "I'm sorry, my dear, but your face! Shall I say a little about me, so you know that I'm unshockable — and that I've tried almost everything anyway?"

"I think I'd be very happy to have the spotlight somewhere else for a while anyway, please." It would be a relief — and she wanted to know more about this woman who was at least keeping Alphonse a little content.

She'd known that Isobel's life must be very colourful, but to date she'd had only snapshots, from the Morkuda events a while ago, and from Alphonse's conversations when he thought he was being reassuring by telling her what a free spirit Isobel was. That hadn't helped at all, of course. You could get more jealous of a free spirit than about someone clinging — she knew Alphonse would have dealt with that easily, after all. That had been his biggest problem with Liqiang — she'd known Alphonse had loved him, but knew he wouldn't allow himself to be tied down.

"I mostly top, and I'm mostly straight, but I'm not so committed that I stick with either of those things. I'm going to guess that you're straight…"

"As a die, I'm afraid." That was a little unlike herself, thought Claudia, but wine and engaging company — and, well, no girl's talk for a long time.

"But you're a bottom, if I'm not mistaken."

"Yes, that's something I was surprised to learn. I guess the love of my life was teaching me that, but Peter encouraged me to be much freer with my instincts — and I was, and had a wonderful time for a while."

"And now, only this…" Isobel gestured around the house — and they were both snorting with giggles.

"I know, I feel like such an ingrate."

"But you love him."

"I do, but I expected that to mean monogamy — but I wasn't even that with Jack. I mean, I thought I was in my heart, but even then, I had these strange feelings for Alphonse — and I was also being much more adventurous than I'd ever thought I could be. Even Jack organised a group for me, which was spectacular."

"Was that why it fell apart? A lot of men can't cope. They're not careful about what they wish for."

"No, no, it wasn't that. I still think it was a poisonous mix of pride and misunderstanding — and we went our separate ways."

"Are you in touch?"

"Indirectly, yes, there are business connections. His new partner works for us. I like her — and she's very good — so now I can't avoid knowing how the bastard is." She laughed, but it was hollow.

"Would it have worked? I was in love with Will, not that I realised it at the time, but what I did realise was that we weren't suited, however wonderful I think he is. He's very happy now, isn't he, and she's well-matched to him. I have the picture of a very capable, even powerful, woman, with quite a narrow, well-defined kink."

"That's Martha exactly, and I love her, but she'd been a play partner of Jack's in Singapore before I met her."

"Wow, I have to tell you I'm hearing regrets. Does he still have his tentacles around your heart?"

"No, not really; well, maybe a little, like Will does around yours. But what about you and relationships, or is it all just play?"

"I call them arrangements — that's a friendship where other things happen — and that works for me mostly. Well, I thought that's what I had with Will, but I found I wasn't being honest with myself. But it's certainly what I have with our mutual friend — but your relationship with him isn't so simple, is it? Am I a real problem for you? I wouldn't want to be. It's not why I see him, but I am hoping I'm helping. He's very self-sufficient generally, but I like to be there when he needs company." Now Isobel was laughing quietly to herself.

"You are going to have to explain yourself. What's funny?"

"I'm being unfair. He's perfectly lovely, he's everything a lover should be, considerate, attentive, and very skilled — and with a lovely body." She paused expectantly, eyebrows raised. "Recognising the picture?"

"Is this where vanilla gets mentioned?" Isobel was nodding. "Well, to defend him, I have been involved in a mini-orgy with him on Peter's old boat, but you're right, he's normally just indescribably sweet." Now she knew she was looking rueful. "But it's a long time since Morkuda."

"And you've no one else."

"Good Lord, no." Then she snorted. "I'm sorry, it's ridiculous to be so dismissive about that."

"Especially since you've just admitted to enjoying at least two gang bangs."

"It sounds terrible when you put it like that. There has been far too much alcohol drunk today, Miss Allen. But I have to say, I'm glad. Now can you show me how the chaise works?"

11

It was the perfect way to wake up, thought Alphonse. She was still there but obviously preparing to leave. He could hear the shower running in the bathroom. She'd slept sweetly beside him; he'd been dreamily aware of her embrace sometimes through the night — just as he'd enjoyed fondling her skin in his half-waking moments, and now it was… After six, when he looked at the bedside clock. He was nervous about the impending day, with the additional discomfort of having no clear tasks for the morning ahead — no one would arrive before lunchtime.

Suddenly she was sat on the bed beside him, wearing the cotton bathrobe, her half-dried hair tousled, face naked of make-up. It made him realise how artfully subtle she was in preparing her normal look for the day — but it was still a sweet face, and she seemed entirely comfortable to be with him undecorated. "I won't escape Raymond's technology, you know. Does he tease you about who comes to your room?"

"No, he doesn't tease me. I have nothing to hide…"

"So, Mrs Brodie's visits in Morkuda?"

He laughed. "Is nothing sacred? I know he knows, he just doesn't tease me, though."

"And me being here?"

"He will probably let me know he knows." He thought a moment. "And, if he's worried, he'll probably tell me how many attempts Lijun made to contact you in the night. Are you worried about that? He obviously still wants you, you know that."

Her face was suddenly serious. "He wants me for two reasons: one, he doesn't have an alternative, apart from his own right hand; and two, he can't have me. Ah, the chivalry of men's desires!" But now she was smiling again. "I have one question for you."

"Yes," he said tentatively, not knowing what was coming.

She pulled the duvet down, bent down quickly and kissed his sleeping cock. "I woke at five and was tempted to have him again, but I thought I should let you sleep…"

"I appreciate that… I think. And your question?"

"May I have him tonight?"

"I think he'd like that very much." He pulled the duvet back up, aware that his cock was now beginning to grow.

She laughed. "He would always like that, of course he would, but I'm asking you." She held his gaze.

He sat up and kissed her lips. "I should like that very much." Then he hesitated. "But will you text before you come?"

"Ah." She smiled knowingly. "You think you might get a better offer?"

It wasn't said in a challenging way. "No, it's not that. But, with Lee arriving this evening, I might…"

She leaned forward and kissed him. "I'm teasing. Of course, I'll make sure you're free. I can always have Lijun."

"Oh, he's probably arranging to have a younger model flown in anyway now."

She suddenly looked pensive. "You're almost certainly right. 'Many a true word,' don't you say?"

He reached for her hand. "I would love you to be here tonight, please."

"That's settled, then. Now," she stood up, threw her cotton robe off, and twirled around, "you get one last admiring look at my peachy little bum," she twitched it at him, "and then you do your homework." She was slipping on her dress — no underwear. "Allen Chou Li has some important clients arriving today. The charming and urbane Mr Newman needs to know their names and their businesses. All in the files I've sent you, with photos — mind you, they all look like criminals in those." Then he got her charming little laugh, barely more than a giggle. "Still, many of them probably are."

"I'll do my work," he said, affecting weariness, "and Mei's file's even bigger, but…" He nodded to the armchair on which a bra and panties were still carelessly draped.

She smiled at him. "You can put them in your laundry please, and Raymond's cameras aren't going to pick up that I'm naked under this." But then she turned round quickly, lifted the skirt up, and flashed her arse at him. "Unless I do this, of course." And it was such a sweetly incongruous gesture from this normally so serious woman that he laughed.

Then she was quickly gone. Yes, he had work to do, but he caught himself already looking forward to the evening and, pulling the duvet back, his body was growing enthusiastic too.

***

He'd been serious about Mei's file being thicker, but he'd met more of the people. There were some, as Daiyu had said, seriously unflattering photos but, in the main, he felt comfortable he'd retained names and faces — and the relevant property projects — getting those wrong would be almost as embarrassing, as well as commercially inept.

Daiyu's clients were less relevant for him in business terms, but he found himself studying hard — in order to please her, it dawned on him.

But there would also be a large number of normal guests that Raymond had targeted. They could have filled the place for the week, they'd run excellent publicity campaigns and offered good deals to the Psamathe customer base, but he'd agreed with Raymond and Teddy that they would ramp up slowly to let the staff get up to speed. There would be some travel writers through the week, but that was never as hard as dealing with the property press. They would all write glorious puff pieces — provided they were convinced the place would deliver on the promises they would make on its behalf. And Alphonse, moving though his gloriously opulent villa, felt entirely convinced that it would.

Business began at lunch time. They'd given the main meeting room over to displays of resort photos and plans of future designs. This was Daiyu's half, and they'd given another half to Lijun, who was showcasing not just his resort designs but also several construction projects, some of which were for the Senlin group — Mei's and Alphonse's customers.

Mei, Daiyu and Lijun would funnel their contacts in to meet Alphonse, who would then chat briefly to them on the sheltered terrace outside. If they warranted a longer conversation, he would invite them to sit — and one of Teddy's staff would immediately appear and offer drinks. It worked very smoothly but, by five o'clock, it was beginning to become wearing and he was hoping for a brief break when he ushered the latest of Daiyu's guests off to his room with his wife — but he found himself suddenly face to face with Lee — Shen Liqiang.

It was a shock, especially as Lee was so stony-faced. No parting was easy, but he'd convinced himself theirs had been civilised. But now… not even a handshake.

"Am I spoiling your party?" At least it wasn't hostile.

"No, of course not. I'm delighted you could make it." He got a very sceptical frown from Lee. "No, really, I know how much it meant to you, how much you put into it. What do you think?" He gestured around but, when he turned back, Lee was still looking straight at him.

"Do you have many other people to see now?"

"Maybe, but what's up? I've done enough to keep Mei and Lijun happy. I can leave now." He was aware that he'd omitted Daiyu's name out of some strange feelings left over from the previous night. "Do you want to talk?"

"We have to," he said ominously. "Can we go to your room?"

"Of course, but I'll warn you, I'm in the main villa — just to show the place off to the important guests, you understand."

Lee's half-smile was wan, barely even polite. This was obviously serious, and probably beyond personal, which had been Alphonse's initial dread.

The butler was in place when they got to the villa. They agreed on gins.

"We need an hour, Harry, please." Harry, that approximation to his name was how Teddy had introduced him, was plainly local. He simply bowed politely and left through the main door after serving the drinks. Alphonse gestured to Lee to sit. "I'm getting the feeling this is important, and probably confidential."

Lee snorted lightly, it was a sweet gesture of his that Alphonse liked, and sat back, holding his drink. "It's certainly both of those things. Cheers!" They drank, then watched each other for a while. "I don't know how to start, my friend, but I'll probably take a lot off your mind if I tell you it has nothing to do with us — well, it has a lot to do with us both, but not our relationship, as it used to be."

Alphonse tried not to react — but he felt intensely relieved.

But that feeling disappeared in an instant. "My father has cancer."

The nameless hole opened up suddenly in Alphonse's life, just as it had done when his mother had told him oh-so-calmly about his father. This would hurt so many people. "Prognosis?"

Lee drank. "Not confirmed, but not hopeful."

Alphonse stood up, putting his drink down. "Lee, I'm so sorry. Can I hug you?"

The first look was sharp, it seemed resentful, but then it rapidly softened. "I thank you, my darling man, but that won't help me just now. You and I need clear heads. This is the movie reel of politicians at a funeral."

"That implies things are already serious. How is he?"

"He's feeling a little weak, and there's a lot of pain, but we only had the diagnosis this week. His treatment starts next week. This wasn't why I was coming originally." Another wan smile. "I wanted to see our project, our baby. You've done a wonderful job, but I am a little distracted."

"Of course, you are. It's such a shock."

Lee drank again, deeply this time, "It's not the only shock."

Just stay calm, thought Alphonse, Lee was seldom melodramatic. He'd even handled their parting remarkably well — well, better than Alphonse had been expecting.

"Of course, I don't think it's such a shock for you."

He looked slightly surly now. Alphonse guessed what was coming, but he should let Lee speak.

"I have a sister, apparently." This seemed to be affecting him even more than his father's illness. "A very successful little half-sister. How long have you known?"

"I've known for a while, Lee. Is that really important?"

Lee, ultimately, was always reasonable. Alphonse knew he had to let the emotions subside. Lee finished the gin and held up his glass. "I'd like another, please." Alphonse waited, not moving towards him. Lee stood, moving towards the bar. "I don't get drunk, Alphonse, you know that, but I do need another one."

His tone was calm and reasonable now. It would be proper to be host. "I'm sorry, let me get it for you."

Lee smiled. "And only fifty-fifty with the fucking tonic, please." And they hesitated, caught each other half grinning, and then laughed. Alphonse refilled the glasses, but put just tonic in his own. Lee took his glass and went to the sofa again. "My father only told me this week, at the same time as he confirmed his cancer. My mother had told me he was having tests, but she had no idea what it was."

"Does she know about Mei?" It struck Alphonse suddenly. This would be a lot for the poor woman to absorb.

"He says he'll tell her. I've no idea if she'll be surprised by that, he's lived a roguish life for many years, but…" He was obviously finding the next thought difficult to express. "The thing is, Meitang doesn't know, does she?"

"I'm pretty sure she doesn't, but there are others who do."

Lee looked shocked. "How many?"

"So far as I know, it's very few. Peter and Claudia in my circle, but Chou Daiyu has guessed — or maybe she just heard a rumour from Yang Lijun. But I don't think Mei herself knows. I think she would have given something away. We've been working very closely for eighteen months, and it's never come up. Is your father going to tell her?"

"No. You are. That's why I'm here."

Alphonse froze. It was his usual response to the outrageous. This seemed so absurd. Questions flew up like shrapnel from a bomb. It was impossible for a moment to organise his thoughts. Better to ask something, but make it intelligent — and sympathetic.

People that mattered to him were in crisis. His mind went back to his last meeting with Wengwei — what was he planning for Mei? Would that now accelerate? Would he go public on paternity?

"I'll do anything you need, of course, but what's the thinking behind it? What else is on his mind?"

"It's early. In his own mind, he's still immortal. He'll be back running everything after his treatment, he thinks. The doctors have a different view. But at least he's not being blind to the situation." When he looked up from studying his glass, his eyes were wet. "He's telling me he wants a committee of three to run everything for him, Liuwei, Meitang and me. He will work through us, and we will take up all of his contacts, including the financial, the legal, the political..." He paused, looking hard at Alphonse. "And, he didn't say it, but I suspect the criminal." He shrugged. "Anyway, he says there's a lot he needs to explain to us — but especially Meitang, he said. He tried to tell me it was because she knew so little, but... what was on his mind, do you think? What did he say when he asked you to Shanghai?"

"Well, he was asking more than he was saying." Alphonse was hesitating. Wengwei had clearly been identifying his long-term successor, but not explicitly. There was no need to tell Lee that. "But he did confirm that Mei was his daughter when he asked how she was doing. I told him she was very good, and he seemed happy with that, almost as if he were thinking about a senior position long term."

"A senior position?" Now Lee looked rattled, "She already has property under her control, her legal father has done nothing for years." He looked around. "And she has my fucking resorts! What more… oh, no. He couldn't, surely."

"Lee," Alphonse said sharply, "I don't know where your mind's got to, but it looks like it's wrong and it's unhealthy." Unhealthy, yes, but probably not wrong, he thought. "If he has to think about succession, and he obviously should now, he wants to look after family, and he seems to be including Mei in that, but he needs to know who he can count on. I've just told him she's very good."

"And ruthless." There was a little spite in his look now. He'd sensed Alphonse wasn't being open.

"That came up. It was his word, not mine, it seemed important to him — and she is."

"More ruthless than her brothers, apparently. He says he worries about us." Now there were tears. "He calls me in, tells me he has cancer, says I have a bastard sister I never knew about, and then tells me she's a better leader than I am." He breathed in deeply and got control of himself — that was more like Lee. "He actually said that: you're not ruthless enough, my boy, not wuqing! Sometimes I actually hate him," now the soft eyes looked to Alphonse again, "but he may not be wrong, my friend. I'm certainly not ruthless enough to have that conversation with Meitang. I wish you luck with that." Then a slow wicked smile spread across his face. "At least I'm ruthless enough to make you do it: come in, Meitang, sit down, the man you've called father for thirty-five years isn't your father, but your real one is dying." And it was the first time Alphonse had seen a cruel look on his face. "I'll leave you to it. I know you won't let the old man down." He downed his drink quickly and left.

Alphonse sat and tried to organise his thoughts — and his feelings. Shen Wengwei, crude, forceful, cunning — and yes, ruthless, having that in a successor would certainly be important to him — nevertheless inspired respect, even admiration, in Alphonse, and a strange affection. The man had imagination, and vision, and courage. It was hard to imagine what it had taken to create the empire he had. And now he would have to leave it. Alphonse had lived through the pathetic shafts of hope that had shone into his father's life in those last six months.

Perhaps Wengwei would recover, but, in the meantime, plans had to be made. He took some time standing outside, watching the sky turning purple as the first stars appeared over the calm sea. Around him the lights were already on by the garden pathways. The moon was rising, as it had done before humans, as it would do after humans — but Shen Wengwei had something that should last beyond himself, for a little time at least. The night sky he always found difficult to confront. But especially so tonight.

And he had to talk to Mei.

It was six thirty. He had to catch her before dinner, unprepared as he was.

He rang her room. "Hello?" He could hear Lily giggling in the background, Mei was calling 'Shh.'

"Mei, it's Alphonse, can I speak to you before dinner?"

"Oh, must be important." But from the audible rustling and distant noises, she was being distracted.

"It is, quite."

"That's an English way of saying something, isn't it? I'm guessing it's serious. Should I come to you now?"

Thank God! She was sharp enough to get it. "Yes, please, if you could."

"Five minutes."

It was ten, but that was very good; she was dressed and made up for dinner — and he assumed he'd caught her playfully naked when he'd rung. In his mind, though, dinner for either of them was unthinkable. He tried not to look too gloomy when he ushered her in — and tried asking 'may I get you a drink?' with calm levity. But he obviously failed.

"Just water please — and you'd better come straight to the point."

He didn't bother with the water, just gestured to her to sit down.

"Lee was just here. His father is very ill."

She gasped, plainly shocked and overwhelmed. "What is it?"

"Cancer."

"Is it serious?" She paused. "Stupid woman! Of course it's serious, or you wouldn't be talking to me like this. What is it? Where is it? Are you saying it's terminal?"

"He still thinks he's immortal, apparently. Lee is not so sure." And he could see her trying to dodge the same shrapnel of thoughts that had hit him earlier, trying to find that first valid but sensitive question. "Let me help you. If you're like me, you don't know what to ask first." She nodded mutely. "He's already thinking about how to run his business while he's undergoing treatment but, if I'm interpreting Lee correctly, at the back of his mind is what to do with Senlin when he's not there."

Her mouth was open, she was shaking her head. He went to her sofa and sat beside her. She looked disconcerted, seeming unsure whether to move further away or to fall into his arms.

"Shen Wengwei thinks very highly of you and he wants you to play a big role in Senlin in the future. I know it seems crass to think that's important in this exact minute, but I couldn't avoid thinking, when I was listening to Lee, about me and our business somewhere in the background of my thoughts. But, in the end, this is important to him, whatever we think."

He couldn't tell if she were feeling numb, or contemptuous. He'd never mastered reading Mei's expressions.

"I'm just saying, all sorts of thoughts go through your head at times like these. A lot of them you're not proud of."

She turned to him, sighed, and smiled. "Thank you for saying that. I am worried about him, mostly, but I admit that these other selfish thoughts came into my head. I'm glad I'm not a freak. Then she smiled at him. "Or maybe we're both freaks. But I am sorry. I hardly know him, but he's been wonderful to me. I hope he gets better. Do you remember, when he asked me to see him at Morkuda? He gave me a big hug. It meant so much to me." She seemed to drift off into her thoughts for a while.

"Mei." He reached out and lay his hand on her shoulder. "I haven't told you the hardest part yet." She turned to look at him, looking curious and incredulous by turns, these were finally responses he could read. "Have your parents spoken to you about your childhood, about your early years?" He could find no way into the topic; he was hoping blindly that she might have some awareness.

"We didn't talk much. It was a cold house. Why are you asking that?"

"Were they close to the Shen family?"

"No, not at all. They never spoke about them. It was strange, my father had a big job in the corporation. They didn't speak… Where is this going, Alphonse?"

"I hope you'll forgive me for this someday, Mei, but I've been asked to tell you that your mother and Shen Wengwei were very close once."

She moved away slightly, pulled her legs up underneath her, and stared at him, expressionless now. When she spoke, her voice was flat and toneless. "If you give me the full picture of this, there won't be anything to forgive, but you can start by telling me why it's you who has to give me this message — these messages, I should say. Are you saying I have a different father — and he's dying?"

He nodded slowly, thinking to embrace her, but she sat like stone. This was the Mei he remembered from their first meeting, tough and self-controlled. "Shen Wengwei has been telling Lee this week, and making plans for the time when he is being treated, and that starts next week. He wants you to be involved in that future. He'd called me to Shanghai two months ago to talk about you. This was before the cancer diagnosis, but I don't know if he'd already been feeling ill then. I told him you were doing extremely well, that you worked very hard, you were a superb negotiator, and that you can make big, bold decisions." He hesitated. "Look, I can't fudge this, Mei — he asked if you were ruthless. It seemed to matter to him, and I said you were."

He couldn't tell if the points were sinking in, even her face was motionless — and he couldn't imagine how she was processing her thoughts.

"And he told you he was my father."

"He did…"

Now there was a flash of anger on her face, "But you fucking well knew." He said nothing, stayed impassive. Now she screamed, "You fucking well knew! Who the fuck else knows? How long have you known? How could you not tell me?" Now there were tears in her eyes, but she wasn't moving.

"I can and I will answer all of those questions as best as I can, but I'm feeling rudderless in this. I can only offer to do the best I can for you."

"Like keeping massive fucking secrets from me."

"It wasn't my place to tell you, but it seems I'm the only one who can."

She sniffed, then waved a hand wildly at him. "Tissue, tissue…"

He grabbed the box from the bar, she pulled the top few, dabbed her eyes and blew her nose, then seemed to deflate. "And you're the only one I can shout at…" And her face creased into a small smile. She slid towards him. "You're also the only one who can hug me right at this minute." She let herself be wrapped in his arms. "I can't even tell Lily, can I?"

"You can tell her Shen Wengwei is ill, you'll need some reason for looking upset. In fact, you'd better tell

her now. I assume she was going to dinner with you."
He could feel her nodding against his chest.

"You're right, but can you ring her? Say we have
things to discuss because of it?"

"Oh, sure, and have somebody else screaming at
me."

She hugged him tightly. "I wasn't screaming." He
said nothing, but hugged her tighter. "Well, only a little
bit. But could you call her?"

"In your room?"

"Yes," she mumbled. "Two zero seven."

Lily picked the phone up quickly and remained,
fortunately, incurious when given a 'something big is
happening in the business' story.

He had himself put through to Daiyu, hoping she
wouldn't ask questions. "It's Alphonse. I have a
business emergency. I can't make dinner. Can you cover
for me? Say I'm talking to Europe." He added 'yes,
please' when she asked if she would see him later and
hoped she would understand. Well, she would think the
wrong thing at first — and Lee would probably miss
dinner too, but he felt relieved he would have her to talk
to later.

"Who were you calling?"

"Just Daiyu. Someone needs to know why I'm not
there. Lily seemed OK. But we have a story to get
straight — and you have some very difficult feelings to
deal with."

She sniffed again. "Yes, and I have to be a big girl and get the story straight before I deal with the feelings." She looked up, her eyes still brimming. "It's OK, pragmatism before self-pity. Ruthless Meitang!" And she seemed to sink into herself for a while, then looked up at him. "I'll cope, Alphonse, but you can fucking cuddle me for a while, before we talk. Tell me I can do this."

And she could, he knew that already.

It was two hours later when she left. They'd talked a lot about business, and how she might interact with Lee and Lou — he assumed Lou had been told by now. She should try to sit down with Lee in the morning — 'he's a wonderful man and his problems are as big as yours. He'll be a superb ally if you can work together' — Alphonse had said that with a large measure of hope but he trusted Lee to be reasonable ultimately. She should also call Wengwei in the morning and arrange to see him later in the week.

They talked about death, and what his father had been through.

But they spoke hardly at all about her parents — 'yes, that will be difficult, but I don't have to think about it now.' The cold detachment was not an attractive trait, but it would be an essential one.

She seemed almost relaxed by the time she was ready to leave. They'd settled at the opposite ends of the sofa once she'd had the long cuddle at the start of the conversation but now, as he stood up when she did, she moved into his arms. "I've never thanked you enough for all you've done for me."

"You've done a lot for me. We're building a brilliant business here. I hope you still have time for it."

"Oh, I can't leave all this. I'm part of it. It's part of me. But there was something else I wanted to say. There's an embarrassing night we never speak about."

He laughed loudly. "Morkuda, you mean, with Isobel."

"It's not nice of you to laugh."

"You're right. But I don't feel embarrassed. It was a lovely night."

"That's all I wanted to say. I don't like it that we don't acknowledge it. I'm not asking for it again…"

He hugged her tight. "But it is a beautiful memory."

"Yes, so I wanted to say thank you for that too." She looked up and kissed him.

And then she left, as if that closed a chapter.

He texted Daiyu and Peter. He knew Peter was travelling but didn't know where he was. He was welcoming Daiyu at the door with a chaste kiss when his phone buzzed. He looked: 'Peter.'

"I have to take this, sorry."

"I'll come back."

"No, no, please stay, you should hear all this anyway." He gestured to the sofa. "Peter, hi, thank you for calling, where have I got you?"

Peter was at Heathrow, but he could listen, even if he couldn't talk much. He was a little shocked by

Wengwei's illness — Daiyu had managed to stifle her gasp as she heard — 'he did seem particularly keen that I go to Shanghai this week' — and they covered all the ground of the organisational implications — with Peter his usual calm self — arranging to talk later in the week.

"Wow!" said Daiyu, as he put the phone down. "I came along all buzzing because it's going wonderfully well here, but this kind of dwarfs that. But Mei seems to have taken it in her stride, you say."

"Yes, better than Lee, but come here."

"Are you threatening to become unprofessional?"

"Only moderately, to start with. I thought it was your idea anyway."

"Oh, and that's gallantry, is it? I've been better treated by Chinamen." But she was teasing and stretched out to lie on his chest. "You know, I obviously didn't foresee this, but I thought you might need someone to talk to sometimes."

He stroked her arm. "Thank you. Do I ever need it now! I'm glad Mei has Lily. I think she'll be sensible about what she says. It's Lee I'm worried about."

"Shouldn't you tell him about how your talk went?"

"I should, shouldn't I?"

"And you haven't eaten. And he wasn't at dinner. See if he'll come — and order a sandwich."

"Promise you'll come back later if he does come?"

"Of course." She sat up to let him call. He rang the mobile. Lee would be there in ten minutes — he thanked Alphonse for calling.

Daiyu hugged him when they got to the door. "I know it's very important for the two of you — but I won't complain if you don't take long." She smiled and kissed him, then left abruptly.

It was late when she came back. He and Lee, old lovers, seemed to grope their way back cautiously to a friendship while talking through all the possible outcomes. Lee had agreed he would talk to Mei in the morning, and thought it was a good idea she should call his father — 'it'll be hard to say our father, but the sooner I do it, the better' — Alphonse had nodded. Lee was a big person. He thought Mei would have bigger problems with Lou. Lee laughed as he agreed. 'Even I have big problems with Lou, as you've seen, I'll probably work better with Mei.' Alphonse had already thought that.

They managed a big hug by the door as Lee was leaving. "I miss this," he'd said sorrowfully, "but I knew you were right. Although I still love you a little."

"I do love you too, you know," said Alphonse, squeezing his hand. And he meant it, but he'd felt no lust as Lee had left.

He'd not felt much lust as Daiyu had ordered him to bed immediately on her return. "Conversation's the main thing, my man, especially after the day you've had." But she reached for his cock, nevertheless. "He and I might play later."

"When you're sitting on my face?"

"Yes, but you can't talk when I'm sitting like that, so tell me now, what did he say? How is he?"

And he talked, and she asked more questions — about Lee, about Mei, about Senlin, even about Peter — and they fell asleep before they could make love.

12

I've just got back from Sandra's. I'm aware that I've put too much gin in this glass, but I've spent two hours jollying her along, hiding my seething anger at Gerry, so an hour to myself now — with a gin or two — is a well-earned relief.

I had a morning call from Daiyu — yes, she seems to be enjoying parts of the trip more than I had intended her to, but I can hardly blame her for embracing my lifestyle — but the big news is about Wengwei. And, of course, about Mei. The beauty of communications with Daiyu, and I'm talking both verbal and written, is how perfectly concisely and accurately — and honestly, of course — she describes situations. So, I think I have a clear picture of what's happening. Clear enough for me to have texted Mei to tell her I'm planning to be back on Sunday if she wants to meet up. I got a 'yes, please;' laconic, even by her standards.

And clear enough communications from Daiyu to let me know that she's had two nights with Alphonse already and may well have more. If she manages the week, that will be more than I've had in six months. You can't really tell with people, can you? I thought she was cooler than that.

Claudia's cool. That was a fun afternoon yesterday. It was after six when I left. It had all got a little giggly — we'd had the appropriate alcoholic accompaniment to Hannes's divine lunch — when I was showing her the chaise. Neither of them had spotted how you could click on the small panels to get the hooks to spring out, nor had they pulled on the concealed shallow drawer just under the seat. The ropes and canes were obviously untouched — I'd had the drawer fitted with locations for everything — it must all stay tidy — and be put back correctly. I know, I know, I am very OCD like that. The mini-triumph for me was when I asked her to lie over the end. She looked puzzled, 'please indulge me,' I'd said, 'I'm not doing anything, just checking a point.'

And she looked perfect. Her bum in exactly in the right position.

"Perfect!" I even said it.

She stood up quickly. That was about the fourth time today she'd looked embarrassed, but she's very sweet, she knows she shouldn't be flustered, so she soldiers on and sees things through, even out of her comfort zone.

I smiled at her. "True confession time: I got Andreas to show me some of the clothes you leave here. I told him I wanted to see colours and styles, but I was really just after your measurements. I'd guessed you and Peter might be a little into playing this way, so I wanted to make sure your bum would be a perfect height for..." I paused. "I don't think I need go on."

"No!" But she was smiling now.

I bent over the end. "You see, it's just not quite perfect for me, I'm a little shorter. With your toes on the carpet, as they were just then, you'll be at the perfect angle — and if you want your wrists tied," I clicked a hook open again — oh, such a wonderful mechanism, perfect fit, almost invisible, I do that so well, or rather, my cabinet-makers do, with my design, though — "you should be perfectly comfortable with that too. I'm not going to ask to confirm you're into all that, because you'll get all flustered again and try to deny it…"

But she laughed. "No, I've had too much wine to deny it now. I used to be very into that for a while, as I discovered rather late in life." Then she'd looked a little thoughtful, "It doesn't feature much now. Are you still?"

And I told her about Conrad's party — but admitted that I, too, lived a quieter life these days. Well, quieter in respect of playtimes; in work terms I'm completely absorbed — I tell you, it would overwhelm a lesser person. I'd gone through all the UK projects with Merle this morning. To be fair, current distractions notwithstanding, she's pretty much keeping on top of everything, but there are prospects in the pipeline it was useful to firm up on. But then I went to see Sandra.

I had to travel south of the river, somewhere in Clapham — she normally comes to see me, of course, but she was still not as well as she should have been. She looked washed out and a little teary. I had been there before, I've no recollection of why or when — I think I may have been making sure she got home safely — probably after a night when she'd done me a favour.

It's a small flat. It has what's laughably called a second bedroom which is only a storeroom for the gifts she's received, but it's fairly new and clean. Her problem is that the flat is Gerry's. And she showed me a letter that she picked up from the coffee table. It was from his solicitor, telling her that he was very happy to keep her as a tenant, but it was time she paid rent. It was more legalistic than that, but that was the simple message.

I read it through twice. When I looked up at her, the big fat blobby tears were dropping into her lap. "I know it's not much, Sades, but I just don't have a regular income. I can't afford it."

"And he's got the nerve to ask you to his parties — and put you in hospital with a bill that must be three months of this rent at least."

"Yes, but he hasn't paid that."

I tried not to look shocked. He'd let me think he had. A little "Oh!" squeaked out of me.

"Conrad did," she said, sniffing, "but I can't expect more help from him. He fills his parties with the young and glamorous — not old slags that are only good for dirty old perverts. I know I still play, Sades, but I dope myself up to deal with it. I haven't really had fun since that lovely young man of yours, Will. Are you still in touch?"

I was just trying to stay calm. I was burning with anger. It was better then to make cups of tea for us — everything's in one main room — and talk a little about my world to distract us both until I can think clearly. I give her a bit more of Will's story. I helped him a lot back then, but she had an important role too — I don't suppose his Martha will ever appreciate that. Although Will's likely to have given her a complete description of his education. He's probably the most honest person I've ever met. I've sometimes wondered if she is as honest with him, but she probably is. I don't think he'd love her otherwise.

Love! What a weird creature that is to Sandra and me. We both feel it. Well, I still do, but I think my friend feels she no longer lives in the same country. She was very pretty when I first met her. There were lots of men who told me they loved her — but none of the ones she fell for, they were always the abusers — but she never got herself too tied down. I always felt a little uncomfortable; she seemed to like men who shared her among their friends. I think she always thought she was enjoying it — 'lots of chunky men, Sades' — but it never convinced me. I don't know what I should have done — we've had a lot of fun times, and I wasn't even thinking about my own life's future. I had work, getting ever more satisfying — and rewarding — I knew that would always be there, but most relationships quickly became either painful or, worse, boring. I was giving them less and less thought, so I certainly didn't have Sandra's future, emotional or financial, in my mind. We weren't even close then. But somehow, we've become so now.

Closer than I'm comfortable being. And I think that's where Conrad must be — six days in The Argosy can't have been cheap. And would probably have been enough to clear his conscience. Gerry, of course, doesn't have one. And he's her landlord. Author of what is, effectively, an eviction notice.

But what am I? What can I do in this?

I need another gin.

13

"Isobel tells me I've had more nights with you this week than she's had in the past six months. I don't think she's happy." But Daiyu was smiling.

"Are you happy?" He thought she probably was, but she remained curiously inscrutable — and he hadn't worked out if that was her nature or simply how she was protecting herself from him. They had developed a ritual every morning. She would shower early and then sit on the side of the bed for a conversation about the day ahead before going back to her room to prepare. Leaving discarded underwear draped on the armchair was part of the routine, as was her habit of throwing the robe on the floor and wiggling for him — he'd protested: 'No peachy bum?' as she walked back to the bathroom on the second morning with the robe still on.

She reached for his hand. "I am happy, actually," she said, but her face was serious.

"What's up? Worried about Isobel?"

"No, it's not that…" She looked distracted. "I'm sorry. I shouldn't put it that way." Then she laughed to herself, the little laugh he'd begun to find enchanting. "I will say that she put so much stress on the fact that you two had an arrangement, and not a relationship, that I began to suspect she was hiding some feelings, so I'm not entirely innocent. I thought she might react, but I've been here every night anyway."

"So, what's troubling you?"

Now she squeezed his hand. "Look, I think we now have what she would call an arrangement. It's been a hectic week, it's been lovely to fall into bed with you every evening and tidy up all the meetings and conversations and plan the next day like this every morning…"

"And flash me your bum!"

"My bum's actually had much more close attention than during those quick flashes, Mr Newman, but I had been warned about your preferences. I'm very sore, you know."

"You should have said!"

"I said I was sore, not that I hadn't enjoyed everything." She had a look of sweet indignation. "That's the point."

"What's the point?"

"I've been enjoying everything, but I don't want you thinking I'm making a play for more than an arrangement…"

"But?"

"Yes, always a but. The nights have been lovely, but they've actually been very brief. Now, Mei's gone to Shanghai to see Wengwei and Lijun leaves today, as do my last clients. So, could we sit at the same dinner table tonight and not spread ourselves around?"

"Raymond will be around…"

"I know that. I'm quite happy about him joining us. I wouldn't want us to look too serious and self-obsessed anyway. But I would like us to come straight here after dinner, there won't be clients to entertain in the bar…"

"Will Raymond still be with us?"

She smiled, and slapped him. "I know your other ladies like multiple partners, but I'm afraid I'm a little boring. This has been an adventurous week for me, and I don't have any new treats and secrets to spoil you with, I'm afraid."

"Well, you've exhausted all of my very limited repertoire as well. So, why are we going to bother?" And she slapped him again, harder. He pulled her down quickly on to him and kissed her. "Can I make this easier for you? I would love an evening together for us and yes, let's finish dinner early — and then, in the morning, let's stay here for a while and not send you off on your CCTV walk of shame. Can we do that? You can spend a little more time on your favourite seat."

She cuddled into him. "I have two favourite seats. I'm surprised you hadn't noticed."

"I thought you liked the one where I couldn't talk."

"I love that one." Her hand had moved to his cock now, and he'd already been half-erect. "But my other favourite is here — and, fuck it, I'm going to enjoy that one again right now." And she threw a leg over him quickly while still holding him, rubbed his stiffening cock-head a few times on her moistening clitoris and then slid carefully down on to him. When she had all of him, she sat up and threw the robe away, put her hands on his shoulders and shook her breasts at him. "Just a quickie now, please — but much, much longer tomorrow."

He loved her smile, he was already finding it dangerous, and he loved the febrile gasps of her orgasms, the grown-up sisters of her little laughs, and as his fingers now found her clit, with her grinding down on him, he knew she would be quick. He looked up at the closed eyes, the huge smile and the shaking head. She was on her way and moving her hips to squeeze him, he knew he was coming with her, and was still pulsing as she slumped on to his chest.

But she sat up quickly. "That was very naughty, Mr Newman, we have a business to run." But she laughed and bent down to kiss him again. "I don't know whether to thank you for your speed, or apologise for mine. But I am so looking forward to going slow tonight." She kissed him again, then almost leapt off the bed to run the shower again.

Their ritual gave him half an hour to himself to reflect each day on the progress of a very hectic and very successful week. Daiyu had been thrilled with her clients' reactions; their property division's own guests — his and Mei's — had been generally appreciative but often guarded — 'just reserving their positions for future discussions,' as Mei had rightly said.

She had done well. She'd had a surprisingly positive conversation with Lee on the Monday — he'd heard that from each of them separately. He'd had dinner with Lee that evening and the man was too good a person to be negative or destructive about the new situation. He seemed to have accepted straight away that he would have to get on with his new sister, 'and she seems to have grown up a lot while she's been with you, my friend,' he'd said. Alphonse was glad Lee was seeing that. He found it hard, working so closely with her, to get a sense of how she was progressing, and some of her more aggressive approaches worried him sometimes, but never her judgements.

Lee had spoken to his father and brother. The first conversation had gone well, and he'd been asked to thank Alphonse: 'he admires you, you know, even though you're only a poof.' They'd both laughed at that, it was a welcome sign that he and Lee were good together again. But he doubted whether he'd had a truly open account of the second conversation. Lou was, of course, extremely unhappy.

He'd been rude and angry when Mei had called him the next day. She'd told Alphonse that evening, but she seemed surprisingly relaxed about it: 'he has to see me Friday anyway, we're all three, spending time with Wengwei, then I will talk with him on his own.'

She'd been teary on the Monday evening, telling him about her Wengwei call, but she'd given a heavily edited account of it — which is what he'd expected. He asked if she'd called her parents. 'I rang my mother' was said tersely — they were in Alphonse's villa before dinner; he hadn't wanted to pry, but he did want to give her the chance to talk if she wanted to and he'd guessed, at that point, that she did. 'She didn't say much to me but I could tell she was very upset — and she obviously won't find my father very supportive.' She'd drifted into her thoughts at that point. 'I've told her I want to see her for a long chat on Saturday, just the two of us — it's only ever the two of us for chats anyway, but the fact that I said that made her flustered. At least she now realises that I might know something.'

She'd agreed with Wengwei that they would tell almost no one: 'We all know you run the property division really.' Alphonse had stopped her at that point and told her that she'd effectively been making all Asian decisions in the past year, with him only overseeing them, and that her profile and reputation among their Asian base was already high. 'That's what Wengwei says. He says he's been telling everyone lately that I run property and I have a strange European assistant to help me.'

He'd laughed but told her that it did feel like that sometimes — and that he was proud when it did. And he truly was, and he felt very confident she would do very well, and he told her again — at that point, he could see, she was fighting back tears. 'That doesn't mean,' he'd said, 'that it's wrong to expect a cuddle from a friend now and again' — that had triggered it, she'd fallen into his arms, sobbing. He was glad, sure that it would help her — and it seemed to; she soon sat up again, sniffing and waving her arm in what had become her 'tissues, please' gesture. He'd laughed and fetched the box — and she'd been laughing herself when she'd blown her nose and wiped her eyes. 'I need to get ready for dinner now, but thank you a thousand times again' and she almost danced off.

For the rest of the week, she was her normal self, even her 'fucking Lou' aside when they'd briefly caught up on Tuesday had been spat out with a wry smile — as if she'd expected no better — and neither would he have done. Lou would be the difficult, shaky leg of the tripod in the interregnum, but she would easily cope with him when she ran everything. Cope with, or dispose of, he'd thought, maybe ultimately putting him in her official father's office to take over as the nominal head of property.

Alphonse had been giving thought to how he would manage without so much of Mei's time. He was very stretched already, he'd need more help, but that was tomorrow's problem. Today he had only two more property meetings in the morning and a review with Raymond and Teddy in the afternoon. He expected them to have a long and self-critical list of what still needed to be done, but he could hardly find a fault — 'you're very good, boss, but there's still a lot you don't see,' was Raymond's consistent rejoinder if Alphonse ever gave him a compliment.

But his mind drifted to Shanghai. Peter had called the previous evening. He'd had time with Wengwei that afternoon: 'It's his pancreas; they're trying radio to shrink it to make it operable, but I think he knows the prospects aren't good. He seems very keen on his daughter taking over eventually. What do you think of that?'

Peter never gave away his own view when he asked a question, and Alphonse had never tried second-guessing him anyway — 'I learn more from misunderstood questions than from anything else, my boy' had been an early learning for Alphonse. But there were two questions in what he was asking, and both needed an answer. 'I'll have to find someone to manage property, I'm already stretched, but Phil and Eddie are coming along well, I think.' He'd waited — he knew Peter had been keeping a closer eye on the guys running London and New York while he'd been spending so much time in Asia. 'I agree with you. I don't think they've had quite the development support your young lady has received, but they're good. But what about her running a big corporation?' — that was the second question.

'It would be a huge leap for anyone, but I have been very impressed.'

'You told her father she was ruthless'.

'That was his word, but I agreed. And I think her brother sees that, too.'

'Lee, you mean, obviously, not that spoilt little shit.'

Alphonse had guffawed at that point. Peter was seldom so crudely critical. "There's something on your mind, isn't there? Is it anything to do with you spending time with a man confronting mortality?"

Peter had seemed to reflect a while. "You've probably got a point. I was impressed at how brave and philosophical he seemed. But you're right. He and I seem to have become very strange partners. Obviously, we're almost managing property together, and for all your fulsome comments about your ruthless young lady, I regard you as uniquely responsible for anything that happens in the sector around the world, so you do need three regional heads, and I would like you and I to be face to face more often."

"I understand, but that's not it."

"No. It's Wengwei. He wants me to help guide his family through the next few years. I was very touched, and I told him so, but I also reminded him that I am a businessman too."

"What did he say?"

"He laughed and said we'd work something out, but he wanted it to be a businessman, and not one of the thieves or murderers or politicians who constituted his entire circle of friends in China. I laughed then — and said it was interesting that the politicians occupied the last step before hell. 'No, no,' he said, 'that was the murderers, the politicians already in it.' The illness isn't dampening his humour, nor his resolve. I've had to promise to come back with a scheme in four weeks — of how I can help — and what I'd expect for it. Give it some thought, will you? When are you in London again?

Can you get Hayley to book us an afternoon together? She'll need to tie it in with Claudia, she's good on this sort of thing."

"Of course." And they'd signed off, with Alphonse feeling that mortality had insinuated its way into Peter's thoughts. He'd talk to Claudia about that when they next spoke. But before then, he'd have to get over the suspicion he always had, that Peter tried to place them together to entrap them somehow.

***

The day went well. The first meeting was with a man from Manila about a property deal there. The man had seemed relieved that 'your assistant' — 'my partner,' Alphonse had corrected him — would not be there. The man had tried to wrap up the deal with a handshake, but Alphonse knew that Mei had a better grasp of detail on the purchase, and that could wait.

The next meeting was about a Shanghai development that Lijun would build and Alphonse had several 'whose side are you on?' thoughts about Lijun during the conversation — and it underlined how important it would be for him to find another Mei for the region.

The afternoon was only an hour with Raymond and Teddy. Teddy was almost explosively buoyant about the guests' reactions, only to be brought down by Raymond being unnaturally dour: 'Do you know how many

158

millions we've spent? It's not just to give you an easy job. Of course they love it. How are you going to make sure they never want to go anywhere else, though? There will be twelve more of these they can choose from in four years' time.'

When they parted, Teddy's ebullience undiminished, Alphonse's questioning frown to Raymond — he thought he'd been very harsh — got a sly 'don't worry' smile in response.

Then later, at dinner with Daiyu and Raymond, he found them both teasing him about his Christian ways. Teddy and the chef came briefly to the table between the courses — Alphonse looked around to check how other tables were being served but everything looked smooth on what was the busiest night so far as more guests were being admitted — and, as Teddy retreated after one brief conversation, Raymond said, 'It really is going very well, boss, but you have to keep setting higher and higher standards. The competition ain't sleeping. You two should look at the new PanSeason hotel near Teluk. It's very good.'

And Alphonse hadn't known whether to be more alarmed by the rising competition, or Raymond's simple apparent assumption that he and Daiyu had become a pairing. There was no question about how it had struck Daiyu who, for the first time in Alphonse's experience, looked flustered. Raymond was smiling knowingly: 'You good people can tell me it's because I've got CCTV and laundry lists, but you two have an aura when you're together and you might want to be careful when you meet up with the other people who love you. I'm just saying.' He smiled broadly at them. 'And to be honest, I'm more worried about that than I am about the competition — but I do have to keep the managers striving.' And he left them quite quickly after that with a 'car's at twelve for you tomorrow. Be ready, we have the villa booked for paying guests.'

They were soon back in the living area, with Alphonse putting 'only water, please' on the table for them.

"Flabbergasted?" he asked as he sat down.

"A little," she said, turning sideways to look straight at him, "but I meant what I said earlier. This is an arrangement. I am absolutely not falling in love or anything like that. Right?"

"Right! Absolutely! And when I get home tomorrow evening and my neighbour, with a week's worth of jealousy, comes down to see me and makes demands of me, I just invite her in and deal with her. Right?"

She turned away from him, looking pensive. Then a thought seemed to strike her. "She told me that's less than once a month."

"And that's true," but it would also have been true to say that it happened every time they were in the same place — that was simply very seldom. "It is just an arrangement."

"Do you have many arrangements?"

Now was the time to be careful, but they had to be clear with each other. "I think you know all I have. I have an arrangement with Isobel. I had an affair with Lee which finished three months ago. And I have an odd relationship with Claudia Brodie where there are deep feelings, one of which is guilt; one, that we give in to only very rarely, is lust, and one of which, I'm afraid, I have to call love, for want of a better word."

"And me?"

She stayed still, looking calmly at him now. This was strange. In similar conversations in the past, the partner, man or woman, would either flounce off emotionally, or throw themselves into his arms. He had never done either, he reflected; in the rare situations he'd been in Daiyu's position, he'd stayed calm and tried to get clarity.

"I'm going to admit now that I'm not happy with the word 'arrangement.' Even Isobel deceives herself about the feelings that underpin whatever it is we want to call it."

"Call it with her, or call it with you? Look, I don't want to be difficult here. I just think we should know where we stand."

"That does go for me too, you know. And, thanks to Raymond, we both have to recognise that there's something. We can tell ourselves that we've helped each other cope with the stresses of the week by lying in each other's arms every night, but I've wanted more each time. I've loved making love to you."

She smiled. "And I've loved you fucking me. Should we restrict ourselves to that?"

"I'm getting a sense of role reversal here."

"Maybe. But we're both having an unusual week. I haven't felt emotionally threatened — OK, until just now, I admit — but I don't want that spoiling my week of lust and adventure."

"Adventure?"

"Bits of it were new. I think I've discovered the most effective way to silence a man — and I've always resisted that other thing until this week. But Isobel had, well, I was going to say she'd warned me, but the fact was she'd seriously recommended it and she made me curious."

"And?"

Now she was looking into his eyes and smiling. "And those were genuine screams of delight. OK, I'm still a bit sore, but I am still going to want everything — and twice, so you can be slower the second time. Take me to the bedroom, we'll deal with all the feelings stuff in the morning."

14

"You look tired," she said to Peter as she kissed him at the car — the alarm and camera had told her it was arriving. Hannes was dealing with the bags.

"Oh, I got a bit of sleep, and it's always easier coming home. But it has been emotionally stressful. I'd love to say we have a new opportunity, but really, we just have another headache. Are they all here yet?"

"They're not coming until tomorrow."

"I thought…"

"My darling man, they'll get through enough of your booze tomorrow. Even Jo's mates switch to wine when they come here — and you've made Abbi's girls addicted to bubbles. I wanted this evening for you and me." She took his hand, "Come on, five p.m. on Friday, officially the weekend."

But he held her back and pulled her to him. He looked somehow touched. "Thank you," he said with a look of surprise. "I love them, and I love them being here, it makes the place come alive in the way that it should do. But I'm delighted that we can have some time to ourselves." And he kissed her, longer than he'd done in a while, and she held him tightly. "Come on then, lots to talk about."

163

She'd had the sense, since their meeting in Morkuda, of a strange bond between Peter and Shen Wengwei. They'd both created huge business empires, she imagined that gave them a connection — and Peter, for all that he knew a great many people, had no one she could identify as a friend. The closest people to him were Will, who was like a son, and Alphonse, more like a younger brother, or maybe just a cousin. She wondered sometimes if his experience of his best friend stealing his fiancée all those years ago had somehow blocked him from allowing friendships to become too close. So, Wengwei as a friend, it seemed so unlikely in so many respects, but Peter had juggled his schedule to be in Shanghai when Wengwei asked to see him, without, so far as she could tell, offering anything beyond it being important.

Yes, dying would be important, she thought as Peter, plainly very moved, spoke more about it.

"I'm not questioning it, my darling, but do you know why you feel this extraordinary bond? You've not been in the man's company more than, what, three times? And do you know why he puts so much faith in you?"

He'd leaned back at that point. They were at the garden room table, the doors opening on to the birdsong dancing in on the warm spring evening air. It was time to let him think.

"I suppose," he said at length, "I should pick at this until I can answer those questions. This will take a lot of our time…"

"Our time?" she was surprised.

"I'll need your help. I have a very strong sense of wanting to do something for a man I have an odd affinity with, who may be dying, but we both know, he and I, that whatever I can do is best underpinned by a commercial basis to the relationship. Our property area works like that. We also manage the largest share of his fund money, and our control of that is absolute, but if we're going to help his little triumvirate manage his empire successfully, that contribution needs to be recognised and in that, as in many things, he and I see the world in similar ways. We both are very reluctant to share any control of what we've built, but he's managed to do that with me, with property and funds, and he's found I've helped — maybe that's why I'm the only one he can trust. I had dinner with Lee after I'd spent the afternoon with his father, and it was very touching. He seems keen for us to help too." Then he smiled. "It may just be that he's trying to put off the evil day when his little sister takes over the running of everything — but I truly think he's more mature and constructive than that. His younger brother, of course, who now calls her the bitch-bastard, he tells me, is much less grown-up about it. And it may be that Wengwei wants us to help there too."

He stood, walked to the doorway and sniffed at the air. "Do you remember, when we were selling bits of the business, how we were going to use all that time we would gain for each other?"

She laughed. "It's been one step forward and two back ever since — but this dwarfs anything that we've taken on so far."

He turned his back to the garden to look at her again. "It needn't... It mustn't... It can't."

She stood up, went towards him and put her arms around him. "Eyes open, my darling, it very well might — but that isn't going to stop you, is it? This seems to have the force of a dying wish."

"It's something other than that, I think. We both think of what each of us has put together as having a life force. Now these are both peculiar entities, you could argue that neither of us has enough focus in our businesses, but we both want the spirit of them to endure — and I'm going to have to face into what Dickinson Enterprises is going to be and how it can be sustained, just as he's trying to see Senlin beyond himself. So, it's an interesting exercise for me."

"That's a pretty maudlin perspective."

"I'm afraid he's confronted me with the inevitable. But I'm home with my darling, and I'm peculiarly happy. It's making me look at life, rather than death. Let's face into it." He held out his arms to her, she stood up and went to him in the doorway and let his arms envelope her. "Well, that was me. How was your week?"

"I've had a splendid week." She looked up and kissed him lightly on the lips. "I haven't travelled; well, one day in town and two in Surrey isn't travelling — not with Hannes driving. I've even had time on my own business. And I was here when Isobel came back with her London business head, Merle. Wow, that is a very beautiful woman, I can understand poor Will being very struck, but it was a very professional visit; all taking photos and measurements and asking me to look at pictures of rooms and furniture pieces to assess what appealed to me. It was almost like a psychological investigation. I was impressed. It was totally unlike the Sunday visit. That got a little alcoholic, I'm afraid, but I do have something to show you later." He raised his eyebrows. She was glad she'd blurted it out; she'd been so undecided about the chaise. If he expected nothing, she could say nothing — or she could decide that it was the stimulus their life needed. She no longer knew whether his indifference was a slow wilting into older age or a response to her passive lack of enthusiasm for a physical connection. And most of the time she was unenthusiastic, or maybe distracted was a better word. There was always so much to do, but on the two nights she'd spent in the blue bedroom the chaise had seemed to, what was it? — to either challenge or seduce her. She'd found herself, between bathroom and bed the night before, drawn to it. It seemed to invite her to lie over its end again, as she had done with Isobel — and then she'd wriggled and slid her pants down over her arse, wondering what it would feel like. After a moment's reverie, she'd stood up quickly — and then felt ashamed of her embarrassment. It should be part of their lives, but she could tease him with it for a while.

"Something I'll enjoy?"

"Oh, I very much think so." Although she was inwardly hesitant, and glad he hadn't made an immediate connection to the chaise. His embrace seemed to sense her doubts; there was a small physical retreat. He would never expose himself to the risk of her physical reluctance.

His "Well, it sounds like that's for later," had a ring of caution, at least — if not disbelief — and that almost quenched the little flame she'd been kindling in her moment on the chaise the previous evening. But only almost — and meantime there were other things to discuss.

Not the Far East, however; in the two calls she'd had, it sounded like Alphonse was coping well, in spite of the new challenges of Mei's situation and the absence of Isobel for the week. He'd been guarded enough about the help Daiyu was giving to make her at least conjecture on what might be happening. She hadn't liked to use the word 'suspect,' even to herself.

But she'd spoken every day with Tania. There was so much happening in the US with two acquisitions in the pipeline — and even her own consultancy business, Brodie Gunter Jeavons, was blooming — her London trip in the week had been to look at new office space with Alan, who remained cheerful at being the third name on the nameplate in spite of him doing ninety percent of the work these days. 'It's a brand,' he'd said when she'd offered to change it.

Tania had teased her when they'd discussed it: 'What do you mean, I'm not doing so much? Have you checked billings — and how much of our business is coming from my group?' They'd laughed, as they usually did, before the 'honestly, whatever Alan thinks is best — I'd have a slight preference for keeping the continuity of the brand name,' which only amplified Alan's view — a view entirely supported when she was sat back at the table with Peter, picking at the cold plates Hannes had laid out and drinking Sancerre.

The consultancy name had been her final business point. "Can I come on to something a little delicate?" Of course she could, that was just a figure of speech, they both knew, to signal a change of theme and tone. He nodded, sipped wine and leaned back. "We talked about Gerry Calvert when Isobel was here last Sunday…"

Peter looked pensive.

"You're not saying anything."

"Yes, then."

"Yes?"

"Yes, we did. What's on your mind?"

"Well, you said you'd stopped him coming to parties."

"Yes, I told you why that was."

"But you also said you'd stopped doing business with him. It wasn't for that reason, was it?" She knew the question would sound naïve, and she expected him to laugh at it, but he seemed to become very thoughtful.

"It's an aspect of business you and I don't talk about much, the twilight areas. His business started in shipping, although he's well diversified now, but he got started in the nineties when the wall came down and he made lots of Russian connections — and a decade later when their economy collapsed, largely because his new friends had been stealing all the country's assets, he was instrumental in helping them place their money elsewhere. We had been using them for logistics in several areas, but Henderson came to me one day…"

"Oh, that man!"

"I know what your feelings are. I don't have to go on. He'd picked up enough to worry me on all the other stuff and we quietly changed logistics providers. That's all."

"So, there's a lot more to the story."

"There's as much more to the story as you want to hear about. I don't think it helps us to enquire. Why are you interested?"

"Oh, I suppose because it's affected Isobel so much. How he's treated her friend has made her so angry and she talked a lot about it. Although I have to say, it was a boozy afternoon and I'd not had a let-your-hair-down girlie gossip for a long time. But it stayed with me, I suppose, and I remembered you saying that you'd stopped doing business with him. You also told Isobel, if you remember, that you would help her if she needed it on this topic."

"I did, didn't I? Is she seeing that as more than politeness?"

"She isn't. She's not asking. But you're never just politeness. And it had stuck in my head. I'm interested, I suppose. What was it?"

He took a slow sip of wine. "I'm not going to get away without satisfying some of your curiosity, am I?"

She shook her head. "I shouldn't be as naïve as I am about the twilight stuff."

Now he did laugh. She looked at him questioningly. "I'm sorry, but that's exactly the point Wengwei and I were discussing about Mei — but she needs to know because he's dying. I wasn't planning on leaving you just yet."

"No, please don't." An impulse took her to sit on his knee. "Am I too heavy?"

"Lighter than an angel." His arms were round her waist — and he kissed her tenderly. He looked thoughtful when their lips parted. "I should say something, darling, at least so you know how I keep us out of danger — but it means I'm going to be talking about friend Henderson."

She groaned. "I think you're telling me I have to be a big girl."

He looked uncomfortable. "I don't want to put it like that, but there are some things that need to be kept as tight as possible."

She stood up and held out a hand to him. "Look, I just had a feeling about the way it was discussed — and it had me wondering about what the man was capable of. But there's nothing I need to know if you don't think I should."

"No, it's one of those areas I've been meaning to talk about. Of course," and here she got a sly smile from him, "it doesn't encourage me when I get your usual reaction to Henderson's name."

"Oh, you're a big enough man to get through that, Peter Dickinson. In fact, you can tell me I'm being childish about it and deal with your brat later on the chaise…"

"I was hoping… I admit, it's been on my mind this week in my quiet moments, but shall we tidy this up first?"

"Yes, please, but tell me I've been a naughty brat about Henderson first."

He smiled slowly. "You've been a very naughty brat about Henderson — and on many occasions. I would think that needs at least twenty."
She found, to her great relief, that the prospect was beginning to excite her. "But are we going to the sofa first? We have some twilight stuff to discuss."

***

He was heavily asleep, but she was still trembling. She was on her side, looking at his serene face in the lamplight. The pains were delicious; there had not been a time since Jack when her arse had smarted like this, and if, in those wicked times that she now allowed herself to remember, she'd been more deeply thrust at, or more roughly handled than she had been tonight, they had come somehow in a rising sequence of events that had, in its strange way, prepared her.

Tonight, had been very different; this man, whom she loved so warmly, and who had treated her in their time together with unfailing gentleness — she smiled here, studying his face, and thinking of the very first time in the cellar — had finally given in to an inner devil that had now thrilled her. She'd had to provoke him — and before he'd fallen asleep, he'd been so lovingly solicitous — but the look of serenity was at least partly provoked by her insistence that she would want at least as much again when her skin had recovered — and that she'd just enjoyed the most thrilling night of her life — and that might almost be true, she thought.

But what a strange evolution the evening had been. It was almost as though, after he'd talked about all the dangers in the fringes of his world, the skirting of criminality in some of the foreign ventures — and the confrontation with criminality in the case of Calvert —
'we got as close as we needed to the laundering to stop us enquiring further, but there was undoubtedly much more' — that he seemed to have reached a point, finally, of seeing her as an absolute equal — and therefore someone whose needs and desires had to be met, and not merely pandered to. "You understood me so well on that first night, you stupid man, much better than I

understood myself. So, why do I have to wait for years for you to thrash me and fuck me as hard as you can. It's what I desperately want — and what you, you fool, are only hiding from yourself. Take me off my fucking pedestal and stick your fucking cock in me everywhere — but only after you've adored my arse and caned me!"

He'd been taken aback — and she worried for a while that she might have got it wrong — for him, and therefore for her but, after a deep breath, his cold 'just put yourself over the end of that chaise and be prepared to regret what you've wished for' had made her thrilled to obey.

And now, with the pain still screeching across her arse, she couldn't think she'd had so much as an instant of regret.

15

I'm not sure my neighbour will really want to spend his Saturday evening with me after the week he's had, but I've told him in the text, I'm seeing Mei tomorrow morning, so I would find anything he knows useful.

He probably thinks I'm just going to grill him about his week with Daiyu, and there is, of course, something in that.

I'll catch up with her on Monday morning. That will be an interesting meeting!

He is, of course, amenable. I pick up his text when I land.

Of course? Of course! Our arrangement is beneficial — for us both. I make no demands on him — well, almost none — nor does he on me. Even this evening is about helping him manage his property business when the role of his Far East business head, which is what Mei effectively is, is about to change — while she is also dealing with some dramatic changes in her life's landscape.

At some point I know we'll have to deal with this new arrangement in his life. It's obviously developed more than I expected it to. Do I mean expected — or intended? You see, I really didn't intend it. I just thought they could help each other a little. I just hadn't realised how much. Oh, well, Isobel the philosopher and philanthropist — always there for other people. If Alphonse and Daiyu are going to be a problem, they're tomorrow's problem. There are more urgent concerns.

I go to his apartment. It makes sense. He's three floors below me and we're going to eat in the restaurant down on the fourth floor. He'll have had a plane ride lunch and not much breakfast. I appreciate the openness Daiyu and I have — and I did give her some graphic descriptions of his preferences — which are, after all, not very exceptional — but I wasn't looking for the text I picked up after his message when I landed. He'll have told her he was going to have to see me and she obviously felt she had to tell me everything before I met him. Yes, thank you Daiyu, you're a real friend. But, when I reflect a little more in the taxi from the airport, she is the one who talks about 'the inefficiencies of tact' and it makes me smile. She is a friend, but I'm glad she's sore!

He invites me in. That's strange, I find I'm stepping in nervously. I get a big hug. I'm not quite ready for that — he's been fucking my friend and business partner this morning, you have to remember, but he's got the cool to ask me in to sit down and have a drink.

"I've booked for eight o'clock," I say. "They're busy. It's Saturday."

His arms are around me, and he kisses my lips — only gently, not at all passionately — but lips, nevertheless.

"Shall I call them and ask them to send something up? Our concierge can collect it." I hesitate. He doesn't. "We've got far too many things to talk about that we can't discuss in a busy restaurant."

He's right, of course, but it would be pointless to protest because he's calling them anyway and it's quickly organised. He's busy getting drinks and I'm sat looking at a view that's very similar to mine, but, I admit, I'm feeling awkward. "Champagne," I say, as he puts the glass in front of me. "Do we have something to celebrate?" He sits in the chair at the end of the coffee table and he has that smug cat smile on his face. I shouldn't be annoyed, but I am.

"Could we get the Daiyu thing out of the way first?" he asks.

"If you think that's appropriate." I'm not managing this at all well. I probably sound frosty.

"I think she'll say this to you anyway, if I don't, but it's been a very successful week — and we helped each other a lot. And yes, we do appear to have developed some sort of an arrangement — I think that's how you'd describe it."

"You slept with her every night. I hadn't expected that."

"Would you have slept with me every night? If you'd come, I mean. I was hoping you'd be there, remember?"

"So, you just went with the surrogate instead!" He looks a bit pained by that — and I'm instantly sorry I said it — and I say so — I am big like that.

Then I go on. "It would be completely wrong of me to get jealous or critical but it's obvious it's affected me — but I will get over it, you know I will, and I would hate it to influence what you two decide to do."

"We're both worrying about you."

"And that's why you spent the morning fucking her, is it?" Oh, I can keep the thunderbolts coming, even though the eye of the storm has passed. He's trying to decide how serious I am. "Oh, I'm OK, at least I'm not worrying about what you're concealing. My friend, I'm afraid, values honesty in our relationship just a little too much — I've had plenty of gory details — but she doesn't think you're rough enough, either." I laugh and, after a moment, he does too. "Although at least you've left her uncomfortable, I'm very happy to say." He is looking a little awkward now. "Look, it is sort of what I'd intended, I just hadn't thought you'd get quite so involved — but it's happened. You now have another arrangement in your life and I'm going to assume you'll meet occasionally." I'm expecting him to nod, but he doesn't. What's that about?

"We've said we won't, until we've spoken to you."

I explode. "Oh, for fuck's sake! You great boobies! It's up to you two. I have to get over it and get on with it — and I will. Jesus, I went to a party a friend organised for me in London and I had a wonderful time, thank you very much, including a little rough sex and some fabulous tongue treatment. We three are grown-ups, or we should be, you're just getting a little emotion and jealousy from me at the moment, but that's trivial compared to what others are dealing with. Can we move on? You've had to deal with Lee, and we both have to deal with Mei."

"But you're all right now?"

"Of course I am. I'll have a hug later, thank you very much, but you've got a lot to tell me, I think."
Now he is nodding slowly — then he gets up and comes to sit beside me. That's better!

***

I'm in my bed. No, I didn't stay with him. He sort of suggested it, but I knew I'd be restless first night back — and I certainly wasn't going to fuck him. That's funny, isn't it? I'd had at least three different men at Conrad's party — and that's not counting Conrad's playtime — but I'm not going to fuck a man who was fucking my friend this morning. I know people who would, it's a jealousy salve — but I see that for what it is.

I've told him to keep tomorrow night free, though. We don't get many opportunities. He's travelling again next week. And I'm lying here, sleepless, and worrying about him.

I'm sad about Wengwei. That's silly, isn't it? He's a tyrant who's fucked up his sons. Mei's probably lucky

179

she's been a safe distance from him, but she may be turning out to be more like him. Alphonse talks about her a lot. They're very close. But not in that way, the Morkuda night was a one-off for the three of us — and she and I have had no times together since then. Days, yes, the work partnership demands that — and I can see why she impresses him — and how she's learning from him. If she can acquire that smoothness of his, she'll be formidable. I think the old man is making the right decision, but I'm wondering how she'll be tomorrow. Imagine, you're thirty-five and you're having a meeting with the man you now have to acknowledge as your father — and he's probably dying. But I'm sure she'll cope. Now I'm not sure why I've suggested we meet. Nah, I think I'm important to her.

***

That's how it seems in the morning. Eventually.

She comes to me and, after a big, long hug, we seem to be beating about the bush, talking desultorily about the Phuroc event until I finally realise, she wants to make sure I'm OK about Alphonse and Daiyu. You see, she is more sensitive than she first appears. I know you may accuse me of belabouring the point, but good tops are empathetic people — and, although I don't know what she's been getting up to — not much, I suspect — I did try to stress that point when we had all that time together on our first Far East tour.

When I finally work out she's worrying about me, in spite of everything else going on in her life, I'm touched. I take her hand — we're on the sofa now — and tell her I'm fine. "They've both been communicating with me this week — more than I truly wanted, if I'm honest." She smiles here. "And Alphonse and I spent yesterday evening together. We're all good, and we're all worrying about you."

There's a long silence now, with her looking out over the harbour to Kowloon. We're still holding hands, but her fingers are twitching like spider's legs. I wonder whether to hug her, but I think it's my place to wait to be responsive.

"Do you think I can do it?" is what she finally says, without turning to look at me. I'm surprised by what seems like such a solipsistic perspective. "I would hate to let anybody down." Now I feel guilty for my crass assumption.

"I think you're amazing, and I know Alphonse does, but whether that's enough to enable a young woman to run a major Chinese conglomerate, well, I don't honestly have an idea. How much help will Shen Wengwei be able to give?"

I'm flustered about whether to say 'your father,' but she solves my problem. "Maybe not much. My father is very sick. He told me when we were on our own and said I had to be ready quickly. He is going to introduce me to everybody — but he has also asked Peter Dickinson to

*help me. He saw him the day before." That surprised me,
although I don't know why it should have done.*

"And your brothers?"

*"Liqiang has been wonderful, I think — I need to
be careful, of course, but I have a good feeling about
working together. Liuwei is an arsehole. I told him that
yesterday, Baba said I could."*

"Baba?"

"Papa."

"Now you have two papas?"

*"No, Zhao Zhang is Fuqin, my father, he will stay
that officially. And Shen Wengwei will be Baba when it's
just the two of us. But it's nice to call him Baba when it's
you and me talking." This is the soft side of Mei — it is
almost always concealed.*

"What about your mother?"

*"We had a long talk yesterday. Fuqin wasn't there,
obviously. It was easier than I thought. I've had several
days to get used to it. And when I see Baba on my own,
I understand how a woman could, you know…" That
was a little beyond me. I found the man coarse and
crude, but I don't have a daughter's eyes — and he's
plainly being very loving and supportive. He must have
made up his mind that she's tough enough.*

*"How open are you about your life when you talk
with your mother? Has she asked about marriage and
grandchildren?"*

"She used to, but, of course, even without knowing all this now, I knew that she and Fuqin weren't happy, so she couldn't tell me marriage was desirable."

"But does she know you're…"

Now she turns to me, puts her hands on my shoulders and looks very hard at me. "What am I, Isobel?" Then she smiles — it's quite sweet when she does, it's just infrequent. "At least you've helped me enjoy men a little." Now the smile is becoming a little sly. "I have been a very good girl. I've been eighteen months travelling with the most attractive man I've ever met — and I've often thought how an arrangement with him would suit me. What do you think?" But she's giggling now — although, if she'd really made a play, I think he might have gone along — he is only a man, after all. But at least that tells me that they're both taking work very seriously. Running Senlin Property Asia is already a huge job — and that's what Alphonse has effectively had her doing.

"But I haven't said I'm gay to my mother — but she is not the beaten-down little housewife I always thought. Their affair went on for years, even after I was born. She stopped it in the end. But she did admit that Baba was being pretty naughty in many other places by then."

"And Fuqin?"

"I suppose I should feel sorry for him — but he was always so cold to me. I understand why now — but I was the only real innocent in all their arrangements. Never mind. Look forward! That's what Alphonse always tells

me. But what about this Peter Dickinson thing? What do you think?"

I'm groping. I don't know what to think. I'll probably talk to Claudia about it. I have to call her anyway. I had a text thanking me for the chaise. That did make me smile. But Mei has asked a difficult question now.

"I have a thought on that, but I'm not sure how much use it will be. What did Baba say?"

"Can you tell me your thoughts first?"

This is a smart lady. Of course she's right to ask, she doesn't want me fitting an answer around what Shen Wengwei has told her. So I dive in. "I know some men — no women until now," and I take her hand from my shoulder and kiss it lightly — and proudly, "some men who run very big businesses — and I know a few men who actually own very big businesses — and there is something different about them. If this happens as Baba is planning, this will be your business to own and run. Lee and Lou will own big shares, but you will be the Shen Wengwei, or the Peter Dickinson — and I'm thinking of two other men I spent time with in London. They all seem to have an absolute faith in themselves and in what they do. Some of what they do is not nice, maybe sometimes it becomes illegal. They will probably tell you that deniable is more important than legal. They do listen, but they seem to have a different ear, none of them is ever fooled by bullshit." I squeeze her hand and smile. "And neither are you. But they all approach what they do with an unshakeable faith that what they're doing is right. And if it ever turns out wrong, they always believe they will somehow make it right. It's much deeper than self-confidence, it's an absolute conviction about themselves — and us little people either don't have it, or, if we think we have, we're deluded, and that's worse. That's my view anyway. But what did he say?"

She smiled slowly. "He just said 'trust only yourself.' He said it several times, like it should have big letters: Trust Only Yourself! — And he said that was how Peter saw things also. I think you were close." But there's a tear welling up, and she sniffs. "I'm sorry. It was wonderful being with him. I felt I'd walked into a most beautiful garden, and he made the sun shine on me — but the night and the rain will come too soon." And she falls on to me, sobbing, and it takes a while to pass.

But pass it does. This is Mei in my arms. I soon have her brave face again, and after some tissue-work on nose and eyes, the conversation continues — and keeps surprising me. "So, I have Peter to help me, and Alphonse will still be on property, so I still see him. But I have a favour to ask."

"Of me?"

"Of course, of you." OK, I'm ready, what's coming now, I wonder. "Can we have an arrangement?"

I'm quick. "Of course we can." I think that's what I feel, but there's no point in looking doubtful — not with her current situation. This may just be a reaction to all she's going through.

"This isn't a sudden thought, you know."

Now I do start to look doubtful — but that's wrong. "It doesn't matter, my darling. We've had some wonderful times, but I thought you'd moved on."

"Oh, Lily's fun — and I didn't know where that was going, but that's more of an arrangement now. Well, it may not even be that, really. It's probably just sex — but it helped me through the week."

Yes, Mei, if you were a real top, you'd give more than you took, but never mind, let's see how she wants to manage this — although my mind's finding it hard to engage with the idea at the moment. "I'm saying yes, because I think you need something like that. But I'm also saying yes for me. I like how we play." I have made her more fun, more adventurous, more experimental. "And I like being part of your life. I'm assuming, especially now, that you want someone you can trust and share pillow secrets with when things get difficult."

"Well, I like how you play with my body too. But, yes, I'd like someone I could really trust to talk to sometimes."

"You can have that without an arrangement, you know."

"I know, but I want the clamps and plugs as well. I was learning a lot — and I don't like masturbating." She's laughing now.

So I laugh. "I'm not proud of where this discussion's got to. We were supposed to be talking about running a huge business, about finding out what your family is, and coping with your real father maybe dying."

"Yes, but I can do all that so much better if I know you're going to spend the night with me sometimes."

"I'll be thrilled to do it." And that's not so far from the truth — and it's what she needs at the moment.

We cuddle together on the sofa and finally, with the arrangement secured in her mind, we can talk about the other things: about Shen Wengwei — 'I'd never thought about losing someone before;' about Liqiang — 'he has always been friendly to me, but it was difficult at first, although he did manage to tell me that his father, our father, thought I should ultimately be the boss — and he told me he understood why, I thought that was very big of him.'

I thought that was very big of him, but, from the little I know of him — well, it's not so little, I was helping Alphonse through that — that sounds like him. He doesn't have that all-devouring ego that the others have. That's obviously not the way I put it to her earlier, but she has it. It doesn't matter how you put it — maybe her father's 'trust only yourself' is the best way to put it — and she will, but I don't mind helping.

I think she might have stayed, but once I'd committed to see her next Saturday — she'll be coming back from Shanghai — she seemed more relaxed about leaving and getting back to work. Yes, it's what we do on Sundays.

***

She got a flight back on Friday evening and came straight to me, which suited me. I'd been fretting about maybe having to get back to the UK again — but I'll return to that later.

She was overwrought, definitely tense: she projects that cold emotionless persona when she's like that, I've learned. But she'd texted from Shanghai airport to ask if she could come, so she clearly had some needs.

I didn't think sex would be one of them — she'd had plenty of Lily in Phuroc — but after a perfunctory kiss at the door it was 'please come to bed with me first.'

Now, what was unusual was not that she came quickly, although she was very shrill, but she insisted on making me come before we got down to talking. Her partner is not normally a priority for her — yes, we know a lot of men like that, don't we?

I could have waited. I knew she had a lot of emotional baggage — and so did I after this week — and anxiety too.

But she's my priority. I had to get her talking.

In truth, she had no real surprises for me. She'd spent a lot of time with Wengwei, some with Lee — and she'd even had dinner with Lou. The latter is the easiest to report on first; it was not a success — but I admire her for trying, and she'd done it on her own initiative.

188

I'm surprised he agreed but, listening to her, he'd obviously thought he might make some points of his own about how the future would look. He has even less understanding of Mei than she has of him — and he appears to have no understanding that his views are of no account. So, she's trying to keep him on board, for her father's sake — but it doesn't sound like it's going to work. She won't give up, though.

It sounds like she was getting somewhere with Lee. She thinks he's got his mind around being the number two of Senlin — after all, he still has the original business to run and Senlin Group will look like some sort of holding company. They will want to keep a low public profile anyway. But he was getting a little sensitive about how his role in that would be described. I think he'd at least got her thinking about that — until they talked to Wengwei. That had been unpleasant, apparently, at least at first. The enfeebled lion had still managed to roar — for him, for all the people they did business with, there had to be one person they looked to — and that would be Zhao Meitang. Lee had looked a little beaten-up at that point but his father then included him in a review of all the people they would interface with — and who he would introduce Mei to over the next few weeks before his health failed.

"Has he accepted that he's not getting better?"

"No, that's the strange thing. He plans for it, but he still acts immortal." *She's caught up in a little Wengwei-*

adoration at the moment. I hope she comes out of that — I guess he's betting she will.

But what he talked about then was a surprise to Lee, as well as Mei. They keep a large legal department busy, she'd expected that; the political connections are few, but very important, and very expensive — her finance head would explain all that, and how it was kept entirely legal.

The next section amused her. They were together in his office in his own house but he'd dropped his voice to a whisper — she could only think that he didn't want even his wife to hear: there were some old friends, he had called them, who had helped him a great deal in the early days. Their work was no longer important, or even necessary, for Senlin, but they were kept on retainer, in case of emergencies. He would introduce her to the most important two next week. Here he'd changed a little and looked in a kindly way at Lee and said, 'I'm sorry, my son, it can only be one person, that is all they will understand,' but then he'd got a little fierce again. 'And if anyone tries to speak to you, you must be absolutely clear: one family, but one boss, understand,' and Lee had breathed deeply and said, 'I understand, Father, really I do. Will you give Lou the same message?'

Wengwei had laughed aloud at that. 'No one will talk to your brother anyway. No one will take him seriously. You should be flattered I'm saying you could be a danger. But you won't be!' and he'd fixed them both with a watery-eyed stare and waited until they'd nodded.

On their own, the next day, he'd made her go through everyone she knew in the corporation — it wasn't that many — and give her views on them. She'd protested, her knowledge was so superficial — here he'd threatened to get cross but I could tell from how she was telling the story that he dotes on her and is relieved that he has someone he can trust to hand on to — 'you meet someone in jungle, you make up your mind quick, that's survival; lions don't ask questions.' And by the time she'd gone through twenty names, he was smiling benignly.

But then a strange thing happened: 'You're worried about something, aren't you?' she asked me.

"Well, I'm worried about how you're going to cope."

"No, it's not that. Well, it might be a bit, but something else is going on with you. Is it Alphonse?"

"Good Lord, no, no. I admit I got a little possessive, but we've worked all that through." I got a sceptical eyebrow from her. "I do mean all three of us. No, but there is something else. Let's get a drink and sit and look at the harbour at night."

And we went to the sofa and I told her about Sandra. She hasn't replied to my texts — and I'm worried. I'm even more worried now I have more background on Gerry. I'd had a long phone call from Claudia during the week, telling me a lot that Peter had told her. And the more I told Mei, the more she wanted to know. But she was better prepared than I had been.

I work for clients, I get paid. Usually on time but in ten percent of cases there are difficulties — but I have a sixth sense about when to expect them. It's more difficult for me out here, of course, but Daiyu has a similar talent — a feeling for the local clients. The point is, however, that I don't give any thought to where the money has come from. Mei is more sensitive. She was anyway, she says, but her awareness has risen since she's been working with Alphonse — it meant that the discussion with her father started with a level of appreciation, on her part, of the dangers of some sources of money. Wengwei had patted her knee at one point and said, 'That man is teaching you well.' It's not something Alphonse has ever spoken to me about but, listening to Claudia, it's a major concern for Peter.

'If they're worried about money, they try to guide it into funds where they can quarantine it,' is what she'd said. 'Trying to unpick a property deal would be a nightmare.' If the authorities come for someone's investment portfolio, at least it can be separately identified — not that they've ever given any back, apparently, although some jurisdictions have come calling. I'd asked if that made him complicit in money laundering. He tries not to worry about that, he just doesn't want GKD, his investment business, getting a reputation for being soft with the authorities — his clients wouldn't like that — and there are very few accounts that are entirely clean.

For me, I finish a project and money is in the business within thirty days. I work for an eclectic bunch of clients, increasingly from outside of the UK, and I get paid from a wide variety of places. I sometimes find out more about what the client does — I often meet them after completion — and in very few cases is it straightforward. I've even had a London barrister pay me from an account in the Cayman Islands. That was a long time ago and I quickly decided that I had no business pursuing enquiries like that — well, that was his advice, to be fair. I'd met him a number of times after the project. I'd guessed what his tastes ran to — my first leather outfit dates from then. He liked to be petted after I'd caned him (yes, after he'd promised to be a good boy — it was that silly) so conversations moved on to other areas. I asked about the Cayman Islands and the first thing he said, in a nice way, was that I would be better off not enquiring. His affairs were, of course, entirely legitimate; he had funds abroad from international work. But his smile was telling me that I should be content that I had clean money in my bank account. He asked about other clients, but he was doing it in a helpful way — and I'm not naïve, it was useful that he allowed me to be a little curious.

On a separate occasion, after an extensive playtime — never with penetration, though, I simply had to help him masturbate afterwards — he told me what he'd sometimes paid for his pleasures. I was surprised — a couple of grand upwards — but I do it for fun. I don't take a moral view of prostitution. I just prefer to make my own choices.

But for my business, his advice was 'just take the money and don't ask, no one will come after you, you're way down the food chain.'

That's not the position Peter or Wengwei can be caught in and, after the conversations with Claudia and now Mei, I can understand that.

And I can understand that they also don't take a moral position, they just need to be certain — or as near certain as they can be — that they're insulated from the more dangerous sources. It's why Peter made sure he doesn't work with Gerry any more — and Wengwei's 'old friends,' who are now mostly retired, or dead, have their riches carefully placed elsewhere. He still advises them, and that will become Mei's job. I think she's quite excited about meeting the old rogues — but they have killed people in the past — 'Baba didn't want to tell me, but I made him. He says it was a long time ago.'

I don't think my view of the world was changed by either conversation, the shapes and colours stayed the same, but everything came into a much sharper focus.

And that made me call Boris. I couldn't think of anyone else I could ask to look for Sandra. He was wonderful. 'Of course I look, where she live?'
That made it much easier to join Mei in the bedroom again.

***

It was early morning when the text came: 'I find her she OK, I call you tomorrow.'

'Tomorrow?' was my first thought, but it was still Friday for him, so now I could feel relieved, but I'd woken Mei, whose arms now came around me. We didn't touch the toys and lube, carelessly abandoned by the bedside last night — she has become surprisingly adventurous, I'm delighted to say. It was I who declined the strap-on. We were fully engaged with plugs and dildos and I didn't want to break the rhythm — but this morning we just rolled together touching, kissing and cuddling — and coming, giving ourselves those long slow ones where it's probably several but it feels like being taken continuously by waves in the same warm sea.

But some switch seemed to click inside her at nine o'clock. 'I have lots to do, do you mind?' I just laughed at that and she looked a little hurt at first — then she laughed too. 'You think — typical Mei, don't you?'

I do, and I told her and I kissed her, but I also said she had to be like that. She has huge responsibilities now. 'I'll come again soon,' she said but I told her to put no pressure on herself. I'd had a lovely night — and we had an arrangement. And I meant all that, but I was also happy when she'd gone and I could return to my other concerns.

Boris may have found Sandra, but she still wasn't responding to my texts — still, it was the middle of the

*night back there. I couldn't ring Boris again. He'd found
her, she was OK, why was I worried?*

***

*Because it turns out she's in the fucking Argosy again.
That's why I was worried. It's mid-afternoon when Boris
rings: "Why the fuck didn't you say?" I scream at him
when he tells me — and I have to apologise immediately.*

*"What you do? She safe there." He's not even
indignant when he says that, and I'm saying, "Of course
she is, you're absolutely right, I'm sorry, I'm so grateful
to you."*

*"It's no problem, she your friend, she my friend,"
he said, which is all very reassuring, but now I need to
know what's happened. And it's unpleasant.*

There had been no lock on the door: "Broken?" —

"No, just taken out, hole where lock should be."

*There had been some damage. "not much, just like
someone show what they could do."*

*She was on the bed, unconscious, but from the pills,
he thought, not from the blows to the face: "look like
they just slap her a bit, shut her up maybe."*

"What pills?"

*"I don't know, I take to Argosy, they say she be all
right."*

*He's told Conrad. Conrad's paying again. I
criticize myself for thinking about that aspect of it but,
although my business is doing well, those bills could*

196

quickly eat a big hole in my current account. And my business accounts have to be kept straightforward — Will sees them; well, his people do. I can't think a big hospital bill would go unchallenged. It crosses my mind briefly about what he'd make of this.

About Sandra, I mean, not about funny money moving around. It strikes me, having listened to Claudia and Mei, that he must know a lot about funny money, if only just to make sure Peter's operations stay clean. The whole Merle affair had blown up when he'd found her husband, his boss at the time, doing some dodgy deals with Gerry.

Boris is trying to reassure me she's safe. But she has nowhere to go. It seems obvious to me that Gerry has sent someone to frighten her out of the place. I'd better talk to her before I talk to her brother. But he won't be able to find her somewhere to live, even if she were prepared to let him.

And Gerry is unspeakable. And probably irredeemable, but I might have to give it one more try.

"Isobel, I'm so glad you called. I was going to ring you later."

I admit, I'm taken aback by this, but I'm determined to stay cool. Just telling him what I really think of him isn't going to help me or Sandra. "I'm surprised you were going to ring me. What do you want?"

"Well, you got me first. Shouldn't you say — although I guess it's the same topic. It'll be my renovation projects, I'm sure."

You arsehole, I think. We both know it's not that but that's his usually vile way of reminding me I have commercial interests but I've already made up my mind that we'll finish these commissions professionally and then have no more to do with him. "Don't be smart, Gerry, it doesn't suit you. The projects are all on track and on budget. I'm calling about Sandra."

"Yes, of course you are, and I have a piece of advice for you on that."

"You have advice for me?" *I'm surprised.*

"Yes. Deal with it as you want to, but keep the gorilla away."

"What the fuck are you on about?"

"Conrad's man, you sent him round there."

How did he know that? "Yes, I was worried about her. You're evicting her, she has nowhere to go."

"I leave all that to Donald, he runs London property. I just told him I wanted sensible returns on everything, he has to act on that, and he has people to help him. That's where you're creating a problem. They want revenge."

"What are you talking about?"

"Donald's two boys; he'd sent them to encourage her to pay or leave, they got little sense out of her, she'd taken too many of her happy pills, so they tried their own way of leaving a message when the gorilla arrived."

"I didn't know…"

"Assumed you didn't. I don't suppose Donald will follow it up with any of you, but that's his business —

but she should definitely stay away and find somewhere else."

"She has things there." I'm just making assumptions. She'll have picked up some valuable items over the years.

"You'd better get it cleared out this week. I don't want any problems with Conrad — and I'm fairly sure he'll want none with me — and you and the gorilla won't want any with Donald's boys. They'd be better prepared next time. Goodbye."

And that's it. I'm feeling dirty for even bothering, but at least I know now that Boris missed out one part of the story — and I'm rather amused by what he must have done. It's obviously best for Sandra now if we put Gerry behind her. But she needs somewhere to live.

Right now, Boris is the only one I could trust to help. Merle would be condescendingly difficult and delegate it to one of our girls, who would be useless.

I'm not sure how much he understands — phone calls are difficult when someone's English is so poor, but he seems surprisingly cheerful about helping. Whether he'll be able to work out what's worth keeping, I've no idea. His 'don't worry, I sort everything' reassures me — but not much. Now I have to get on to the difficult bit.

"She has nowhere to go, Boris. You can take her to my place until I get back but it's too small for me to have someone else living there. Does Conrad have anything free?" I'm pushing it a bit with my excuse. I'm a Samaritan, but not a particularly good one. And the

woman has done a lot of favours for Conrad over the years — just less so recently as he's engaged younger resources.

But Boris surprises me now. "It's no problem, she have spare room here, next to me on top floor, have to share bathroom. OK?"

Well, she should be grateful, but people can be very funny about generosity. "That's very kind of you. Are you sure?"

"I sure, no problem."

"And Conrad? Will he mind?"

"Of course he mind."

Is this linguistic confusion? I wonder.

"But he away two weeks. We find something different then, I think. I talk to him."

"You're a treasure, Boris. I can't thank you enough."

"No problem. Call me tomorrow afternoon. I have her here. When you come back?"

"I'll make it in two weeks, then. I'll look out for somewhere small to rent for her."

I'm mostly relieved. We've solved the urgent problem, and I guess I'm resigned to having to help out with rent for a while. How have I become responsible? Most of the people I know, the ones who have the resources to help in situations like this, are content to leave it to the individuals to sort their own problems out. Some are like Gerry and quite capable of provoking the situations that harm the helpless. The thing is, when I'm criticising myself for being too soft, even for encouraging dependency, I do wonder whether I'm being exploited by manipulative victims. Somehow, it's more transparent and acceptable in playtimes — and if you suspect a bottom is being just that little bit too self-centred, you usually have a remedy in your hands: hit harder — or refrain altogether.

But here is real life. I'm not accusing Sandra of just letting someone else solve her problems for her. Not accusing, but it is a thought, and on my down days, which are rare, I can put a lot of people in that category.

But she is a friend — and she needs someone — and it sounds like dear Boris will help for long enough. Then maybe I can work something out with Conrad — but I think his Arab friends want someone younger than Sandra. And in two weeks?

Fuck it! She has to manage something for herself!

But Boris does seem keen to be helping. I wonder.

<h1 style="text-align:center">16</h1>

Claudia was amused by how solicitous he'd been the following morning. It had started with him bringing her tea in bed — that was a first.

She'd deliberately overdone the wince as she turned on to her back to take it from him — and then laughed when he'd looked concerned. "I'm teasing," she'd said as she'd taken the cup. "I'd forgotten how robust I was."

"Was I very bad?"

"Oh, you were dreadful." But she was smiling as she said it. "I've never seen you like that. Well, I didn't actually see you, of course, I was pinned down by this unspeakable monster behind me having all his evil delights." But she wasn't going to extend the tease very long. "My darling man, I am still a bit sore, but it was a thrilling night for two reasons." Now the worried, furrowed look eased into one of puzzlement. "I had a wonderful time. However serious and respectable I've become, I am still the woman whose inhibitions you unlocked all those years ago — but, all this time, I've been wondering how I unlock what's inside you. You've always seemed so considered and controlled — even when I've been getting you to come. That was the first time I'd felt something wild in you — and it was glorious."

"It wasn't too much?"

"Oh, for God's sake, no! I want it again — and again. Just not today, maybe," she said, and, when he'd frowned again at that, "but I am going to show you your handiwork — and it's my arse that's sore, not my pussy. My pussy wants your cock again while you're telling me once more what a glorious arse I have." She'd felt nervous about how slutty to be for him, but staying loving and lovely, which is how he often told her she looked, had never seemed to unleash him — not like last night. And in the morning, it had worked again. "I'm ready now," she'd said, as she turned and lifted her arse, "but I'll be very happy if you lick me first." And he had done as she'd raised her arse as high as she could — and he'd licked and stroked and played, just occasionally letting his stiffening cock bounce against her legs, reassuring her that he would have her, could have her, until she found herself shouting, "Stick him in me, for fuck's sake, stick him in me." It seemed to work so well for him: she felt his hands gripping her hips, avoiding the sore spots on her arse, but feeling him pushing faster and faster — she knew he was close — and so was she. As soon as she touched herself, she felt herself coming with him.

They'd slumped, smiling, into each other's arms and she'd drifted off into a brief sleep for a few moments, waking to him kissing her forehead and stroking her hip.

"I'm extraordinarily happy," he'd said. She'd kissed his lips lingeringly. She was too.

It had been the start of a wonderful week for them — a rare week with them both at home in Barnes, with Abbi and Jo lingering through to the Tuesday, after their friends had left, eating dinner together on the Monday as if in some unconscious ritual of inclusion for Peter to induct him, finally, into their family.

Claudia had been almost as touched as Peter was when Abbi had hugged him as she'd been leaving on the Tuesday morning. But, as Abbi had hugged her, she'd whispered, "I love it when you're happy, Mum," and they'd both burst into noisy laughter.

She'd hugged Peter and said, "I'll explain later," as Abbi treated them to a sunny, conspiratorial smile.

Sometime later that day, Peter had asked if they could have a China day on Friday. She'd been happy to move appointments. China had been on her mind — how could they help, how would it help them — but the Friday night experience was still alive for her, and would have been even without the constant physical reminders, so she felt bold enough to demand, "But the same again in the evening, please, after bath-time and, for the avoidance of doubt, I want Peter the Monster. I shall want you everywhere — and the chaise should be the centrepiece. I'm not even going to pretend to be bratty or anything like that. I love what you do with your hands and the cane — and I especially love what you do with your cock — and your little electric friend."

He'd smiled. "I thank you very, very much for such a detailed briefing, but if I think of any embellishments, you will be subjected to those too."

She'd looked seriously at him. "I'll be thrilled with everything — but just the two of us — well, and toys, and your dirty mind."
They'd hugged for a long time. He seemed happy, and somehow relieved. Maybe they were turning a corner.

***

She surprised him on Friday. They were breakfasting together, a rare treat, when he stood to slope off to his study. "We're starting promptly at nine o'clock."

He looked startled. "I have to…"

"You have to be in the library at nine."

He seemed to relax. "Thank you. It's been feeling like a dentist's visit. I need that prompt." This was unlike him. He was normally so disciplined and would always face into the difficult issues first but she'd sensed his reluctance and had decided to tackle it formally in their agreed meeting, avoiding the temptation to circumvent the looming problems in what was proving to be one of their most relaxed weeks together.

He came into the library at nine. "Gosh!" The furniture had been moved and she'd had Hannes put a flip chart side-on to the two displaced sofas.

"To my mind, we need to be clear about four things: what does Senlin do; how do you train Mei; how you make the trio work; and what's in it for us — which comes last, of course."

He sipped the coffee he'd brought in and put the cup on the table in front of him. "Thank God, you've given it some thought. I've been struggling about how to approach it. What you're saying makes sense to me, and I certainly can't offer an alternative."

"Good. Now the first topic is the biggest and most complex, but the blueprint essentially exists..." She'd spent much of the week studying the activities of the core Senlin business. "No one in the West would grumble about double-digit growth but the share data is starting to look worrying, so it needs a fresh impetus. There's plenty of cash, of course, to finance acquisitions, but that needs a clear head and a lot of energy. Does that sound like Liqiang to you?"

He looked pensive. "Well, it's a good team running the business. It doesn't look like Wengwei's let them get complacent. As far as Liqiang himself is concerned, well, what do you think?"

She smiled at him. She was used to this by now. He made her commit to her own idea first. "I'm OK about the clear head. I think he's very bright, but I'm not sure about the energy."

"Do you think that's been affected by his distractions over the past year or two?"

"Maybe…" And she waited.

He smiled. "Maybe, but it shouldn't have been?" She nodded. "I think I agree with you. We have to get him focused. He's got to be their Tania out there and I'm not seeing that level of energy. I think we pincer this one. I'll ask him to tell us his plans in four weeks and suggest he talks to you in the meantime so you can seed a few ideas."

"OK." She was nodding slowly. "And?"

He chuckled. "Yes, and. And you can test out the dynamism of his responses."

"He'll know we're working together on this."

"We'd think he was stupid if he didn't, but he'll trust you a little as an ally. I think he felt quite close to you in Morkuda, didn't he?"

"I think so, and he'll know we want it to work. Did I pick up in the middle of that that we're in China in four weeks?"

"Can you manage that?"

"I'll have to shuffle a bit, but yes." She still kept a clear picture of her diary in her head even though work had grown complex — but Abbi and Jo needed less attention these days. Well, she thought, avoided more attention would be more correct. "Can you leave Mei that long?"

"No, but I'm at a loss anyway about how to approach that project anyway."

"Who taught you in your early days?"

"Ha! Well, nobody, of course. I got lucky with a few things and took it from there."

"That, my darling, just will not do. We all see behind this front of louche amateur dabbling — and I know how much time you spend on analysis and phone calls. I don't suppose it matters exactly why you're so driven, but how you make it work does matter. I've got my views on that, and we should see if they tally with yours, but even when we've done that, it still leaves us with the question of what's right for Mei and how we can offer anything to her."

He looked uncomfortable. "She's not me, even if we can agree on what my formula was — or is. And I was starting small, as her father was, and even, to use another example we've spoken of recently, Gerry Calvert." He grunted quietly. "I don't like that comparison. I'm not even sure I like being bracketed with Wengwei, but even if we could analyse them accurately, it doesn't mean we have relevant advice to give to someone who has to take over what is actually an established conglomerate."

"But your new friend obviously thinks you have worthwhile advice and guidance for her."

"I think you've put that well. We need to restrict ourselves to those objectives: advice and guidance. We can't make choices for her, or let her try to copy what we've done. At least Alphonse feels she tackles things in her own way." He smiled. "He says she used to embarrass him with some of her approaches until he realised how effective she was — and she would cast her net wider than he would and go faster if they could access more funds. But she never proposes bad deals."

Claudia nodded, unsure of how much to say but relieved that Alphonse seemed to have had the same conversations with Peter as he'd had with her.

Peter seemed to have stopped to think. "What I used to like to do was confront people with the unthinkable, with the borderline absurd. Once it had worked a couple of times, they began to treat my ideas a little differently, like they were expecting the radical.

"I got Henry and Tony started when I saw they were trying something very new with funds, and Alphonse always looked in new areas. We've never tried the 'copy but better' route — always go for the different. Does that make sense?"

"Completely. I think that's why Tania does so well with the Group. She looks in new areas. They must link in with the rest, but she won't touch anything unless there's a different approach at the heart of it." She paused. He was looking pensive. "What's up?"

"My mind went back to that wretched Calvert. You could say that even he's put an operation together that is based on new approaches and unorthodoxy but, without looking too closely, I suspect a great deal of it is illegal. That's almost a given with his Russian connections."

"Does that bother you?"

"Somebody else's problem. It's only my problem if I get tainted by association. We try to keep clean by having clear principles but, however transparent our reporting, I couldn't swear that we're blemish-free, could you?"

She shrugged. "I think we're close to that in the Group, but I think we're admitting that the money that comes into property and funds might have some dubious sources. We don't do any more than ensure it's clean when it enters our system, do we?"

He sighed. "No, we don't, but I made my peace with that pretty early on. We have at least two major client organisations investing in funds whose ultimate beneficial owners are in prison, but the connection can't be established across the murky organisations between them and us. And there's a lot more grey stuff, out there." He paused and smiled at her. "Does it bother you and, second question, in your Senlin research, have you seen anything that looks suspicious?"

She wasn't troubled. She felt sure Dickinson stayed ethical, but she had grown aware that other organisations they dealt with seemed to bend rules. "It's funny you should ask. I'm sure we're clean — as are most of the people the Group deals with — but I wondered how Senlin progressed so well in the early days." She looked at him questioningly.

"I think we're being left with plausible deniability by that old fox. He's told me about friends who helped him in at the start. He kind of left it with me to work out how much I wanted to know. He said he'd told me as much as he'd told Mei, but that these people were entirely independent from him now but received innocent retainers for possible future services — and presumably to keep quiet about past ones."

"Is that as sinister as it sounds?"

"Probably. And there's no point in me being mealy-mouthed about it with Mei, but we're mostly out of danger now. The government connections will see to that. Wengwei assures me that those are based more on principles than people and old connections now, but he smiled when he told me that principles were more expensive."

"Does that mean we're comfortable with the Senlin set-up now?"

"I don't think we're challenged ethically, but they haven't reshaped the core business enough, I wouldn't think. You made the point that double-digit growth means you don't look enough at new businesses but share declines tell you you're making mistakes or getting complacent. They, well, I should say he, seem to have been happy to cash-cow their main business and get into property and funds. I did ask him if that was mainly to get things further away from government interference — he just smiled. But they do need to ask themselves if the old core will continue to be the engine, in which case it needs looking at closely. That will be the first test for her: how she sees it — how she approaches it — and, if she thinks changes are necessary, how she gets its business head…"

"You mean Lee…"

"Exactly — how she gets her business head to expand in new directions — and whether they'd have enough freedom from interference to make sensible business decisions. I'd like to get Wengwei's views before we dive in, I hope he's well enough in four weeks. What's up?"

She was beginning to feel uncomfortable. "I'm not disagreeing with your analysis at all…"

He smiled. "Well, I'm mostly just repeating what you've been saying."

She felt gratified by that observation. "I just worry that you'll be spoon-feeding her too much — if she's as good as we need her to be, she'll be developing her own thoughts anyway. Let's ask her to talk to us in four weeks about how she sees it developing. She may come up with better thoughts than the ones we've just been having. I think we're agreeing that we wouldn't find it acceptable to just get projections from the status quo, right?"

"Right, and maybe that's the step into our second point. How do we train her…?"

She was happy with the two hours they spent. "You can get back to work now," she said decisively, standing up and pulling another well-filled sheet off the flip chart. "I'll put these into shape and send you the notes this afternoon."

"Is that where I end up with more action points than you?" he asked. She could have been annoyed, but his smile told her he was joking. He had plenty to do, some of it awkward — but she was getting used to the idea of having to engage Henderson again for some of the researches. Her most difficult task would be working on Lee, hoping he would see the opportunity and not retreat into resentment.

Difficult as that might be, Peter's task of dealing with Lou was a bigger mountain, but at least they had identified options — of which the fall-back was letting him replace Mei's official father as nominal head of property. But their fingers-crossed hope was that he would show aptitude and application on the fund work in the time they would ask him to spend in London and New York with Henry and Tony — who would surely see the advantages of having a well-connected Chinese super-salesman, if that was what he could become, pulling more business in throughout Asia. But he would have to show competence and commitment, and not just use his old connections. The prize for him would be a greater level of autonomy from his sister. If anyone could get him working in that way, Peter could.

17

The messages I've been getting from Sandra and the calls I've had with Boris have allowed me to feel that she's settled safely. But Sandra has complained about sharing a bathroom and about the wrong things being brought and the wrong things being stored and her racism about anything but British white seems to intrude into her texts — I suppose our interactions before were heavily circumscribed by their circumstances. I'm getting to know more about her now.

Boris, I suspect, would rather lose a limb than admit he was confronted by a problem he couldn't solve, but his mastery of his new language is so primitive that he can't conceal that there are issues. 'Maybe you ask her no use Conrad bathroom — I no think she understand me,' was just one point that had me alarmed.

The idea that I might just relax at home after flying in on Saturday afternoon was obliterated by that — especially with Conrad due back on Wednesday.

"I cook you," is Boris's offering when I call from the car on my way in from Heathrow and tell him I'll be there around seven.

"You're a darling," I tell him — and nowadays I think he is — "but it sounds like I should take her out and talk to her."

He doesn't resist — which confirms my suspicions. These become convictions when she and I are eating. I can't ask her much over dinner. It's noisy but I wouldn't want to risk any of her special topics with anyone within earshot, but she has the air of a sullen ingrate as I attempt to distract her with tales of Asia. I just talk about everyday life, trying to avoid anything that might smack of glamour. I wait until we're back in Conrad's front room — I sit on the Pam and Paul chair, rather than contemplate anyone else on it, and Boris has served us two whiskies — before I begin to question her about how she's getting on now — I'm leaving the difficult topics until later: where she goes next; how does she support herself.

But even the current circumstances are described with no more than perfunctory politeness: 'It's OK, but I couldn't use that bathroom,' isn't, for my money, an adequate display of gratitude for a man who's saved you from another severe beating and provided you with temporary luxury on a scale you never enjoyed unless you've been providing deviant services to some of the dwindling band of rich men of your acquaintance — and their luxury accommodation is one night only and doesn't include breakfast.

"Look, I'm not saying it's bad," she finally admits when I look theatrically around this large, elegant room, "but, fuck it, Sades, I've got to get out soon anyway. What the fuck do I do then?"

It's a fair question, and I've maybe not been giving her enough slack — but why do people find it so hard to own up to feeling worried?

Scrub that question — I just never would; talk like that makes you weaker. Not merely appear weaker. It actually makes you weaker. 'Solve your own fucking problems!' Isobel Allen, twenty nineteen, and you get that piece of wisdom for only the price of this book. But Sandra isn't solving hers. That's why I'm here.

"I'm assuming that you've got nothing put by."

I just get a hard stare from her.

"We're not contacting your brother?"

"And give him one more chance to gloat and moralise?"

There's a long silence now. She's worked in the past, but mostly in retail, and that can never sustain her lifestyle — and she's too feckless to keep a regular position anyway. "I know you're trying to help, Sades, and I'm sorry to seem so ungrateful, but I'm scared shitless now. I don't know what to do. I don't know what's going to happen. There aren't so many parties for me these days, and they're not so much fun anyway. That's why I get off my head quicker to dull it all. Even I'm not crazy enough to let nights like the other night happen unless I'm out of it."

"Well, short-term, Conrad's your best hope. He may have a property vacant, but it doesn't sound like you're making yourself a welcome guest."

"Why? What's the hulk said?"

"I think he feels he has the top floor and he can say what happens there, but the rest of the house is Conrad's — and you're not Conrad's guest."

This appears to shock her. "Oh, I thought you'd fixed it with him."

"Look, precious one, I was in Hong Kong, failing to get any replies from you to my ever more frequent messages. Boris was all I had — and it sounds like he got to you not a moment too soon. What's he said to you about what went on in your flat?"

"He just said some guys came in and wrecked it."

I'm exasperated. I don't want it to show, but she doesn't seem to be piecing this together. "They were Gerry's men — or his property man's men — making the point that your letter was an eviction letter. You can't go back there."

She just says, "Oh," absently. I can only think she hasn't thought it through, like you sometimes don't when problems are too big. She'd rather dwell on not wanting to share a bathroom with a strange man than on the fact that she has nowhere to live.

"Shall we see what Boris knows about Conrad's properties?"

"Could you do that? I find him a bit creepy."

I take a deep breath. I know how Sandra's lived, and the sort of men she's had. Boris is an angel. I figure it's better if I encourage her to socialise a little.

"I'll ask him. But you'll fucking well stay here while we talk to him." I've just lost it a little bit. Shit!

But it actually seems to have a positive impact on her, as though reality is slowly dawning and she's realising there are few good choices for her at the moment.

"OK, let's ask him in. And can we get more whisky?" Her glass is empty, mine has barely been touched. She does know how serious things are.

I go and ask Boris if he can bring us two more whiskies. I don't know why I'm being circumspect with him. I only realise why when I ask him to sit down with us when he's brought the drinks — and he looks raptly at Sandra! The poor sod seems to have some soppy chivalrous feelings for the distressed damsel. Oh, dear! But maybe that's useful — although a moment's reflection tells me that Boris is actually more important than Sandra. I need to look out for him. He's certainly that for Conrad and — after what he's done for me these past few weeks — probably for me as well.

"Boris, we're trying to work out what Sandra can do when Conrad is back. He won't want her here."

"She in my flat. She my guest." There's a sort of indignant pride in his assertions — but now it's awkward for him. "Only my guest no use Mister Conrad's bathrooms." He's turned to look at me now, as if it's my fault because I've not made the situation clear to Sandra. He's refusing to blame her.

"Well, you won't want her as a permanent guest," but from his look, I rather think he just might, "so I was wondering if Conrad has any of his properties empty for a while." I know he has some blocks of apartments. I

also know what one of them is predominantly used for, and I don't want Sandra in there.

Boris is pursing his lips and shaking his head slowly. The pussy block — Conrad's term — has high turnover, I believe, and frequent vacancies, but gallant Sir Boris does not want his lady in there. "If they empty, then already cleaned for sale or…" He's struggling.

"Long-term let?" I'm having to help him here. He nods. "And Pimlico isn't suitable?"

"No! Not suitable." He says this almost aggressively. His dream girl must not be so sullied.

"What's wrong with Pimlico?" asks Sandra. "I've always wanted to live north of the river."

"It's for hookers on short-term lets," I explain — and she gives Boris a strange look, as if she's finally appreciated how he's seeing her — or not seeing her, and what he's trying to do for her.

He looks at me. "We talk Mister Conrad on Wednesday, yes? Maybe he have idea." I nod, but it's a long shot. To Sandra he says, "You have bathroom, it yours."

For the first time she seems to engage. "But what will you do?"

"I use other bathrooms. I know where he no look. I leave no mess behind. Don't worry."

And after she frowns at first, her face relaxes into a smile. "Well, thank you, Boris. Thank you ever so much, that's ever so sweet. I'm sorry to be so awkward."

Suddenly the hulk is all bashful and is looking at his toes. "Is nothing. No problem."

Well, we seem to have solved the short-term issue. Maybe now I can get home and find out why I've had four texts from Merle during the day.

***

"All the projects?" I'm shrieking. This is not a cool response. "When did he tell you?"

"Wednesday, but I didn't want to say anything until I'd got the full picture and seen what I could rescue, but now I've spoken to Michael and it's worse than I thought. Shall I come round?"

It's eleven on a Saturday night and I'm tired and I've been drinking — but I know I won't sleep with this on my mind. "Yes, I'd be grateful if you would."

She's five taxi minutes away but she'll be half an hour. Merle won't come out without looking wonderful. How big a disaster is this? I don't like the hit to my reputation — I never lose business; I drop clients. But it's big for Merle — and when I finally do come back here to live, I want a large organisation to run. I've grown.

I decide that coffee is a better idea than more scotch — and I also resist the temptation to get into pyjamas. This is a serious business conversation.

It's three when she leaves. Wow! We have covered some ground.

220

The business is gone. That's certain — and I wouldn't have taken on any more projects with Gerry anyway. I'll just need to limit any fall-out with other clients whose opinions Gerry is trying to poison with his 'Isobel Allen is permanently in Asia stories.' I'll call Alphonse in the morning.

I wasn't as surprised as Merle had been to be told that Ellen was also behind the decision. I had to tell Merle about Conrad's party and how Ellen had been treated — no doubt I got the blame for that, but I suspect it was pure Conrad — he was getting revenge for what had happened, in his house, to Sandra. Bless him! I'll talk to him on Wednesday. He needs to know in case Gerry tries anything else; I wouldn't put anything past him! He may not have wanted to have gone this far, but he hates to back off. He did use to enjoy his playtimes with Merle and they will obviously stop now. Well, he will always hope, men's vanity is endless, but she'll find plenty of new offers for that still-pretty bottom.

It was that topic that took us into the whole area of her relationship with Michael — and his relationship with Gerry and that business. My business, and the impact of Gerry's actions on that, we dealt with very quickly. She's obviously spent three days spinning like a top, trying to recover it, so when I tell her, after the initial shock, that I don't give a fuck and I'm glad to be rid of all the Calvert crap, I get a big hug and some weeping. By the time I make the Ellen connection for her, she's laughing about it with me. I think I can detect considerable relief in her voice that she won't have to please Gerry any more.

I should qualify that. She's as manipulative as any bottom, and she never does anything unless she really wants to, but she's never seemed too fussy about who comes over her arse; she just wants the circumstances and the environment to be right and the spanker acceptable. Gerry, with her, has almost always been considerate — but that's rare for him. But there will be others for her, just not Will. Yes, we touched on that too, we always do.

But I made her talk more about Michael, and it's every bit as complicated as I assumed it must be. He still loves her — duh, even I knew that, and I hardly see him — and she still likes him, finds him fun sometimes, although they spend very little time with each other, and then usually in company. But he didn't want to get divorced and made her an offer she couldn't refuse. He bought her apartment and gave it to her, all tidied up legally — and contracted to give her a huge allowance. She got coy on numbers, but it sounds like two hundred plus. Wow, again. It seems Gerry pushed him to keep the relationship going and appears to have made funds available.

That was where it got interesting again. I wanted to know what Michael did. After his disgrace, he couldn't find a mainstream job again, but he seems much wealthier these days. I touched a nerve. She's smart enough to understand that she knows as much as she needs to know. 'Gerry's businesses are very international, Michael has to travel a lot — and I never meet any of the people he deals with,' is what I got, expressed several different ways. I wasn't prying particularly but it's obviously on her mind — together with the 'what happens now' question. She's wondering how much fall-out this will have on her and Michael. Not a lot, I wouldn't think. OK, this is a big hit to my London business but there's enough to keep her and the others busy. And if I'm guessing correctly about Michael, he's too involved in twilight stuff for Gerry to risk anything there — and I think our Michael is smart enough to make sure he couldn't be disposed of without some considerable risk to Gerry.

I wonder. I'm thinking ahead as Merle and I are talking. We have a meeting with Claudia in Barnes on Tuesday and she mentioned that Peter might be there. I get the impression that my little chaise project has been doing wonders for them — just the way she talks about him these days tells me that.

But, tonight, I give Merle a big hug as she leaves and tell her we'll be fine. I'm actually quite proud of how she tried desperately to sort the mess out and, as I wave the taxi goodbye, I have a flashback to Ellen's disfigured face as she left the party and I actually laugh out loud.

But I do have a lever with Conrad now. Yes, tops can be manipulative too!

18

Peter was back early. A few weeks ago, she felt, he'd have made no effort to get back for their renovation project meeting — and she wouldn't have wanted him to. Now there was a long kiss when he came in — and they'd already made love in the morning.

His 'have I got time for a shower?' she met with a nod and smiled at his back as he turned to the stairs. Making love? Yes, even a delightful little quickie was making love, and all their body parts had wanted to — her mouth had coaxed him quickly into life and she'd straddled him and enjoyed those brilliant blue eyes smiling at her as she came. He'd followed quickly.

"They're staying for dinner," she called. He stopped halfway up the stairs. "Isobel is close to Mei. I thought she might have some useful insights."

"Ah, good idea." He was nodding, but he still paused. "And?"

She smiled up at him. "You miss nothing, do you? She'll have Merle with her."

He looked puzzled for a moment. "Oh, isn't that Will's great love?"

"Before Martha, yes."

"Before Martha, of course." But he smiled slyly and went on upstairs. A similar comment a few weeks before would have had her worrying about Peter's first great love, the one who went off with his friend — but she, having died, could never be revisited but the ghost could still haunt. But Claudia herself was feeling very warm and secure these days. And Martha should, too, she told herself. Will was the most honourable man she knew.

Peter, bless him, was his perfect gentleman self when the ladies arrived: effusive with Isobel; courteous with Merle — however indecently beautiful the woman looked. And dressed just under the boundary of too much. Claudia reserved judgement on whether there had been a calculation about a report of the evening going to Will. Yes, her gender was that conniving — and Merle's marital status was unusual, if Isobel was to be believed. And Isobel was always to be believed.

The sketches and computer pictures looked wonderful. Peter dutifully asked questions but she could tell he was completely committed to the proposals — and Merle had fabric samples that she showed them in all lights. The late spring evening had plenty of natural daylight in the garden room and the north-facing rooms with closed curtains showed the full artificial light impact. Isobel had artfully left just enough choices in her proposals to let them feel they were participating, but the basic schemes were left unchallenged. She felt excited. So, evidently, was Peter but, she had to admit, that was unsurprising. He'd been pushing her to take ownership of all the changes — she'd been the reluctant one.

They'd been an hour, which had passed very quickly, when Peter suddenly said, "I hate to be rude, but I think we've covered the big stuff here and I have to ask Isobel about some Chinese business. Do you mind if I steal her?"

"Go ahead," said Claudia. It made sense. There was nothing in those discussions that should concern Merle, who took the chance, when Peter and Isobel had left them, to ask about Will — but Claudia was ready for that.

She could understand why Will would have fallen for her. The woman was gorgeous: tall, slim, flawless skin, fabulous chestnut hair and a lovely mezzo voice — and there would have presumably been other dimensions, knowing what Claudia knew about Martha's tastes and how, she presumed, they would have figured in any life with Will. But Will had moved on. It didn't seem that Merle had. There was something wistful about her, but Claudia didn't want to get drawn into a conversation like that — that would require deep friendship, not mere passing acquaintance.

Peter wasn't long. In business mode he could extract the essential extraordinarily quickly. Hannes appeared with two new flutes, having opened the champagne for the two ladies only moments before. Peter raised a glass. "I think I can speak for us both. I am absolutely thrilled with what you've presented.

Thank you both so much." After a sip, he went on. "I took you at your word, Isobel, the budget is cast in stone. I trust we weren't seduced into alternatives today that would breach what was agreed."

Isobel reacted theatrically. "How even dare you, my good sir? The budget is sacrosanct."

"And the timing?"

"There you meet with good fortune." She glanced sidelong at Merle.

It was the smallest movement of the eyes, but it prompted Peter to ask, "There's a story, ladies, may we hear it?"

Isobel remained unfazed as always, but Merle was taken aback. "It's a sordid saga, I'm afraid, and Merle won't thank me for opening up about it, but you may have some useful advice if you don't mind us giving it an airing." Now Merle looked distinctly uncomfortable. Isobel squeezed her hand. "Trust me darling, we couldn't talk about this with more discreet people than Claudia and Peter and they may have some views you'd find useful."

Calvert's name had piqued Peter's interest and he had many questions about what had gone on. But before he'd asked too many, he turned to Merle, beside him at the table, and took her hand. "I remember hearing about your husband's position, and not just from Will." He let his eyes catch hers for a long while at that point. It was his sympathetic look, not his interrogatory. "Sometimes people, particularly finance people, get caught in invidious positions and there are no good options. I'm certainly not going to make any judgements, but I doubt whether working for Gerry lets him sleep peacefully at night."

"I don't know how he sleeps," she said awkwardly.

"No, no," he said quickly, squeezing her hand again. "I'm sorry, I didn't mean to imply anything by that beyond speculating that it must be uncomfortable working for Gerry. We severed contacts a long time ago." Now he addressed them all. "I'm not talking ethics or morality or anything like that, just plain practicalities. We've been talking a lot lately about what goes on beyond the boundaries of our organisation and we can't be too squeamish, or we'd do nothing. I just try to be sure we're legal everywhere ourselves, and that our direct contacts are clean enough that we can't get embroiled in anything. We do OK, but there are no guarantees. I just suspect that Gerry is closer to indefensible stuff than we are but, I have to say, he's never been caught, whatever dark suspicions hover over his operations."

"From the little I get to hear, I think you've made a wise judgement." Merle had clearly decided she was in company she could trust. "When Michael was getting difficult about a divorce, he got very generous if I promised I would stay together. Not live together, just stay married. We tied the arrangement down legally. I pushed him quite hard — if he could afford that much, then a divorce could have been much more lucrative than I'd been led to believe. But he made a very convincing case that it was Gerry backing the deal that made it possible for him to offer so much, so then I asked more about Gerry. I mean, I know he's always had a bit of a thing about me but," and here she shrugged. Claudia had heard enough — from Isobel, even from Will — to be able to piece the story together. "Well, that made me ask about how secure that was and then it got a bit strange. He said that Gerry couldn't afford to lose him but that, if anything strange were to happen to him, his solicitor would be in touch with me."

"Didn't that make you nervous?" Claudia would have expected Peter to ask that question light-heartedly, although she was aware of how serious it was, but he was looking intensely at Merle.

"Should it have done?" Merle asked blithely.

"Not especially. It sounds like your Michael knows what he's doing. And I'm certainly not the person to offer any advice on managing divorces." And now he did seem more relaxed as he laughed at himself. "So, here we are, four singles, but only one of us was too wise never to have made the marriage mistake. Were you ever tempted, Isobel? Were there any offers you wished you hadn't turned down?" The question jarred only momentarily with Claudia, but she realised that Isobel, of all people, would be capable of responding in the right spirit.

And she was, and the digression into Isobel's greatest escapes took them right through to coffee.

After they'd waved the ladies goodbye — Peter had insisted that Hannes take them — Claudia asked, "What was that about? That 'didn't that make you nervous' question. You were serious, weren't you?"

"Ah." he hugged her tightly to him and smiled. "I drop my guard a fraction and you spot it."

"I think Isobel caught it too. What is it?"

"Are we going to bed?"

She smiled. "We are, but you're telling me more before anything else happens."

"What!" It was mock horror. "You expect things to happen twice in one day?"

"Of course, but I want some explanation first."

He shook his head lightly. "I'm afraid it's more speculation than explanation but sometimes that's all we have to go on. Come on, upstairs."

He wasn't being evasive. He very rarely tried that with her, even in the early days, and leaving his bedside light on when she snuggled into him was a sure indication that he would continue the story. "The first thing I should say is that you should warn Isobel to be careful. It sounds like Merle's husband has got himself covered — and, with that, Merle's probably OK. But Gerry got into Russia early. All credit to him, I think he was prepared for what might evolve, but his businesses seem to help his new friends move their money around more easily and, within a few transactions, the money looks almost clean. But the accidents that befall some people are as untraceable as the sources of these funds."

"That's a little more than speculation, isn't it?" She knew he wouldn't dramatise.

"I'm afraid our mutual friend…"

"Henderson?"

He chuckled at her, but winced when she pinched his skin sharply. "Yes, Henderson. He has information on a few hits that, shall we say, are too close for comfort to Gerry's operations."

"You mean Gerry fingers people?"

"No, no," he said emphatically. "I doubt that, but I suspect he's sometimes in the loop when his friends want to act. I think he just solves his bigger problems with money, but, lower down his organisation, well, who knows with the sort of people he has acting for him. But he's always going to be a few steps away from culpable action. He's got it well set up," he sighed, "but I don't want us to be within a million miles of it."

"But weren't you saying that some of Wengwei's old problems got solved in a similar way?"

He sighed deeply. "Ah, but that was in another country…"

"It does trouble you, doesn't it?"

"Along with many other things, yes, but I don't think it would help to delve too deeply into how things got resolved in China thirty years ago. I'm just going with my sense of how Wengwei is. I think he's very clever and very forceful and, yes, unscrupulous, but I just don't think he'd let his problems get solved that way. Having said that, if problems are solved that way, and

that creates opportunities, I think those are opportunities
he would seize on. Of course, that begs the question of
whether he might indicate to the less moral in his
network that some events might be exploited
advantageously."

"You think he would?"

"I like to think not, but I'm admitting it as a
possibility — and deciding not to pursue it."

"I'm glad it's your call."

"Are you comfortable? You're in this too now, you
know."

"I know. I had a long conversation with Lee this
morning. Can we talk about that over breakfast?"

He pulled her to him and kissed her forehead — and
then chuckled. "Well, I'd rather not do it now. But, are
you comfortable? You haven't answered my question."
It was unlike him to even hint at uncertainty.

She kissed his lips. "I trust your judgement even
more than my own, my darling man, you know that."

"Yes, I do know that," he said, and turned out his
light. It hadn't been uncertainty — but she liked him
asking her.

***

With so much having gone on during the day, she'd not
had time to reflect on the conversation with Lee. Now
was the time, before sleep took her, to let her

impressions form, while her memories were still quite vivid.

She felt she had a bond with Lee. She felt relieved, as her shoulder touched Peter's back, that it was more than a shared love for Alphonse. And she was pleased she didn't balk at using that word in her own mind when she thought of him. And she smiled in the dark as she realised that he, too, would probably use the same word still to describe his feelings for her. She also felt that Lee had come to terms now with his own feelings for Alphonse — and he was certainly more concerned with his family and business priorities. Whether he would be able to deal with them adequately was her major worry and the morning phone call had generated more doubts than answers.

At least he had asked for the call. She had, it was true, sent an email offering to discuss how they had gone about redefining and reshaping the Group in case that was relevant for what he might want to do with Senlin Industries, the core of the Shen family businesses. He had responded gratifyingly quickly which, in itself, didn't resolve her doubt about whether he was genuinely curious to learn, or simply being ably political.

But he'd seemed impressively eager to understand how they'd looked at where they would be competent to grow into, and how they would fill in the gaps in their expertise in order to become more coherent in how they approached their markets. He seemed to have a sharp and appreciative business mind.

But when she'd moved on to what he might do with Senlin, he seemed to have given embarrassingly little thought to how that might evolve and, while he was plainly well aware of the financial performance of the business, he seemed to lack awareness of its deteriorating market position. He was showing, to her mind, too little curiosity and it wasn't apparent that he had anyone in his organisation challenging him to approach the future differently. He reminded her, in a strange way, of Arthur Gunter, Tania's father, running a large and historically successful logistics company showing potentially fatal signs of complacency. She'd talked to Lee about that. It was too late for too much tact. He'd seemed taken aback but arranged another call with her for the following week, when he promised to have given her challenges some more thought.

He hadn't convinced her. He should have been thinking that way himself, but she'd left him with the thought that he should look for some challenging thinkers in his existing business. 'Look for the malcontents,' she'd said. He'd been rather rueful then — 'We tend to force malcontents to hide, or at least stay silent,' had been his response. 'But I will look, I promise,' had been his commitment. 'Oh dear,' she'd thought as she'd put the phone down. 'You should be doing this for yourself, Lee, not for me.'

It will be an interesting breakfast conversation in the morning, she thought, as she snuggled sleepily into the slumbering body beside her.

19

Alphonse was normally comfortable with his own company but, staring at the lights of Kowloon again, it struck him that his usual conversation partners were less available to him these days — and too busy for a casual disturbance; Peter and Claudia, in particular, seemed intensely preoccupied with their China connection — and with each other, was his new impression. And Hong Kong was not London. There were fewer opportunities to socialise with old friends or casual business contacts.

He'd been spending more time talking to Daiyu. And a sly waiter's reference to her as Mrs Newman on their last dinner date had given them a private joke that she'd begun to tease him with.

I believe you're neglecting your wife, Mr Newman, dinner this evening would not be amiss.

— had been the text.

She was always aware of his itinerary — all the Asia time was booked through their shared office — but her awareness of when he needed company was unnerving.

An excellent idea, Mrs Newman. Mandarin? It's a short walk if you're still working.

Of course I'm still working! See you at 7.30. I'll book, but the husband pays!

So, she'd booked in his name, of course, and he was surprisingly relaxed about that. He was there a few minutes early to politely reward her perpetual punctuality. He greeted her chastely, although tolerance would have been extended to a more western greeting style. He let the waiter position her chair.

"Were you under instructions to call me?"

"No," she said, mock indignantly. "I think Isobel's view now is that I shouldn't be given any encouragement at all after the Phoruc week. And her diary for the next Psamathe opening week is blocked in bold type and capital letters and highlighted in orange. I think I'm being given a message." But she was smiling warmly. "Of course, she has her avid admirers among our client group, so you wouldn't receive the undivided attention you had in our week together."

"Am I allowed to say I enjoyed that very much?"

"You are, as long as you're not just being charming." Their eyes lingered a moment on each other's. "Do you know what you're having?" she added quickly, as if they'd strayed too close to a more difficult topic. But then she touched his hand lightly. "I was just guessing that you are suddenly on your own more these days and… Well, maybe you wanted company. It was a low-risk guess on my part. No feelings would have been hurt if you'd said you were busy."

Now his hand touched hers. In a short time, this had become his easiest relationship. Time with Mei was always intense, her commitment to work and to learning was ferocious; time with Isobel was always challenging as she tried to ensure he was managing his life appropriately; there was a difference in Claudia that had crept into the last few conversations — she'd seemed somehow more contented, which pleased him, but also deposited a burr of discomfort in his stomach. But meeting with Daiyu, and this was only the third dinner since Phoruc, was simple, somehow. He'd realised, the last time, that he'd been gently prodded through the evening as she attempted to assess how contented he was — and he'd found, as she made no attempt to prolong the evening, that he'd been disappointed she hadn't stayed. It had just been a dinner with a very close friend.

"Well, I'm going to say, without any attempt at being charming, that I was delighted to get your text." He got a knowing smile from her — yes, he could have texted her — and he pondered briefly on his own inhibitions, realising that he didn't want her to feel their arrangement was deepening, even as its importance was becoming more obvious to him. Was that because the others were less available? He looked at her, and asked her to order for both of them as the waiter hovered — no, she was lovely to be with — and he let himself be enchanted by an ordering process that seemed as unnecessarily lengthy as it was unhesitating.

"Am I going to be confronted with a mountain?"

"No, I just wanted to know what was good today. We're sharing three courses — two of your favourites and one surprise for you. Well, maybe it won't be a surprise. I mustn't forget how well-travelled you are," here she smiled slyly, "or how open to different experiences." This was the unexpected side of Daiyu; he'd always seen her, before Phoruc, as so serious and professional, strait-laced almost, but, once she'd stayed that first night, he'd seen the playful side — and the openness and tolerance about relationships, and what went on in them. He'd found it easy to talk to her about Lee — and how that would have affected his family relationships — and she'd had a healthy curiosity about what they did. But that hadn't led to her questioning his nature — she didn't need a simple label for him.

"Have you heard from Isobel?" he asked.

"She checks in every other day. This is a scheduled trip, but I think that crisis is still rumbling on." She smiled slightly. "I don't think she's entirely averse to drama — but it is impacting her London business. Won't you have to go back soon, by the way? Ha, that tells you I haven't checked your diary that far ahead. I know you think I spy."

"I don't," he said defensively, then smiled. "I just credit you with astonishing intuition, but I don't have a firm plan anyway. My priority is getting organised here. I've already lost half of Mei's time — we need a replacement, especially as the tie-in between Dickinson and Senlin is going to get closer. Peter and Claudia will be out in two weeks, meeting Wengwei and Mei. I have to join them and have a plan for the region. I'm fortunate in that my London and New York guys are working well now."

"Will you ever settle, or will you stay a gypsy?" It was a question he'd been asking himself more recently, especially since his commitment to Asia would keep him predominantly in the region for two or three years.

"Oh, I've always been a happy gypsy." But he knew from the long look he got from her that she saw that for the superficial and evasive response it was.

She took his hand. "You know I wasn't asking that for my own sake, don't you? You just seem a little rudderless at the moment or, and I hesitate to say it, a little overwhelmed. You have the Psamathe vision that you want to see fulfilled, but there are other calls on your time. I'm not one of them, by the way. I'm just having fun helping."

"You're making me sound needy." He wasn't sure that was right, but he was so used to controlling relationships that it felt strange to have someone almost managing him.

"Heaven forbid! Look, I just thought there were a number of areas you might find it useful to discuss, including, for instance, how you might reorganise property out here. I didn't want to prod you into a pit of introspection."

"You have thoughts on property?" It would be better to step on to the dry land of business issues. He would be happy later, he knew, to explore the personal with Daiyu but, for now, she was right. He found her a very helpful partner for discussing any issue.

"Just a thought," she said, clearly ready to divert to less personal topics. "I don't think you have anyone in your organisation in Asia who could step up. But I deal with a small property company here. Well, small by Dickinson and Senlin standards, where the son is just taking over from the father. I think the young man is very good, and he'll soon get frustrated by their constraints."

"Financial?"

"Partly, but also by his father's lack of ambition."

"Are you suggesting I poach him?"

"That wouldn't be friendly. But you could buy them and all their interests. That would keep the father and his contacts, and groom the son to run the region."

"Does Mei know him?"

She hesitated, then smiled. "She thinks he's bumptious and arrogant."

He laughed. "Sounds ideal, thank you. But, joking aside, that's a much better approach than just fretting about inadequate succession in the group."

Without sticking consciously to their self-imposed constraints, they focused on business until the jasmine tea was served. "I really was here to be a resource, you know," she said as she sipped her tea.

"It's been a big help, thank you, especially the possible property angle."

"We have some contracts on their properties. I wouldn't want you to think I was just being altruistic."

She was very easy to laugh with. "Never crossed my mind!"

Now she looked a little serious. "I'd like you to understand that my next point isn't altruistic either."

"Go on."

"I thought you might want to spend some time talking about how your relationships are working out."

He was feeling more mellow now, and unthreatened. "You're right, I do, but why is that not altruistic on your part?"

"Because we're going to be naked in bed for that discussion," she said quietly, "and I've been missing what we had in Phoruc."

He felt much happier than he would have expected to. "I'm thrilled by both parts of that. Finish your tea."

"Who needs tea? Come on!"

***

It was two hours later when she brought a bottle of water back to the bed. She offered it to him first. He swigged and handed it back. "I'm going to prove I was serious by talking to you now, are you ready?"

"Not really," he said, "but I think I have to accept that he needs recovery time."

She smiled, then guided his hand to her pussy. "She doesn't, but I want him that new way next, please. I wouldn't say you'd made an addict of me, but I think about it a lot when I'm playing with myself."

"You play with yourself?"

"Of course. And don't tell me you don't. I'm not going to ask you who think about though."

Now he wondered what he should admit to — and he didn't even have to be tactful. "If I understand you correctly, we've been having identical thoughts."

"Are you saying it's my sweet little bum you've been lusting after? I'm not sure I'll believe you. Fantasies become a little impersonal when you get to the climax. It's just that, when I'm in bed with my arse up and I'm playing with myself, I know that you're the plug I have in my bum."

"You have a plug?"

"Of course. You may have enjoyed me being very tight in Phoruc, but that had consequences, my good man. I'm not saying I've been planning this, but I have been looking forward to it." She was a joy; it was an unexpected uninhibitedness he was confronting. "I had to be given some advice by Isobel once I'd admitted to having been sore. She likes it very much too, doesn't she?"

He guffawed. Daiyu seemed surprised that she'd surprised him, "Are you honestly comfortable talking about that openly?" he asked.

"I don't know. I'm trying to be. Those are my principles anyway. Secrets are shit, in my opinion. And you and I just have an arrangement." That was more wistful than callous. "But I'll admit there's a part of me that was glad you didn't reach for a condom. What shall we call the child?"

She had him! And she laughed very loud. It had only been a millisecond's horror on his face, but it had been enough. She snuggled in quickly to his naked body. "I'm trusting you to be the judge — and I hope you don't feel any pressure from being my only outlet at the moment. I've never been wildly oversexed or promiscuous anyway."

"You been giving a wonderful impersonation of sex-starved for the last two hours."

She reached for his cock. It was soft, but still heavy. "I've not finished with you yet, and I don't need a response on the condom question. I'm trusting you, OK? But I'm not going to get upset if you use one."

He wondered briefly whether he should anyway, just to keep the relationship defined correctly, but there was an innocence about this developing relationship. And that's what it was, no longer just an arrangement. "Well, let me respect your commitment to openness. Isobel is the only other person I've slept with in the past two, no, wait, at least three months, and we always use condoms."

"For oral sex too?"

He couldn't see her face, but he could feel her body tensing for a giggle, so he tickled her and they laughed and squirmed for a while until their limbs wound into an embrace — and he found his cock rising again. As it slid into her pussy, they smiled into each other's eyes.

"Ha, that's reassuring. I am going to get what I want later. But you know I'm committed to the discussions first."

"Well, I think, I'm pleased to say, that you're committed to the discussion second. I quite liked our more urgent priority."

She swung over him to straddle him and tried to look outraged, "Quite liked! Quite liked? You'd better tell me I'm not fully tuned in to English understatement."

"Obviously, or you'd know how jolly good I thought it was."

She wiggled on him. "Well, I can't be that good. The poor little old man seems to be going soft again. Shame, I thought he was doing quite well."

He chuckled at her. "I hope he'll show you later that your plug was inadequate preparation."

She bent down and kissed him. "Promises, promises." She slid off and cuddled him. "But I'm not going to pester…"

"On discussion, or on more sex?"

"Oh, no, you're committed to the latter." She kissed him again. "I'm just aware that people who need or want your time and attention, and who are very important to you in their different ways, seem to be being pulled away from you. I'm the beneficiary of your availability but I'm not seeing it as more than that. But I just didn't know if you wanted to talk about things," she put her finger on his lips as he began to respond. "I'll admit I'm not an independent counsel — I like our infrequent engagements too much — but I have some insights into two of your other relationships. I admit I know little about Claudia, but you seem very close."

"We are, but that's awkward because of how each of us feels about Peter. But I do have the sense recently that she's feeling more settled."

"But it's hard to be just friends."

He hugged her to him. "Yes, it's a little hard to be just friends. But I will manage, for everyone's sake."

"Including your own?"

"Including my own." He didn't want to tell her that holding her as he was made it easier to feel better about that.

"So, what about Isobel?"

"That's easier. I am very fond of her, but that really is an arrangement. You're not seeing it any differently, are you?" He suddenly felt alarmed.

"Oh, no, I don't think so. I think we got the honest response after our Phuroc week. I think she was more upset that she'd miscalculated how far it might evolve than she was hurt by me fucking you every night. Although that did make her a bit jealous and, as I said, she's getting into a little planning now."

"Are you coming to the next one?" He wasn't sure why he'd asked, but he felt the need to know.

"So you can have a threesome? I rather think not!" And he couldn't guess whether there was some real irritation behind the tease. "Besides, you've done threesomes with her already, if I've understood her correctly, which brings us on to the final part of the trio."

"I guess that would have felt even worse if you'd said the third member of the quartet. But Mei is very different. That was a one-off, in very peculiar circumstances."

"She adores you, you know."

"I know there are strong feelings there, but they don't draw us together that way."

She moved her head away from him and squinted at him — without disengaging her body. "I think there might be times when she'd like you to make a move. You're together a lot in lonely places."

"I know that, but she feels more like a younger sister. I defined it that way for myself right at the start and it's made it easier. But I like working with her very much. She's got more energy than anyone I've ever met — and more imagination than anyone except Peter, maybe. I also think she's ruthless."

"I've seen a bit of that. There are some bruised egos around here."

"Any grudging admiration?"

"Oh, a lot of that too. I think the old man's got it right. But that doesn't mean it will be by any means easy for her. Anyway, are you starting to miss her?"

"I'm noticing a gap, but I'm experiencing a little relief, to be honest. She's made me up my game — but I could do with a rest." He chuckled.

She was silent for a while then, after a deep breath, she asked, "What would you say about the fourth member of your quartet of adoring ladies?"

"Ah, your mastery of irony."

"Sorry, Mr Newman, no irony intended. But you don't have to answer." She snuggled into his body, her face into his neck.

"I guess I was being evasive. Am I going to get away with saying that it feels like it's becoming more than an arrangement, instead of less than one?"

She hugged him. "I'm happy with that." She moved and began fondling his cock, which began rising more swiftly. "And you may be delighted to hear that I haven't practised with a large enough plug."

"Oh, should I be careful?"

"Don't even think about it! Show me there's an uninhibited Mr Alphonse."

"Well, show me that gorgeous peachy bum!"

20

I'd had a busy day contacting clients. It felt artificial. It's not my way to call them without specific project-related issues to discuss and I don't like inventing those, but most found a few minutes to chat, or made appointments to do so. One even attempted to book me for dinner and hinted he'd like more time with me, but we haven't finished the project yet and, according to Merle, we've had too many pernickety queries on progress — so he hasn't yet engaged my interest. But it's reassuring that some of them are still trying.

I got a few 'thought you'd left us' comments, so Gerry had been trying to seed rumours but nothing seemed serious — and one or two — well, three exactly, to be honest — had fallen for Merle. Oh, well, I'll let her work that out.

It did mean I was later getting to Conrad's than I wanted to be. Boris was picking him up early afternoon from the airport. I had to leave first explanations to him about their temporary lodger. Boris seemed confident it wouldn't be a problem. I wasn't so sure.

I was right. Conrad never likes to appear unpleasant, but he's comfortable being firm. "This house is my space. I share it on my own terms. I need Boris here to guard it for me — and help manage the guests I invite, who are here for brief, well-defined moments."

I can understand that. I'd hate to share my space and I would have to admit that to him if he pressed me — and making the point that his house is almost ten times bigger than mine wouldn't defeat the principle of his argument.

"What about lending her an apartment?"

That got a funny look from him, condescending really. "I don't send heavies in, like Gerry seems to delight in doing, but I do keep pressure on my property guys to deliver proper returns — and there's nothing in the portfolio she could foreseeably afford."

"Pimlico is smaller." I'm sorry I said that — but at least I get a kindly look from him.

"You know that's not an answer, don't you?" he says patiently. I nod. She can't work like the other girls do. She never has and it's too late to start now. The competition's fierce — and younger. Maybe not prettier, she still looks good, and certainly not kinkier — but I wouldn't want her to explore deriving an income from that. She gets into enough trouble as it is.

"Got any ideas?" I'm getting desperate — but why the fuck is it my problem? Actually, if you're still with me, you understand this question. This problem is a cuckoo nesting with me.

Conrad hesitates. He's clearer and more decisive than I am, but I can tell he's troubled, "Look, I don't mind the short-term interventions, she's been very useful over the years — but she's done nothing with all the contacts she's made. Suzanne's been to three parties and we've already let her take out a three-year lease on an apartment. She'll easily pay her way." He smiles here. "That's thanks in part to your training. I had an email this week from her thanking me — and Dominic sees her every week."

"But Sandra's..."

"Not a hooker, I know. Does she have family that can help?"

"A brother, but she won't go to him."

"But she's happy to throw herself on us?" It's not said with any emotion. This is Conrad: he confronts everything dispassionately; even setting the gang on Ellen would have been a serving of cold revenge.

I risk it. "Well, we have contributed to her problems."

He raises his eyebrows. "I may have created some problems for your business. And I'm sorry, I hadn't foreseen that. I was just having fun at Gerry's expense and trying to discourage Ellen from coming here again — she raises the average age of the guests by five years. But Gerry had already evicted Sandra by then — and dumped another large Argosy bill on me. I don't mind that," he adds hastily, he doesn't want me thinking he's cheap, "but I was hoping for a surgical solution with that; I wasn't getting into long-term palliative care. We haven't identified a way she supports herself long-term."

"I'll have to work on that with her." I haven't a clue what to do, and he's shaking his head, clearly understanding that. "Can you give me a couple of weeks to work on it? Let her stay until then?"

"A couple, no."

Shit, I think. I don't panic, but I don't like the other options.

"But four, yes."

I feel relieved, but I obviously look puzzled.

He grins. "A couple is indeterminate. Four is four weeks today, OK?"

I nod.

Now he looks a little serious, "You do understand I wouldn't have done this for anyone else, don't you?"

"Only Sandra?" But apparently, I'm being unusually thick.

He raises eyes heavenward. "No, dumbo, you." I let out a huge sigh, but he raises a hand to stop me speaking. "And, before you go all grateful on me, tell me you'll have dinner with me on Saturday."

I am grateful, but that's not the way he wants me to play it — and I'd have dinner with him anyway. It's a peculiar little insecurity he's showing. "Is dinner going to involve your favourite special treatments?"

He smiles, "The invitation is just for dinner." He pauses. "Of course, if anything happens, I'll be ready."

Now we've withdrawn into badinage and we're cloaking our feelings. I must admit our last dinner left me thinking about him — and he seems to have reacted the same way. Oh well, that's an interesting one to let develop. Meanwhile, Sandra and Boris are upstairs, waiting to hear from us. "But for now, you talk to him, I talk to her, OK?"

He smiles and nods. "And I'll get you picked up at seven on Saturday."

I nod. But it's as though he's almost nervous about it.

I meet Boris on the stairs. Conrad has obviously summoned him somehow. I can't begin to interpret Boris's face, but I do get a simple, big smile as we pass.

Sandra's in an austere little room on the top floor, but it's been junked out with a lot of her knick-knacks and there's a large suitcase in the corner disgorging clothing like a disembowelled heretic's intestines. The old pine wardrobe barely closes on what's already stuffed inside it. I sit on the little chair; she's on the bed.

She looks better, somehow — apprehensive, but clearer eyed. "How are you doing?" I probably should have started with what's going to happen.

"Do I have to get out?"

Yes, I should have done, "We've got four weeks. And he's very serious about four weeks. He's a very precise man, our Conrad."

She shrugs, looks relaxed. "That's better than I was expecting."

"Any ideas on what you're going to do?"

"Come on, Sades, not my strong suit." She leans back on to the pillows like a beached shipwreck victim

— which is probably what she is, but eating coconuts and waiting for a passing ship isn't a promising survival strategy.

There's no immediate need to panic. And we shouldn't ignore our basic decencies. "You're looking better," I say — honestly.

"The hulk's being very sweet. I don't see him during the day but he always leaves things out for me for breakfast in the little kitchen up here" — there's an open area between the bathroom and her room, done out as a small kitchen diner. "In the evenings he cooks for me downstairs. Funny dishes, but tasty enough. He doesn't talk much. Well, his English is crap, isn't it, but he asks me lots about here — and about me, mostly childhood things, and I babble on like I do and the evenings seem to pass. But I know he was worrying about Conrad. He does think of this as his apartment, but he's very aware it's Conrad's house. And Conrad doesn't want me here, does he?"

"It's not you, Sands, he just doesn't want anyone."

She looks a little faraway. "I get that, I think. I wouldn't want to share. You wouldn't either."

I'm not going to treat that as an accusation. She hasn't said it with that intent.

"Look, we're not going to solve anything tonight — and Boris sure ain't going to cook for you downstairs, not with Conrad back now. Shall we go out and eat?"

She brightens. "Oh, lovely. Give me ten to get changed?"

I smile. "Take twenty. I'll wait in the front room downstairs."

I'm almost down there when Conrad and Boris emerge. It's probably an unhappy look on Boris's face. Conrad just looks relaxed. "You get on, OK?"

"Yes, fine. I'll tell you if you have a minute, but can I speak to Boris first?"

"Of course. I'll be in the office next door."

"Thank you, I won't be long." I gesture to Boris to go back into the room.

He's still standing after I've settled in the Pam and Paul chair. "Oh, please, Boris, do sit down, my lovely man."

He turns a high-back chair by the desk around and obscures it with his bulk when he sits. He knits his fingers together nervously.

"This is hard for you, isn't it?" I'm making a wild stab at this one. He nods. "Have you fallen for her a bit?"

His eyes are fixed firmly on the floor, but he makes a small forward movement with his head. It could be a nod.

"You're a very attractive man, Boris. Do you see many ladies?" Oh, dear, he seems to be huddling into a ball. When I say he's attractive, I should explain a little more. First, you have to like huge and shaven-headed — and inarticulate. But he has this rock-like body, yet a wonderfully gentle and caring manner — he exudes calm and competence, you would always feel protected

— even cherished, I would think. But I'm obviously going to get nothing out of him beyond what I can interpret — maybe some other time, but the current circumstances are too fraught.

"Well, never mind. I'm taking her out to dinner now, we'll try and think of a plan." I stand up, walk towards him and try to take his hands. They are, initially, completely immovable but, as I stroke them, he begins to release and let them hang in my grasp. "You have been absolutely wonderful, and I wouldn't know how to thank you for what you've done for her."

Now he looks up, and, oh my God, there are tears in his eyes. "I want she stay."

Time to get firm. I'm very grateful to him — but I'm even more grateful to Conrad, and we have a deal. "Boris, she has to leave. If you want to see her, she doesn't have to be here — and even if she is here, you have to start something with her. At the moment she thinks you're very sweet, but you're behaving like a love-struck schoolboy."

"What is love-struck schoolboy?"

"You're just making big eyes. Look, if you ask me, I don't think you two are right for each other — you're too nice."

"Too nice." He looks horrified. That touched a nerve.

"Yes, too nice. And, unfortunately, Sandra doesn't get attracted to nice people. It's a shame she didn't see you kicking the shit out of those two men at her flat."

He's looking mystified. "But I very rough."

I shake my head and pull on his hands to make him stand. "Oh, Boris, you see so many things going on in this house, in this cellar, but they're all games, all playtimes, they're just people enjoying parts of themselves. People have feelings for each other but…" And I run out of steam. This is too difficult. Tops and bottoms can love each other — even I've been a little susceptible sometimes — but the roles don't define them.

"I'm just saying, a little rough is fun sometimes. Some people want a little rough. Sandra likes a little rough, but only sometimes. Most times she likes someone who leaves her breakfast and who cooks her dinner."

Something dawns on him. "But she no like just cook dinner."

I'm triumphant. "Exactly. I think you've got it. The important thing is: understand when someone wants rough."

Now he smiles. "And when they want dinner."

"Perfect!" I'm so pleased I stretch up on tiptoe and kiss him full on the lips. He's more shocked than responsive, but at least he's not pulling away — and he does have nice lips. We're still holding hands and smiling when Sandra comes in — and looks surprised. Boris just looks pleased to see her. "I shan't be long," I say. "I just need a moment with Conrad." And I leave them.

I am quite quick. There's no need to tell Conrad that his man has fallen for her, but Boris has gone when I return. We walk to the Queen's Arms and we're sat down in ten minutes.

"You know he's crazy about you, don't you?"

"Of course, but, duh! What am I supposed to do about that?"

"Nothing, just in case you're tempted. You'd only make it worse."

You're right, I'm being disingenuous, even scheming; steering Sandra away from something usually has the opposite effect. And what would that achieve? It would make things most likely worse, but they could both do with a little love. Anyway, the seed is planted. Now we have to get down to her problems.

Two hours later we're drinking coffee and we haven't solved them, just established implacable opposition to doing anything constructive about them — yes, I'm getting annoyed. I understand her objections to her brother — and he would probably have even bigger ones to her. I understand that she couldn't hold down a job, not one that would pay what for her would be a living wage. Merle had, at some point, asked whether Sandra could give us admin support — but I'm too wary of getting into what Conrad is trying to avoid — offering long-term palliative care — and I wouldn't trust her to be reliable, so I don't even mention the possibility. I'm being honest here; I'm not that nice a person. And I think Merle was relieved when I pooh-poohed the idea.

I get the taxi to drop her off and I spend the rest of the journey home in a pall of frustration. I tell myself it's one of those problems to leave alone for a couple of days and wait for a moment of revealed truth — but I know I'm talking crap to myself.

21

Alphonse was almost enjoying the quandary: should he first approach Lang Hua, the man whose name Daiyu had given him, or should he first discuss the idea with Mei? He knew the Lang business, it was big in Hong Kong and had small operations in Shanghai and Beijing — that fitted with what Daiyu had described, and her judgement on what was holding them back was almost certainly correct. He would feel quite comfortable making a direct, albeit tactful, approach. In deciding to talk to Mei first, he found himself smiling about his own motivation: six weeks ago, it would have been a training exercise for her; now he found an element of deference — he would soon have to treat her as the senior decision taker. He wondered how she would respond. He texted:

Having thoughts about managing the region. When can you discuss? Face to face ideal but don't want to wait beyond this weekend.

Ask me to dinner on Friday.

Mandarin 7.30 booked.

It was a tiny thing, but her response had been an instruction, not a request. No, he thought again, it wasn't a tiny thing.

He was seated at what was becoming his usual table: a view of the harbour; a view of guests arriving. She was barely late. His martini had not yet arrived. He complimented her with his eyes — they'd been working too closely for too long for words to be needed — her small smile accepted and appreciated his look. She'd flown in from Shanghai, but she'd certainly come via her apartment to look so poised, and she was dressed for an evening engagement, not a business meeting.

As was he, of course: no tie and a less-structured silk and linen suit.

"I've ordered a martini," he said, as the waiter hovered.

"Just water, please. So, what's this about?"

"Can you tell me how your father is, first?" This was more than a pleasantry — and he was slowly abandoning hope that she would ever find gentler ways into conversations. She looked almost exquisite and many, thus prepared, would have made time to be admired, but Mei, having paid so much attention to how she looked, still had a compulsion to get straight into business. Although, to be fair, he thought, making his usual excuse for her, the issue of how they would manage Asian property and resorts was the biggest issue they had to face jointly.

"He seems worse, but they told him that's how he would feel at this stage, so he seems unperturbed."

"Still immortal?"

"That's what he's still projecting." She paused, considering what to say next, it seemed. This was not unusual. He still felt, her father apart, that he was her only true confidante. Now her eyes were lowered. "He tells me, though, that he's not very hopeful." She breathed deeply. "I'm dealing with that by telling myself it's not what he believes, he's just putting pressure on me to be prepared." Now she seemed to shake herself slightly, sat more upright and looked into his eyes again. "And part of being prepared is getting Asia Properties and Resorts organised for when we can't be there all the time."

"I'm still here almost…"

She held a hand up. "My dearest Alphonse, apart from your resort obsession, you have a lot else to manage in the rest of the world. We're in vastly better shape than when you and I started but we both have to move on now. So, what's your idea?"

He could feel a command in how she'd returned to the topic. He knew he'd made a contribution to getting her to focus and prioritise, but he was seeing more and more of her father in her.

"What do you know of the Lang organisation?"

"Local, well-run here, not really tried to expand. The father is lovely, the son is an asshole. Why?" But he could tell by how her expression changed that she had almost immediately jumped to the point. "Tell me you're not serious." But then she waited patiently for him to make his point as the drinks came and the menus were presented.

"It wouldn't be a bad idea to think about what we want to eat so we don't get interrupted."

"Would you like me to order?" Her smile was teasing him.

He put on his helpless look. "With all that's going on, you still find time to talk to Daiyu?"

Now he got a bigger smile. "Of course, and Isobel too, in case you're wondering. But don't worry, Claudia and I don't talk."

He smiled. He could stand being teased a little. "Do you know the property idea came from Daiyu?"

"Yes, silly, that's why, joking aside, I am taking it seriously — but you've got a lot of work to do if you want to convince me it's a good idea."

"I don't know whether I do, yet, that's the point. I'd just decided to talk to you first before I had any embarrassing conversations."

"Embarrassing?"

"If I get into a discussion with the Langs and then get pulled back because you don't like it."

"Just a moment." She'd hung on to the waiter, with whom she now had a brief conversation before turning back to Alphonse. "Wine or sake?"

"Sake."

And the waiter was despatched. She looked at Alphonse with narrowed eyes. "When have you ever pulled me back from anything? Apart from my father now, you're the only person whose judgement I trust." She sipped water, smiled, and added, "But, as you've just found out, I'm not immediately enthusiastic. I'm still not enthusiastic, I should say. Daiyu told me yesterday and I didn't like it then."

"But if I meet him and still think it's a good idea — because I'm not seeing any internal solutions — would you have a conversation?"

"I agree with the internal point, you know that, so, of course, but with whom?"

"With them both." That seemed obvious to him. He would be their real business head, but, since she'd asked the question, there was a different point of view to consider — and she was gently shaking her head.

"Do you mind me suggesting we start with just the father?" She paused. "Why are you smiling?"

"Am I the only person in the world you would say 'do you mind me suggesting' to?"

They both laughed. "Yes, I don't even say it to my father. Look, there's no point in getting coy about this, especially as we get less and less time together now, but I think you're wonderful and I've learned so much from you, I can't begin to tell you," now he got the sly smile again, "but I've said it now, you've had your mega-compliment. It won't be repeated."

"Well, as a one-off final appraisal as our partnership evaporates, you have amazed me — and I totally understand why your father has picked you." There was a little emotion in her eyes, but her self-control stayed as strong as it usually did. "I would like to make sure that Property and Resorts will give you the minimum of distraction."

She reached out and squeezed his hand. "I'd like it to be a one-hour catch-up, before dinner once a month. Could we do that?" That seemed sensible, but for some reason he was slow to respond. "Don't worry," she added, "I won't be as demanding as Daiyu." And she giggled as he smiled helplessly. Now she was a girl again. "Is that getting serious?"

"It's an arrangement. That's the word we use, isn't it?"

She looked at him slyly. "That's what she's saying too… but I don't quite believe either of you."

He smiled at her. "It seems to have become an important arrangement."

She smiled. "That's what I thought. OK, now we've dealt with the important stuff, you can tell me what you're thinking about the Langs. Oh, but there is one more important thing to add."

What was this little drama, "Yes?"

"I stay the night after our monthly meetings," he wasn't quite shocked, "starting tonight."

"Of course." That seemed more gentlemanly than giving way to surprise.

"I've been terribly well-behaved these past eighteen months, travelling everywhere with the world's most desirable man — who has behaved utterly fucking impeccably, I have to say, but we're moving on now and I'd like us to manage our lives a little differently."

"So, we'll be having an arrangement?"

"Yes, is that all right?" The self-possession she always showed now seemed to falter for an instant.

"I would be thrilled and delighted." That wasn't quite accurate, but this was no time for fatal hesitation. And it would be wrong to ask if she'd discussed this plan with Daiyu. Then it struck him that he would have to do just that. Yes, that had become more than just an arrangement.

***

Mei left before three. She'd kissed him tenderly and said, "You don't want me here in the morning," which had seemed strange but also, as the door closed, accurate. Of course, she would also not have wanted to be there, probably.

They had focused on themselves and each other, apart from the fleeting moment when he'd remembered that the cleaners changed his bed linen on Fridays and the smears and spots of his night with Daiyu were no longer present. Mei had thrown the duvet back quickly and seemed to check the sheet, smiling at him as the fresh linen was revealed, then she quickly stripped and lay there waiting for him. "Are you going slowly because you don't know how he feels?"

He laughed, but felt skewered by her insight.

"Come on, darling man, let me cuddle your naked body. If he does wake up, that will be wonderful, but my distant memory of our threesome tells me that no man kisses better."

He'd loved how she'd opened and moved and responded to every move of his tongue, even gasping 'oh, yes,' as he'd pushed her knees to her chest to lick her other hole as his face was smothered in her cunt's wetness. His attempt to go slow was torpedoed ultimately by her hands pressing his head on to her while she screamed wildly. When he slid up and embraced her, he felt her chuckle deeply as his cock, now stiff, moved snugly into her vagina and she wriggled on top of him to straddle him and take him deeply. He looked up into what now, in a rare moment, had become a soft and smiling face. But now she closed her eyes and pushed down on him, gasping 'oh,' before he was fully in, then opening her eyes and smiling again. "This is a bonus for me. I didn't know if we could, but it is soooo lovely." And she surprised him by coming with him as he grasped her small cheeks and pushed her firmly down on to him to make her clit rub his pelvis.

They'd dozed briefly but woke again soon after midnight and had a desultory conversation. "It feels odd to talk to you like this," she'd said.

"Because we're so intense about work all the time?"

"Yes, and because I've been trying so hard not to find you attractive. And please don't say any stupid sweet thing now about how it's been for you. I completely adore and admire how you've been utterly professional with me. I've never known anyone who can stay so focused, and I've been so glad to see how that works — and I know that's how you'll always be with me," now the wicked smile again, "except once a month." And she kissed him gently, tenderly on the lips. "I only want one thing more tonight, then I'll be gone."

He wasn't completely surprised when she straddled his face. He was a little surprised that his cock responded so well to her hand and her mouth, but he was able to keep enough control as he pulled her clit on to his tongue and soon had her screaming again. But she'd stayed slumped on him, massaging his cock gently, licking his shaft and his balls, keeping him much stiffer than he'd expected until, as she began to take him deep in her mouth again, he knew she would make him come a second time but, as that point neared, her pussy moved to cover his face and her clit found his tongue — and this time they built — or she controlled — their climax together.

He'd stirred to the sound of her in the shower. She'd returned dressed and perfectly made-up again, their usual driver no doubt organised to collect her.

She leaned over to kiss his lips. "These nights are going to be very important to me — more than they are to you, I know — but could we make a schedule please?"

He took her hand. "Of course we can." Then he smiled. "Best not done on the office system though."

She laughed. "No excuses though. Every fourth Friday."

One more small kiss, and she was gone.

How firm a commitment that would be, he had no idea. How practical for him might be even more problematic. But, for a while, she had this big need of him and, while the sex had been fun, it was being close to him that was more important to her — and he wanted to be that for her.

22

I'd texted Conrad that I wouldn't need his car. I would be at his place talking to Sandra anyway. He texted back that he would send the car an hour earlier. That was my first surprise: pleasant. I was more ambivalent about the second surprise: Sandra met me at the front door, not Boris. "Taking Boris's job?"

"I knew it was you. I told Boris I'd meet you and he asked Conrad if we could use the front room." She was clearly excited. "That man is so lovely, can I get you a drink?" all came out as one word, more or less.

"I'd rather you told me what this is about. First, what's Conrad done?" I didn't want him relenting. I knew that would only present a bigger problem down the road.

"Not Conrad, silly, Boris."

Oh, God! Now I'm worried for Boris. I'd not remotely expected my Cupid machinations to bear more than a single fruit, but this feels like it might have festooned a tree. Sandra looks lovelier than she has done in years; younger too. I could do with a minute to digest this, so I send her away to fetch a g and t for me and sit down in what is becoming my chair. The mind adjusts very quickly to new realities so, by the time she

270

returns, I'm upright in my seat, eager to know more about my new challenge.

"I think that's yours." I take the nearer of two identical glasses. "Mine's just water." She's standing, holding the tray and her glass, waiting for me to confirm. I sip and wave to her to sit.

"Does Conrad know about you and Boris?"

This is where her euphoria stalls. "Yes. He's being a bit grumpy."

"Has he spoken to you?"

"No, he's just told Boris. He's said he'll talk to you about it."

Good! I think. I still have a problem, it's just a different problem. One that might easily go away. Leaving me with the first problem. Which needs solving anyway: what to do with Sandra. I'd better find out more about the new problem and assess its likely duration.

"I don't want the gory details but I'm guessing you two," and I pause to create my verbal parenthesis, "have fallen in love." I do try to keep sarcasm out of my voice. I doubt if I succeed.

But she has the decency to chuckle at this. "Oh, come on, Sades." But now she's looking down into her glass, pausing. "But something's happened, yes."

"So, you've fucked him."

"Well, no." Now I'm getting the girlish smile again, the one on her face when I arrived. "He fucked me, actually. What had you said to him?"

So, I am getting the blame. Now I'm beginning to dread talking to Conrad. But I owe her an explanation. Wait, no, I don't! But I do need to understand the problem. "I knew he was besotted with you. I just told him not to be soppy. I know there's a brute in there — I just thought if he showed that a bit. Oh, Sandra, you get so silly at times, you've fallen for monsters — and usually losers."

That makes her thoughtful again. "I have, haven't I? But Boris isn't like that. He can play brute, but he adores me. I have to encourage him to get rougher."

"Oh, Sandra!"

"What's up?"

She's looking indignant. She's a bottom, remember, and what have I told you about bottoms? They manipulate! "You've got to remember, next to me, he's your only friend. You can't play games with the poor guy."

"Who's playing games? I think he's wonderful."

"D'uh! The hulk, remember? That was all of three days ago."

"Is that all it is? I feel he's been fucking me for weeks. I'm quite sore, actually. He's very big, you know." She giggles. Oh, please! I could fill in the blanks, but she continues, "I call his cock the incredible hulk, now; he thinks it's funny."

I might think it's funny someday, but I can't get there yet.

"Conrad's even grumpy about the noise we made one time and he was three floors down." The memory is clearly amusing her. "Mind you, we were on the table in that open area on the top floor. I guess it must be echoey up there."

"Sandra, stop it please." Now she looks a little taken aback, and hurt. There is something of the simpleton about her, if I'm honest. Woah! I must be careful here. Her little girl schtick is how she plays people — Boris included, presumably — and I mustn't let myself get fooled like that. "We have three and a half weeks to solve a real problem. What are you going to do?"

"Boris says he loves me."

I stifle 'for fuck's sake,' but I am very close to losing it. "Be that as it may..."

"Aren't you happy for me?"

I take a deep breath. "Not until we have a means of you supporting yourself. Even if this is love fucking eternal, you still need an income and somewhere to live."

I'm sure these thoughts have been going through her head, but she just sits and looks at me, her fingers twisting around the glass she's holding, waiting for me, the top, to solve the problem for her. Part of me would like to cut her adrift, but I can't, and now there's Boris.

"I could work here... or I could work for you," she says quietly, plaintively.

Absurd ideas, but I've nothing better to offer at the moment, and there's no point in hurting her feelings just because I'm not finding an answer.

There's a gentle knock on the door. I'm surprised. Sandra and I are both guests here, the door's not closed, no one needs to knock. It's she who calls 'come in' and it's Boris who fills the doorway as the door is slowly opened. "Sorry disturb you. Mr Conrad want know when you like leave for dinner."

Sandra has stood up, moved to him and put her arms around his waist. He dwarfs her — and looks uncomfortable — "And I like say thank you, maybe."

Poor Boris, he's not managing this conflict well, and I remember, once again, that he's a bigger priority — and he's more probably vulnerable emotionally than Sandra — why am I thinking that about a heavy who can obviously deal with some very difficult people?

Maybe Conrad has some thoughts. "I'm ready when he is, tell him. Thank you, Boris."
Now an unalloyed smile — I presume that's because I've made no negative comment — "Is pleasure," he says, and he hugs her gently and leaves. She looks after him, and then back to me. They'll be bonking in fifteen minutes is probably what all three of us are thinking. Three days into being 'in love' — come on, you must remember!

***

It's hard to know if Conrad is grumpy. He won't talk about the domestic situation with his driver all ears in the front; information is the currency of staff. He asks very civilly about my business and we're soon at the Dorchester again. When he's ordered two martinis for us, he tells me he's not happy — and you would never know from expression or intonation. "Are we talking minor irritation or volcanic resentment?"

"Never the latter." He smiles. "But I don't think we've moved towards solving our problem."

"Well," I'm rueful, "I think we've allowed an extra problem to emerge, and I may even be a little guilty there." He looks puzzled — as puzzled as he can look, he normally has such a grip on things. "I just hinted to Boris that he shouldn't mope around her, it wasn't doing either of them any good. What's he said?"

"He says he loves her." His eyes move heavenward.

I have to ask. "What's his story?" I've only been guessing.

He shrugs. "Grandparents got him out of Bosnia. But he ran away to go back in to find the men who killed his parents, but he got lucky." I think 'lucky?' but Conrad will tell his story at his own pace. "He fell in with a group who were very good. He was eleven years old but big and strong. They trained him very well but used him as a front in some operations, when it was useful he appeared as a child. He saw lots of horrible stuff and grew up quickly, but for him it was always about justice. I think the group was good like that: first priority, survival; then, justice; never random reprisals. After the ceasefires he found his grandparents again, the grandmother was Romanian, they'd gone there, and he supported them by petty crime but he got picked up by one of my businesses out there and used on what I'm going to call security work." He raises an eyebrow at me, checking that I've some understanding of what that probably meant. I nod. I probably have. "I'm out of that region now, well, except for a medical centre and two schools that I keep going." You get these little surprises sometimes with Conrad — I want to know more but he's telling a story. "I only tried a few ventures when it was opening up but he was on a detail looking after me when a problem blew up and he dealt with it so quietly and effectively I offered him a job on the spot. Not a word of English and he began to negotiate with me." Conrad smiles, raises his glass and says cheers. I drink with him. "I find out that all he wants is security for his grandparents. I'd still be sending money every month now from somewhere in the organisation if he hadn't come to me a couple of years ago and told me his grandmother had died — the old boy had gone a few years before. Boris said I should stop paying and could he have time off for the funeral. That was a problem." I look puzzled. Conrad has a huge organisation. he could easily backfill one heavy for a week. "We think he's still wanted for murder in some places, and I didn't want him caught up with any bent cops or make-a-name lawyers. I have a business that managed it for us — fake i.d. and private jet — he was very grateful, but he'd done so much for me by then." He shrugs. "That's Boris."

I'm intrigued, of course. "But what about him and ladies?"

"I'm afraid his formative years were confrontations with the dark side. He saw lots of rape and violence. I think he used to get enough freebies from girls he helped protect, so he's no innocent, but, to my knowledge, he's never formed a relationship."

"Until now."

He shakes his head slowly. "Until now." And he smirks at me. "And it's your fault, you tell me."

"I just felt a bit sorry for him. He was looking so pathetic around her. I thought one good bonk would get it out of his system, but it doesn't seem to have done. He's got this teenage crush now, making up for the missing years, I assume. What are we going to do about it?"

"We, kemo sabe?" And we both laugh. "But have you thought of anything she can do? Is she any good at anything? Christ, I have enough businesses but I do let my people run them and..."

"You don't want some ditzy nympho making you look ridiculous."

"I'm not saying that." He looks a little irritated with me — that I could impute such a thought to him — and, in truth, he is always careful about how he expresses himself; always calm, always reasonable.

I take his hand. "Conrad, it's what I'm thinking about having her work for me. I don't need a ditzy nympho. And I certainly wouldn't pay enough to support the lifestyle she's got used to." I can see a small smile play on his mouth. "What are you thinking?"

"Could you try her, on admin, or something? Wouldn't she have to work for Merle? I'd enjoy that."

"That's only half a solution. Where's she going to live?"

"She can stay with Boris until we see if it works. I think it's what he wants."

"You're a sweet man, Conrad."

"Shhh, for fuck's sake, Sadie, someone might hear you." We're laughing again. We soon move on; into the dining room, and into another conversation about my business. He's never shown this much interest before. Eventually, I ask him why he's asking now. "Weeelll," he starts slowly. "Two reasons. I hadn't wanted to spoil the social relationship we have with anything business-based. I know your work's very good and my place does need renovating, but..." And he shrugs. I get that, not that we have much of a relationship really but I probably do the best job of handling his more extreme tastes and we wouldn't want talk of budgets and soft furnishings to interfere with that. "And, limited as that social relationship is, it's certainly got much more limited since you've been living out there. How long's that going on for?"

I touch his hand again. "Oh, Conrad, you're missing me!"

I get his irritated look again. My frivolity doesn't appeal, but the waiter is beside us now. We haven't looked at menus, but Conrad picks his up and I know he's going to make quick decisions. I can do that too. And the lady needs to be first; I tell the waiter what I want. "That's what you had last time!" says Conrad, and I can't tell whether that annoys him, or whether he's pleased with himself that he's remembered.

I just say, "And it was marvellous," to the waiter. Whether what Conrad picks is different, I haven't the faintest idea, but I do know that the Bâtard-Montrachet — the Leflaive — is a step up this time. I avoid looking impressed. But I can't help noting that I'm receiving special treatment. And it's not that he's angling for special treatment later, he can have that anyway. He's a very appreciative bottom — and I love our playtimes.

***

It has been a lovely evening. I've learned a lot more about his business — businesses, I should say. I was intrigued about his Boris story, but he just tells me he was more opportunistic then — and less principled. When I asked about that, he just made a face and said that he saw principles and morality as pragmatism in the long term — he just doesn't want to be in unsustainable businesses. I teased him about his oil interests and he got serious for a moment and said he thought it was better to work with people to move them away from dependency but of course that was unsustainable too. I got a little lecture on climate change until he saw my eyes glaze over: 'This isn't news to you, is it?' is what he said. I gave him a tolerant smile as I shook my head and, bless him, he did laugh at himself at that point and say, "Jonny-come-lately evangelists shouldn't lecture to converts."

He looked serious again a little later when the coffee came. I'd declined cognac since I'd guessed what was still ahead of us. "Have you got things with you?" he asked.

"Of course," I said — a big tote is always useful, for work and for play.

"I have a special request tonight." Yes, I was mystified. His tastes are fairly extreme, as you'll see, and I couldn't, offhand, think of anything we hadn't tried. But dealing with Conrad is simple — he just says what he wants, or wants to try, and I've never said no. We have those conversations away from the event itself, nothing interferes with the top and bottom roles when we're playing but his usual approach is to say, 'I thought such and such might be interesting,' not 'I have a special request.'

"Will you stay over?"

I tried not to look shocked and said 'Of course' as a throwaway response. It's not a problem for me — but it is a significant step, and the look that passed between us confirmed that. I decided just to let the evening develop. I assume he just wants to give it a try. I've woken up often enough with Alphonse, he's the most recent, and that's always pleasant. He wakes first and showers, then comes back to bed and makes me happy again. It's very sweet and he kisses wonderfully — and then seems so surprised that his cock rises. Come on, my oral skills are very well developed, but I like straddling him when I've got him stiff, I love watching his face when he comes — so controlled, so sweet.

With most men it's not like that, so I'm no great fan of sleeping over — and I never invite anyone to stay. But Conrad is sweet and fastidious too — although there will be more equipment to put away before we fall asleep. It's not stuff you want to wake up to. But that's where the ottoman at the foot of his bed is so useful.

Yes, we play in his bedroom. Conrad, as I've told you, only watches in his own cellar. He picks up ideas from what other people are doing. I'm sure, a long time ago, it helped him sort out his own particular profile. He's told me he's had some gay affairs in his youth but couldn't make an emotional connection with the guys. It was when an understanding lady identified his anal fixation that he began to enjoy life. Yes, he prefers me that way, but I'm the top, remember; I'll have that if I want it. First, we need to deal with Conrad — but I must admit, this 'special request' is weighing on me a little.

But that concern has almost disappeared by the time I'm lying on my back on the ottoman. I'm wearing a platform bra that shows my nipples, a garter belt and stockings. Comfortable? No, but effective. Somewhere down there he's holding his stiff cock but the important point is that he's licking me. Yes, he's licking everywhere — and I do like it. At some point I will come. He won't, not yet. He's under instructions not to. His hands are off his cock now, I can feel him smearing lube on me. His tongue is gently stroking my clit and I'm on that plateau of pleasure where no orgasm is immediately threatening — although the feelings intensify as a second finger enters me.

The third finger is a danger point. "No, Conrad," I say quite sharply. The third finger stays. I'm delightfully stretched and I always love it — I've just needed to make him take his other hand off his cock. I don't want him spoiling his own evening, so I give him something to think about. "Make me come now, you bad boy!" I order and his fingers push deeper and I get his tongue pressing flat on my clit and...

When my breathing slows — he's still licking, of course, he is very good — I tell him, "I think we'll have a cuddle before your big treat," and we slide on to the bed and embrace. I hold his cock, of course. I control it better than he does, and he's happy being managed. At the risk of being boring, he's a bottom, he's more focused on his own body's pleasure; as a top, I'm primarily interested in his body's responses, in the pleasure I'm giving him.

Sure, he's enjoyed playing with my body, and he's done a moderately good job, but we both know that the important part of the evening is what comes now.

Conrad's older than you might choose, but he's in very good shape. He has a pleasant cock, and it's reliable. I suspect he's using blue-pill help, but who cares? He has smooth, relatively hairless skin and is well-muscled. He's a little too white to be ideal but we keep the lights low anyway.

I order him on to the ottoman. He's on all fours, his cock pointing out nice and stiff, even with no one touching it. Last time I had Suzanne to help me but we didn't really need her. It was a training exercise for her.

I ask him casually, "Did Suzanne's training work?"

"I've been away since then, so I don't know." There's a hint of irritation in his voice, or is it impatience? He's lowered his head to his forearms and is wiggling his arse. I slap him lightly with a bare hand — it's just a message, spanking isn't his real kink — I want to let him know I'm taking my time. Which is what he truly wants.

I remove my bra and drape it over the back of his neck and I begin rubbing my breasts over his skin. I enjoy it, but it has him gasping, especially when I slide each nipple in turn up and down his crack. I slap him again when his hand grasps his cock. He wouldn't make himself come. It's just part of our play ritual.

I reach into my tote and ostentatiously take out a latex glove and pull it on. It's not necessary, I generally prefer without — and Conrad is, as I said, a fastidious man, he'll have had an enema earlier, partly because he enjoys it, but it's comforting to know that I will have unrestricted access — and he will want me very deep, both with the strap-on, if that's what we choose, and later, with the hand.

Yes, we will be going that far, but for now we have a lengthy finger playtime. This may even be the best bit. I've squirted lots of lube on him. It always feels cold of course, and Conrad has an array of little gaspy noises to show appreciation at every step.

I start with two fingers. He's an experienced man, although he isn't playing frequently at the moment, so I can spend plenty time relaxing him.

An aside: I do love playing with the arse — and I enjoy being played with; there's a thrill in the stimulation of all those nerve endings and a voluptuousness in all that progressive stretching. If I'm not talking to the converted, well, go on, it's time you gave it a try. The principal health warning is that a sensitive partner is essential. Conrad's feedback — the gasps, the wiggles, the pushing back for more (slowly, boy!) — tells me that I am exactly that, sensitive (not that self-doubt has ever even coughed outside the door of my consciousness).

I've pushed two fingers in as far as I can. When I use my other forefinger to tickle around the rim, his hand moves to his cock again. He gets another playful slap for that and I leave him for a moment. He groans, but I'm only going to the credenza drawer to fetch a paddle. I slap him quite hard and get a cry of pained surprise. "Too much hand on the cock, Master Conrad, no good will come of it."

I'm not putting too much pressure on myself, but I am trying to gauge what will please him most. There are a number of ways we can play this, but it will be best if it culminates in him coming. Will I come again? Of course, he can eat me later if I choose — and he is quite good — but it's never really the same if you can feel that limp stump dribbling on your leg, is it? How is he responding to, well, it's three fingers now and my other hand is holding his cock gently? He's in a zone of being thrilled but not yet in danger of spilling over. Yes, he's gasping, but with a regular tempo, even as he's pushing back, wanting me to squeeze more into him. This is the point at which I sometimes reach for the strap-on but I'm feeling intimate tonight, and I sense he is too. I whisper to him, "You can give me a little fun now, baby, just make sure you don't come inside me. I make you come, remember that." This is tricky to manage. My arse will excite him, I know, and we finish that way sometimes, to both our satisfaction — but tonight feels a little bit special, and I want to manage his orgasm, but he'll enjoy that all the more if he's thrilled me first. "Time for us to switch places."

I hold on to his cock while I slide my fingers out of him. I need him nice and stiff of course. I kiss him. "I'll be coming when you fuck me, but hang on for your big treat later." Now he kisses me; it's tender, not urgent. He's controlling himself. I can let him hold himself for a moment. I need lots of lube, he may push in too quickly.

But I've underestimated him. Bless him, he slides one, and then two fingers into my arse, one into my pussy and lets his pinkie tickle my clit. I'm gently holding his cock as he's standing beside me, stroking my back with his free hand. We have him under control, but I'm finding this is taking me too high. But I'm here for him, and I know what he and I will both enjoy. I squeeze him. "I want the big boy now, please." I squirt more lube on, while he fiddles with the condom I've left on the bed for him, but he's soon behind me, positioning his cock. I love that first moment when the head gets squeezed in — he's done just enough work on helping me relax. It's a bit of a stretch, but all the more gorgeous for that. My fingers move to my clit.

"Are you allowed to do that?" he asks.

I push back a little. I can feel his belly on my bum now. "You know you won't last long if I don't come soon." He knows I'm right. His hands are tightening their grip on my hips, so I rub myself vigorously and begin to shout even before I'm truly coming, but I need him to relax and just enjoy the feel of me squeezing him and of me shuddering — now I am having a wonderful time. I hope he doesn't come now but I've become very selfishly obsessed with my own orgasm, as you do at these moments. I'll have to trust him to stay in control if he wants more real fun tonight. His hands have eased their *grip. I think we're safe. I can revel in the long slide down after coming — and continue to enjoy that nice cock still filling my arse. Ooh, I enjoy that more than a real top should, but I'm now thinking of him again and I pull myself off him. There are still different options but I'm sure I know what he wants tonight. Now we're standing, his cock in my hand again and I'm looking into his eyes. "Now you kneel again," I tell him and he nods gently at me. I'm guessing right. I can't rush the next bit, but I can't be too slow — or he'll come too early or, worse, miss the moment altogether.*

Oh, I can always make him come, of course, my mouth never fails, but there is a moment we're striving for, something he especially likes.

He's kneeling again now, and I'm applying more lube. I do this for a few people. A charming old boy taught me many years, ago. It was easy with him. He'd been fisting-promiscuous for a long time and was easily slack, so I could play quite comfortably. I was curious enough to enjoy almost everything, and I managed to give him a lot of pleasure and so I built it into my repertoire for special occasions — like for Conrad.

The old boy? He believed that giving presents, quite generous ones, was a substitute for giving orgasms — and that wasn't, even then, the way I wanted to organise my playtimes — tops are sensual creatures too, not prostitutes.

But Conrad's made me come twice already, and I've been keeping him on edge for about as long as he can stand, I think. But now I'm momentarily hesitant. He had a wonderful time last time. Suzanne had been there to stretch his cheeks and that made it very easy to move my hand — in and out, and twisting and spreading — in a way that kept him gasping with excitement, then she'd managed to get beneath him and take his cock in her mouth while she kept her hands on his arse, still stretching; I carried on fisting and began tickling his balls. Oh, my, I'd never heard anything so loud. And she had to let go and put one hand on his cock to stop him fucking her mouth too deeply. I was on the point of pulling out to protect her, but he seemed to control himself enough — and we probably prolonged his orgasm even more. She had to pull away to breathe and swallow, but she went straight back like a trouper. She'll do very well in her new apartment.

But now it's just me. I'm giving him a wonderful time. I thought for a while that he wouldn't manage the full fist, I was easing back, but I got a breathless 'No, no, no, more, more!' and I pushed on slowly past a brief cry of pain and then he could begin to wallow in extreme pleasure. I think he's near enough now. I don't want to miss the optimum moment. I hold his cock. He's still wearing the condom he put on for me — he's a little too squeamish about mess, really, but this is about giving him ultimate pleasure — and that's coming now with those strange ghoulish noises, his wiggling arse and his now shuddering cock. I press my breasts on to his back, I want to feel everything about him coming — and it is truly splendid. I ease my hand out and slide the condom off as I pull my other hand away while he subsides on to the ottoman. He's lying on his side to look at me, so I can kneel down and take his softening cock in my mouth. If I don't, he'll move away quickly to stop himself dribbling, so this is partly for me as well; we should glide down this long slide together until I'm ready to get him to move to the bed and take me in his arms.

We don't talk for a long time. I'm very happy snuggled in to him. His body is a good size for mine. I could get sleepy, but there are things to be tidied away before I can drift off.

But he starts talking. "That was just the most marvellous thing," he says drowsily.

I don't want to get too forensic, but a top has to understand what works and why. "I thought when we both had you last time that you scaled some peaks."

His arms move a little tighter around me. "Oh, that was an amazing thrill, but it didn't match the intimacy of what we've just been doing." And he seems to be threatening to fall asleep with those words echoing in the night air. No post-mortem now, Isobel, let's just tidy up and snuggle in and see what happens in our waking conversation. I ease myself away. He makes a small noise of disappointment but he's too near sleep to protest. I'm not three minutes, well, five, including a bathroom visit, and he's asleep when I lie down again. Or he seems to be, but his arm moves out and he pulls me into him and spoons me. OK, but I almost never sleep like this.

When I wake in the middle of the night, we've separated, but he still has a hand on my waist. When I'm woken by the slanting sunlight in the morning, he's cuddling me again. This is what he wanted — yet I've no idea why. But I'm not so crass as to rush in with any questions. I don't have to. He kisses my shoulder and asks, "Could you do this more often?"

I don't want to appear silly and read too much into this. "I love our playtimes, Conrad. For a bottom you're exceptionally thoughtful and caring, but our paths so seldom cross. I'm happy to look at diaries and plan a bit more."

He takes a deep breath — what's coming now? "I'd like, maybe, to think about doing a bit more than that."

I'm tempted to turn and confront him; something specific is on his mind. I'll admit I'm a little on edge now, but I'll try to stay cool. I wiggle my bum on to his dozing cock — but, for some reason, I'm not really feeling frivolous.

"I'd like us to be a couple," he suddenly says.

I'm shocked. I freeze. I fight to unfreeze myself, pronto. But this isn't a situation I top my way through. I'm not in control here. But I seem to be open to having a discussion. My brain isn't screaming: 'reject, reject, reject!' "I'm going to assume this has been brewing for a while and it's not just the typical male response to a wonderful fuck." I've turned now and I'm looking into his eyes.

He smiles, kisses my lips gently, and says, "Of course, you're right. I have been thinking about it."

Of course I'm right, but I'm still puzzled — and it shows apparently.

"I didn't know if you might have guessed. You always seem so supernaturally perceptive." But he can tell I'm genuinely floored. I can't even begin to get my mind around what he's thinking. What is 'being a couple' to him? I live in Asia mostly. I have arrangements. Well, only Alphonse and Mei are commitments. But now the little creature that sleeps in my head wakes up — you know the one, he has horns and a tail — and he reminds me: 'They're both gay, Isobel.'

Now I kiss his lips. "This sounds like a wonderful conversation for breakfast time — or after we've read the Sunday papers together." I don't actually know if I'm teasing him.

He doesn't seem concerned. "I'd like us to take some time over it. I'd hoped it mightn't be such a surprise, but it's rather sweet to catch you off guard like this."

"You have. I thought you'd just set me up for another fuck this morning."

"Well, I didn't want to rule that out." His hand caresses my hip.

I slap it, playfully of course, and smile at him. "Twice a night? Not if we're a couple!"

But he smiles and kisses me. Jesus, he does understand me uncomfortably well.

I'm trying to hide the turmoil I'm feeling. I have enjoyed the morning fuck, but it didn't distract me as much as I'd thought it would. He was more toppy than usual and that made me think more about his proposition — about how it might be. I had, apparently, not rejected it — and I found myself responding warmly to his guttural commands. Well, 'suck my cock' only does it for me in very specific circumstances but that seems to be where I was. Even though it jarred a little with me, it did make me very wet, and it was making him, when my mouth got there, gratifyingly stiff. He was very close when I felt his hands on my shoulders, easing me up. 'I want us to come together,' is what he said. I moved to straddle his face and again I got given a clear command. 'No, your arse is too sweet, my love, I'm having you that way again, but I come with you this time.'

My love?! Yes, that's what got me. It was still bouncing around my head when he was coming inside me five minutes later. I almost forgot to come myself.

We dozed again a little. I woke still very aware of the rasping feeling in my arse — he'd managed to hold himself back for quite long enough, in spite of how vigorous he'd been. He's woken up now and he's sliding down to kiss my pussy — but I really am too distracted to get the most out of that.

"Ordinarily, I'd encourage you but, fuck it, Conrad, you made me curious. Whatever is on your mind. What's a couple, for fuck's sake?"

He slides back up and smiles at me. I'm not going to say it's a stupid grin — but it is a stupid grin. "I don't think I've ever surprised you before. It's very simple, I would have thought," he hesitates, "but it obviously can't be."

"No, it's not. I sometimes have arrangements with people. They aren't quite relationships but there are people I know and like and like to fuck with, but I'm not 'couples' with them. Well, maybe I am. I really don't know what you mean."

He looks a little perturbed — worried he might have been misunderstood. "I don't want to interfere with any arrangements. I just want to do more things with you, share things with you." He's hesitating again. "Holiday with you sometimes and..." More hesitation. "Spend nights together when we're in the same place."

I don't think either of our faces is showing much at this stage. Mine must just seem frozen, I would think. He has that small, patient smile I see on him sometimes. But I know it to be a face of implacable resolve. He hasn't exactly expressed himself forcefully, but Conrad's convictions are dressed in soft cloaks. I need to take this very seriously. And there are upsides.

That sounds terrible, doesn't it? The man himself is very attractive. I have just not thought for years about living differently.

"Conrad," I say firmly. He settles, his head on an elbow-propped hand, the calm smile a little larger now — he thinks he's won! "I think you're a wonderful man." He moves to kiss but my hand, on his chest, pushes him away. "I just haven't thought about anything like that for years."

"And now you have?" He's not looking smug, I'll give him that.

"I'd like to give it a try." And, you know, I think I would.

23

Alphonse had agreed to meet at the Lang headquarters. It had been set up by Daiyu. The old man's office was small and simple and had a view of only other buildings. This was unusually spartan modesty but in keeping with his company's reputation of fair dealing and good controls.

The man was small, wispy-haired and smiley. "I am very honoured to meet you, Mr Newman. I have admired what you have been doing."

"And I admire your business very much, Mr Lang. We seldom compete directly but I can always see the logic in the deals you do, and you always seem to close at good prices."

The man shrugged modestly. Daiyu had assured him that the man's English was competent, and that seemed an accurate description. It should take them through the first part of the conversation.

"It is an interesting market. There are opportunities at sensible prices."

"Is that why you are less active in Shanghai and Beijing? The prices are not sensible?"

The man grinned enigmatically. "Is that what you find, Mr Newman?"

"Well, we can usually find some sensible prices, but they are buoyant markets." Alphonse was smiling inwardly. The man was being charmingly cagey — he expected no less. "But we have to work hard to find the treasures — and negotiate hard also."

"You are very well assisted in that regard, I believe."

Now Alphonse felt he could risk a smile. "I think you are very well informed. Zhao Meitang is a very able businessman." He had thought hard about how to describe her. He had no feel for the gender sensitivity of Chinese businesspeople. He had not seen any antagonism towards Mei which appeared to arise from her sex — from her approach, of course. She was hard, but would only seem rude to people who were not masters of their information.

Lang was smiling. "I have heard many good things about her. My son does not like her. That is also a good thing." Alphonse found himself chuckling with the old man. "But I also hear she may have more responsibilities in the future."

Alphonse wasn't surprised by the observation. Increasingly the world felt like a country of virtual villages — as if the community of major property dealers could sit around a watering hole and chat of an evening. Even he, as an outsider here, could gather with seven or eight men, mostly men, although Mei was not unique, and talk about their concerns — but not about their deals, of course. But he could imagine the people he knew passing on observations about the Senlin organisation and how it might need to be led.

"She seems to have grown under your guidance, if I may say so. Her father was never so ambitious or adventurous before the relationship between Senlin and Dickinson." At least Alphonse was prepared for any discussions about Mei's father to be about the man in the Shanghai office — even had there been speculation in the village about Mei's paternity, it certainly wouldn't emerge in a conversation like this. "But it is often the way that the next generation is more dynamic than their fathers."

Alphonse had the sense that he was being teased a little. Surely Daiyu couldn't have given the man this much insight into the purpose of the meeting!

"Are you describing the Lang business, if I may ask?"

The old man stared straight at him. "Of course you may ask. It's why you're here, I assume."

There seemed to be nothing to be gained from concealment or subterfuge. "I have been thinking about how we might work together for our mutual benefit."

"My English is, I fear, not so subtle. Working together for our mutual benefit, now that is phraseology that is very imprecise, am I right? I would prefer you said exactly what you wanted. Why are you here this morning?"

No respect would be gained by hesitation. "I see so many opportunities in the region, both in property and resorts."

"Yes, I have been told your new hotels are very impressive and it seems a good time to be making those investments." OK, thought Alphonse, the man was giving positive signs.

"But you are right about Zhao Meitang. Shen Wengwei expects her to work nearer to him and that will be a loss to the property business."

"He is ill, yes?"

Alphonse thought a while. The man would probably expect him to be discreet. It was best to say nothing. "He is looking to the future of his group and how it can be managed as he steps back."

Land nodded impassively. That had been the right way to respond. "So, you lack the leadership resources to manage your expanding empire." He paused. "And you are looking to divest, perhaps? Our capabilities to absorb more business are also stretched, I'm afraid, although my son doesn't wish to accept that."

The man was playing with him, but that was the very least Alphonse had expected. "We're reluctant to slow our expansion. Since we brought Senlin and Dickinson together, our opportunities have expanded with our resources. Our bottleneck is our leadership capacity. Our investors believe in us and want us to go faster, but it's hard to spend money wisely."

"Yes," said the old man slowly, "I could do that, but I cannot access new funds without guarantees which are, to me, unacceptable. I have assumed this has something to do with why we are meeting today."

This was an open door, but there was a lot to consider. "Well, I am interested in why you have not expanded further. Here in Hong Kong, you are the best managed company I or Zhou Meitang have encountered. Is it only a question of funding?"

Lang leaned his head to one side. "You have no children, Mr Newman."

"No," said Alphonse, aware that, in England, that observation would have come with many nuances. Here he could not begin to guess what was in the old man's mind.

"What have you heard about my son?"

"I have heard that he is very bright, dynamic, and very ambitious — and that his judgement in the property market is good, but the last point, of course, is where your influence and education are the greatest."

Lang laughed lightly. "We are serious men, Mr Newman, your last observation was more fact than flattery — but flattery it was, nonetheless. And you could have begun by describing my son as conceited, wilful and greedy and the picture would not have been much less accurate. It is a question of perspective, is it not?"

"But we all have the same perspective on the bottom line, do we not? Yours is a successful and profitable business…"

"But you and my son feel we could grow faster."

That point could hang in the air a moment, thought Alphonse. It would be a classic mistake to feel that every observation required a response.

"And you both may be right." He shrugged. "Perhaps I place too much value on security these days, I have less appetite for risk."

Another point that could hang in the air.

Now he smiled. "I think you are here to persuade me that I can do both, yes?"

Alphonse was beginning to like the old rogue and his fake humility: he wanted less risk, of course; he wanted more growth, also of course; the outstanding question was about name and legacy — how important would that be?

"You are assuming I am not here to offer to buy your business?"

Another smile. "Of course you're not. That would be too crass for a man of your judgement and subtlety — you probably see some value in the networks I have built and in the knowledge I have."

"May I accept your flattery in the same generous spirit in which you accepted mine?"

"I intended that you should. Are we wasting time with pleasantries when the solution is obvious to us both?"

"That we create Shen, Lang, Dickinson and appoint your son as managing director, reporting to a board of you, me and Zhao Meitang?"

Now the old man laughed. "I admire you so much, Mr Newman, the manners of a prince and the morals of a pirate." And Alphonse, in spite of himself, found himself laughing. "But all this is conditional, of course, on you being able to work with my son…"

"And he with me."

"Oh, but you are such a charming pirate, Mr Newman, you have even formed a very successful relationship with Zhao Meitang. She is an impressive lady — but a demanding one, I believe. I am anticipating, you see, that, should we form the right relationships — and, of course, create the appropriate financial conditions — that you would work most closely with my son."

"That is what I have assumed."

"You are happy here in Asia? You seem so European."

"I am European, historically and culturally, but professionally I like to think of myself as global."

"I'm afraid I'm Cantonese — that's what my son calls me. I will call him in soon, but I am intrigued how you will answer the question you have so ably side-stepped."

"I am happy here, yes. My resort project is a passion that binds me here, and the whole business environment is more dynamic, more exciting."

"I was wondering whether, socially, you are able to find contentment. Could you be drawn away by motives other than business?"

It was a valid question. The success of the enterprise would depend on Alphonse's commitment to it — and it made him suddenly aware that he was becoming, in a way, content. He would be seeing Daiyu later to discuss this very conversation — and he realised how much he was looking forward to their time together. "I really am very content, thank you. I'm anticipating this being my main base for three years at least."

The old man smiled as he reached for the phone on the desk nearby. When he put the phone down, he said, "My son will join us in the main meeting room. Shall we go through?"

***

"I promise I'll be more imaginative next time, but I do like this table. Anyway, thank you for coming."

Daiyu smiled at him as their cheeks touched. "You don't seriously expect me to object. But I'll book next time. I'll even pay, so it won't be so lavish."

Well, he thought, that will tell me something — but how soon the next date would be should not preoccupy him before this one got started, although, technically, this was a business meeting, rather than a date. Was she seeing it that way?

"How did you get on?"

"I think I liked the old man more than I liked his son. What did Mei call him? Bumptious and arrogant? Her judgement is good. But that doesn't mean he's not talented. His appreciation of the market is excellent around here, but he'll have things to learn on the mainland — and that's where his dynamism would have to be checked. We're meeting again early next week when we've thought a little more about it — and I've talked to Peter about the idea just now, and I'd already asked Mei to stay until then. Peter thinks the idea's good — but he didn't say that until I told him it was yours."

"Are you teasing?"

"No. I know you impress him, and he thinks you've been close to the market and the businesses for long enough to make a good call. If Mei and I get further with the Langs on Monday, he wants to meet them later that week. He's meeting Shen Wengwei then."

"Is Claudia coming with him?"

"Yes, this is a big thing for them, getting the organisations closer to help with Wengwei's health. Peter likes Claudia's thoughts on organisations." He wasn't sure why Daiyu had asked the question. Were they sinking into the complexities of a closer relationship? Feeling sensitive about what could be discussed? That would surprise him. She normally abided by her 'tact is inefficiency' mantra.

She took his hand. "I am interested in how that all comes together, that's one reason for asking. But I'm also looking out for you. And now you're looking worried." He got her serious look. "I was happy to hear 'more than an arrangement' last time but I made no assumptions about how it would affect the rest of your life. I'm not martyring myself, but I do hope to be the least challenging of your relationships — or arrangements. OK?"

It did make him feel relaxed. "OK, thank you. Will you order again?"

"Only if I'm guaranteed the same dessert." They smiled before she spoke to the waiter. "And I'll warn you now," she said when he'd gone, "I have an overnight bag with me. I enjoyed our mornings in Phoruc too much. But now, tell me about the Langs."

24

I had the most extraordinary video call earlier today. Claudia had rung me to warn me — that was the word she used — that a man called Henderson would be in touch. She was quite blunt. She didn't trust him at all, but he worked on assignments for Peter, who had briefed him on my little issue. I told her I thought that was magnificent of Peter, but the situation was being brought under control. She sounded relieved but asked if I would at least talk to Henderson, since Peter had set it up. I agreed, of course. I was a little intrigued about the whole area anyway, especially after I'd spoken to the man on the phone to set up the video call — I had to go to somewhere near Berkeley Square, it's an office Claudia used to use, because they have 'more secure communications,' is what he said. Anyway, a charming man met me. He introduced himself as Sandy Nicholls and it was his name on the office — Nicholls Associates — he was a cheery, bald and somewhat garrulous man — it's not often I struggle to get a word in, but he was smiley and very solicitous. He's part of Peter's empire, he does recruitment consulting, and he'd been told a little about me, but not what the call was about — but, at that stage, I knew barely more than he did.

The man on the screen looked quite like I thought he might — I'd formed a picture from the voice, as you do. I'm not going to claim a special talent in that regard — I once met a radio newscaster at a party. I recognised the name when he was introduced to me but it took all my powers of concealment to hide the crushing disappointment of having to ascribe this wonderful, sensual baritone voice to this shabby, fat little man I was confronted with. I try not to be a pulchritude snob — I've played with uglier men, I think — but I couldn't put my disappointment behind me, however charming he tried to be.

But Henderson — Rod, I have to call him — was trim, steely-haired, and quite handsome in an unremarkable, unmemorable way. His principal business, he said, was security investigation projects for a few key clients and Peter had asked him to look into the operations of businesses owned by a man called Calvert.

I wouldn't say his tone was unfriendly, but I was feeling the temperature in my room going down. And when, at one point, he said, 'I can see you're feeling nervous, Isobel, but too much ignorance is more dangerous than too much knowledge,' I froze for a second. Nobody had signed me up for danger — but I suppose that's just what Sandra had been exposed to.

He certainly had too much knowledge of me! I always think of myself as quite discreet, but he knew plenty about 'the party scene,' as he called it, and its key players. He tried to set my mind at rest by talking about other people and other cities. But even though he merely hinted at what 'your friends Claudia and Peter' had enjoyed, I'm afraid I found that even more chilling. When I protested about this privacy invasion, I merely got a smirk and a 'you're a big girl, Sadie, you've found this part of your reputation useful, haven't you?'

Before I could argue, I got a 'but of course, you're much better known for your business reputation' — he'd heard only the most fulsome of comments, apparently. OK, that helped a little, but I was still feeling very unsettled. I have to admit, though, that it did make it easier to talk about Sandra's circumstances and what had happened to her.

"I know a little about Calvert's operations," he said, "but I've never investigated him. But I think I know where to look. What do you want to do if I find anything?"

"Look, Mr Henderson…"

"Rod!"

They're usually hitting on you when they do that, but it wasn't worth making an issue about. "OK, Rod, I think I'm working out a solution which just gets us clear of all that shit. It's a chunk of business for me to give up" (I'm terrible for sprinkling my speech with incongruous Americanisms when I'm talking to them. I berate myself for the habit, but choose not to break it!) "but I'm doing well everywhere else — and I'm halfway to an answer for Sandra."

"Are you sensitive in any other areas? Who's helping you? Conrad Kitter?"

That stabbed me a little. "Is that really any of your business?"

"Absolutely not, but it is your business, isn't it? Is there any reason that Calvert might want to attack, or at least make life difficult for Conrad?"

I thought of Ellen, but surely Gerry wouldn't let himself get upset by that. I would guess he'd had a good laugh when she'd come back all distressed, but you never can tell whether he thought he'd been personally slighted. I was nonplussed. I suppose I froze again.

"I know very little about Conrad, except that his operations are almost as obscure as Calvert's, but I can tell from your reaction that you're a little worried. Is there a personal angle? Beyond playtimes, I mean."

Fuck you, Mr Henderson, I thought — but I just let 'he's an old friend' squeak out. I got a silent nod from Rod. He'd obviously read more into it, but protests would only have made things worse.

"I accept that it may quieten down to nothing — although I do occasionally encounter obsessive revenge seekers." He was going to talk now. I felt relieved about that. I was seriously into composure recovery. "I just don't think we should get complacent about it. You're flying back to Hong Kong next week, right?" I nodded mutely. His knowing that didn't help my composure at all but it would have been silly of me to get worried about that, it's something Peter may have said as part

of the briefing. "Well, could you be in Shanghai at the end of next week to meet up with Peter and me?"

"I could, I suppose, but..." I was being unusually lame; that's not like me.

"I'll have done some work on it by then but there's something I'd like you to do for me before you leave London. Well, two things." I'm having an out-of-body experience, looking down on this person masquerading as me having the strangest conversation with a man who knows too much. "The first thing you should do, in a low-key way, is to alert Conrad to what we're doing. He won't know much about me, if he knows anything, but he'll understand what sort of business I'm in. If he wants to flash a red light at us, you must tell me immediately — my contact details, by the way, are on the grey card Sandy should have left on the desk in front of you."

It was there. "Shit!" escaped involuntarily — not cool, Isobel — but I get a smirk from Rod — yes, I'm warming to him now.

"What I'd also like you to do — and here you need to judge how cautious you need to be — is talk to Merle and Michael McKenzie. I have got those names right, haven't I?"

Of course he has. I think he's just prompting me to speak. I'm thinking I should keep quiet; I just nod.

"I'm not saying I have anything, but a number of people can be implicated, and a few can be actually endangered, if things get out of hand. Let's get the

clearest picture we can without arousing too many suspicions. "

"What am I looking for?"

I got a hard stare from him at this point. "What do you think you're looking for?"

And I look down on this surrogate Isobel having this weird conversation and she says, "I think there's dodgy money flowing through the Calvert system and Michael will be a. managing it and b. worrying about it — Merle's already hinted at that to me."

"You see," he relaxes, "you already know more than you realise. If you find out any more, that would be good, but you don't want to raise any undue suspicions."

I drop back down into my body as the gravity of an everyday point pulls at me. "Rod, what's all this going to cost?"

He seems to mull that over a while, presumably about how much to tell me. "Peter's a guarantor of your business. These are his costs, as he sees it. He wants to know more. Look, you're probably right and the solution you've worked out already will probably get everything settled down, but we see enough reasons to worry that we'd rather find out more and make sure we're insulated. I'd be surprised if your Conrad sees it any differently."

My Conrad? My! What the fuck?

***

He doesn't see it differently. I find that out on what, for me, is an evening as bizarre as the video call. I'd texted him and he called back within an hour. I think my account was fairly garbled, but I got Conrad's typically calm voice in response. "What are you doing this evening?"

"Rescheduling next week's travel, it looks like, why?"

"I have a dinner engagement, but I can be home early. I'll tell Boris to feed you and get there as soon as I can."

"You don't have to," I found myself saying — Jesus, what's happening to me?

"Look, I don't want to get things confused. I know you're being cagey with me personally and I respect that, but this sounds important and we should be clear about what we're all doing, so, there's a serious business conversation we really need to have, OK?"

"OK, yes."

"Now, on the entirely separate, but, for me, just as important a point, if you decide you can stay over, I will be thrilled. No pressure, I'm just confirming that I was serious the other evening — it wasn't just a man's typical reaction to a wonderful fuck." And I laughed. It was a nervous laugh — but it was a laugh. "I should be back before ten, see you later."

***

*Boris has made some sort of stew. "This is marvellous!"
I tell him honestly.*

*"I think flavour better with pig feet, but I have to
use fillet," he says and he has a big smile on his face as
Sandra and I laugh. We're into the second bottle — and
Boris isn't drinking. I think I'm being careful, so I'm
quite pleased when he just tops her up and takes the
bottle off the table. She flashes a look at him, but it
softens quickly. Yes, my dear, I think, you're just getting
a tiny inkling of what a treasure you might have.*

*Before he sits down again, he strokes her face
gently. "I like you happy." He smiles. "Just not too
happy." And he has the little girl Sandra taking his hand
and kissing it. Yes, it's a bit sickly, but something seems
to be working here.*

*We're in the garden room. It's only just got dark
outside. I love these late spring evenings. We've been
surprisingly relaxed — I'm making the assumption that
they've had each other between Conrad going out and
me arriving; they looked all freshly showered and loved
up, and I think her drinking was just general bonhomie
— but, of course, it can easily spill over into
recklessness and Boris had probably timed the bottle
removal perfectly.*

*Conrad joined us. I hadn't heard him come in.
"You've been to dinner like that?" Oops, that was a silly
question from me, maybe I had been keeping booze-pace
with Sandra — we had been having fun, mind.*

Conrad stays calm. "No, I've just had a quick change out of the suit. I've put your bag upstairs. I hope that was all right."

I see Boris and Sandra flash a look at each other and I know I colour up, but I try to say 'of course' as casually as I can. Did I really think that my staying over would be a secret from Boris and Sandra?

"I'll have a glass, please, Boris. Some of my Arab friends still live by their alcohol prohibitions." He smiles to himself. "Fortunately, they yield to their other vices — they're being well looked after, but now I need a drink."

He checks the bottle as Boris pours and gives him a little nod. It was a nice wine, but not lavish — I think it's in little things like that where trust is earned. But what do I know? For all the stories I've been hearing this past week, maybe Boris has taken a bullet for Conrad, or dealt with a would-be assassin. Yes, I've obviously drunk more than I thought, and these new fantasies are playing with me.

"Anyway, Isobel and I have things we have to discuss. I'll see you both in the morning." He nods to Boris, but bends and gives Sandra a peck on the cheek. She'd lifted her face as if she was expecting it. Curiouser and curiouser, I think. I stand up to follow him, but he puts his arm around me as I move past him and I get a kiss too. I'm flustered, not really ready for a display of ordinary affection. I walk out towards the

front room with no backward glance. I'll need to avoid Sandra in the morning if I'm to escape an inquisition. Yes, I'll be staying. Just trying the idea out. Becoming a couple? No, definitely not — well, not yet, so, not a completely closed mind either.

***

The most bizarre feeling that grabs me as we sit down — yes, I'm in 'my' chair — is that this is completely normal. Conrad and I are just going to chat as any — yes, fuck it, as any couple would do about some everyday domestic issue.

"What can you tell me about Henderson?"

"Have you heard of him?"

"No, but I'd guessed Peter must use somebody."

"Do you use someone like that?"

"I'm going to say yes, because I don't want to seem like I'm being cagey. There's a man I use who checks out difficult stuff for me and I'm assuming that's what this Henderson does for Peter — but you haven't really told me that yet."

"Are you going to tell me more about your man later?"

He's looking patiently at me. "Look, I don't want us to get distracted, and I'm not being evasive or manipulative." Then he smiles. "Except you always think that bottoms are manipulative." And I have to smile. "I will tell you more later, as much as you want

314

to hear, because it's not fair to proposition you like I have done unless I'm prepared to let you look a little more deeply into what I do. I'm not ashamed of any of it, but you already know that some of it's not for the squeamish."

I can only nod. "Henderson now?" I ask, and he settles back into his chair, ready to listen. He doesn't pose many questions, it's as if he understands everything already.

"You'll be careful when you talk to Merle, won't you?" he says when I get to that part of it. I look quizzically at him. "You probably already know all you're going to find out." Then he chuckles, but looks troubled by whatever the thought was.

"What's up?"

"You might have more luck with Michael. I think he'd be more likely to unburden himself. Did he used to do that after playtimes?" Well, he did, as you know, but there are different thoughts passing between Conrad and me and a silence falls between us. He speaks first. "I may be reading you wrong, but I doubt whether you've ever exploited a playtime."

It's a sweet point to make — and he's right, playtimes are playtimes — for tops and bottoms. Obviously, people tell you things, but that being able to be open is part of what they're seeking usually — exploiting it is just going to make you feel dirty, and make them hate you.

"This is a little different though. We're trying to assess if anything's dangerous — and it's already been that for Sandra." I'm nodding. "But I'm going to have to confess to something here." OK, I'm looking puzzled. "I didn't like the thought of you playing with him."

I understand his point — but that has very complicated implications in other areas. "That's very sweet of you," but we both know there's a more difficult point beneath that, "but I think we've already persuaded ourselves that it would be risky and wouldn't yield much beyond what we already know." We're nodding to each other. "And it's a long time since I enjoyed a playtime with Michael." Now I look hard at him. "But talking about other playtimes is going to be part of the bigger discussion, isn't it?" See, I can be quite brave about tackling difficult issues.

I can't really read his expression as his head moves a little to the side, as if he's trying to gain a different perspective, but then a small smile creeps onto his mouth. "So, you are giving it some serious thought."

I smile now. "Bastard!" I say, and he laughs. "But, coming back to the topic of this discussion, you're not flashing a red light about what we're doing?"

"On the contrary, I'm very supportive. I'm just asking you to be very cautious with the McKenzies." You don't want me playing with Michael, is what I think — but I'm immediately ashamed of the thought. "I realise you talk with Merle most days — but I honestly wouldn't touch the topic unless she raises it." That's a

useful guideline — and I tell him so; he nods. "One thing I'd like to do, with your permission, is talk to Peter Dickinson."

"Why do you need my permission?"

I get a funny look from him, as though that answer should be obvious. It isn't, not to me.

"He will speculate on our relationship. You may not want that."

I'm sceptical, and I don't think it's relevant, it's just becoming obvious to me that his 'couple' idea is becoming a big thing for Conrad. "It really isn't that big a deal. Of course you can talk to him." I've been deliberately ambiguous, not saying whether Peter knowing anything is a big deal, or the potential relationship itself — I'm already feeling a little crowded by the man sat opposite me. Fortunately, he seems to appreciate this.

I will still be staying tonight — I don't do flighty — but I'll be interested in how he plays that later.

Well, dear reader, he was actually lovely. We'd dealt with the difficult business — except that the Henderson intervention is a bit of a non-issue — and we talked in whispers about Boris and Sandra; Conrad seems as touched as I am and he seems happy that Boris has 'found something,' as he put it — but we did agree that we didn't see a long-term perspective.

But that was a funny point, I came back to it later. We were cuddling in bed, naked — I'd had to say 'for God's sake, Conrad,' when he climbed in wearing boxers. 'I'm not expecting sex, but I do want a real fucking cuddle.'

He'd laughed a little nervously and then had to reveal that his cock, at least, was a little hopeful. I smiled to myself. I would have been disappointed without that, but an ugly little thought shot through my mind: what was everyday sex like? Is there such a thing?

I was brought sharply down to earth by a distant sound of an orgasm two floors above us — I hope they were in that open hallway. If not, they were being extraordinarily loud. Conrad chuckled. "I'm not sure if I can live with that long term."

"How long-term do you think it might be?"

"I'm worried Boris is a mating swan, but I don't see her that way."

"You're seeing a looming disaster?"

"I'm concerned about it."

"Yeah, me too. I like your stiff cock on my bum, by the way, but I'd rather deal with him in the morning." His arms wrapped tighter around me.

But it was me who was sitting on him in the middle of the night. Yes, I started it! It was such a luxury: a cock, right there beside me, waiting to be had! And it was me coming loudly, bless him. His cock was the only fully awake part of him — and he didn't come. I quite liked that, I could enjoy him more in my mouth afterwards — even if the cuddles that came then were a mite too 'grateful' — I enjoyed it too, for fuck's sake.

In the morning I was glad we'd been busy in the night. I wouldn't have wanted the 'shall we fuck?' pressure if we hadn't — and I found it quite pleasant to just idly chat for a while. OK, true confession, it was also very pleasant half an hour later when he slid down and began eating me. But I'm not so naive as to think what we're doing is real 'normal,' OK? It was just, all together, nicer and easier than I'd expected.

"I'll call you this evening if I can get hold of Peter, OK?" He was standing up, obviously on his way to the shower.

"I won't be here?" I felt instantly stupid; if that was a tease, it was childish — and I shouldn't be getting serious yet. And I didn't actually have a plan.
But he was cool. "Yeah, I'd be happier with that," he said, and disappeared into the bathroom.

***

In the event, I was saved by Merle. She asked if she could see me that evening. I was glad of the excuse — but did I really have to text Conrad to explain? Not cool, Isobel!

Not cool also described Merle. We hugged lightly when she came in, but there had been something fraught in her expression. When I turned around after closing the door, I suddenly got a much bigger hug. I went with it. She was very emotional. That's never a good place to start a discussion. As her hug slowly relented, I said quietly, "I have no plans for the evening. I'll cook for us if you've got time."

She eased back a little, but kept her arms around me. "I've plenty of time, just absolutely no appetite."

I had a lot of thoughts going through my head — but none that I could share with Merle. I'd assumed this emotional manifestation had something to do with our crisis, and I was on my guard now. "I think I can force a g and t on you."

"Can't we go straight to wine?"

"You drink that too quickly. You look like we have things to discuss. We should keep clear heads." She reacts as I expect. She shrivels slightly. I'm the boss, I'm the top, I control. I need to keep all that in mind as I manage this conversation. It's the way I'll get most out of it — and a number of people who mean a lot to me are being drawn into this. And even Merle means a lot to me. Yes, she frustrates me, she annoys me — but I do love the poor, sad girl. Even I'm sorry she didn't make it with Will — but why that didn't work, why she fled in a crisis, is all part of her make-up. We need to bear that in mind.

I'm hungry, even if she's not. I'm going to make pasta, quick and simple — and she can have some if she changes her mind — and it's easier to keep conversation on the day to day if I'm pottering around in the kitchen. I've made the g and t's, but I could kill for a big glass of red. No, Isobel, clear heads are needed. But we chat office stuff for a little while — she's complaining about *wanting more admin support. Interesting, we'll park that one — but, in truth, I have serious doubts about whether Sandra could do anything useful. Anyway, "You're losing business though, remember?" is what comes out.*

I shouldn't have said that. It's not a worry for me. I'm glad to be out of the Calvert contracts and I'm seeing opportunities elsewhere. But she's crushed by the comment. She huddles into a ball in the corner of the sofa and she's weeping. I resist the urge to run over there. I shouldn't have said it, but still… I need a big girl here.

"That's a bigger thing than you know," she sobs.

I think the story is about to come to me.

Michael had come round to dinner — she'd cooked, I didn't know she could — yes, yes, Sadie the bitch, I know — but he couldn't have a conversation in a restaurant, he'd said. He was even more worried than he is usually. He's a haunted man, our Michael, remember.

By now I'm on the sofa beside her with my arm around her and she's huddling into me. "I knew something was wrong. We talked about nothing all evening, silly memories, people we knew but it was obvious he wanted to talk about something else."

"Neither of you is much good about being open." I think I said it kindly. I meant to.

She mumbled, "I know," and didn't seem too upset. "We've always needed you to prompt us."

"I haven't been there for a long time, my darling. I'm slightly bewildered that you're still together, in whatever strange way you manage that — keeping the same old secrets, I expect."

"Well, I thought that's where we were going to end up last night, chatting, eating, and then parting — but then he opened another bottle and I realised I just had to wait. I was expecting some dodgy proposition with some new circle of his but instead..."

"Shall I open the wine now?"

"Aren't you worried?"

"It sounds like it might help you unburden yourself. Did it work with Michael?"

"Yes, that's why I'm here, and I'd better get it out first before I lose courage." Now's the time for me to sit still and shut up. I can, you know. "He's very worried. There's a man called Zivko. He comes very rarely. Michael has to process payments for him in Serbia to a company called BPI. Michael's used to organising things like that, but the thing is, now Michael's started to look into it, these payments, always set up verbally by Gerry, only happen when something bad has happened."

"Something bad?" I'm not sure I needed to ask the question. No, I did. My mind was going all over the place.

"Michael didn't want to say. He says the more I know, the more dangerous it is for me. But Michael's worried that, with all this stuff blowing up, some people *we know, well, he's thinking about you mainly, but you might be in some sort of danger."*

Now I feel strangely calm — but very glad I have Peter and Henderson and, yes, Conrad around me. It sounds very fanciful. I could imagine Gerry having bad things done in foreign places, but on his doorstep?

"Is Michael doing anything about it?"

"I asked him that. He's tried checking the company out but there's not much on them. Belgrade Private Investigations and an address is all he's got, and he's worried about alerting Gerry. He tried to reassure me that he and I are safe but Gerry's the sort of man who always believes he can get away with anything."

"Well, so far, he has." I don't suppose that reassured her, but I think I have enough now. If I ask any more questions, I'll just make the pair of them more jittery and increase the risk of them alerting Gerry.

"I'm sure there are far worse things happening at the fringes of Gerry's misbegotten empire that need the services of Mr Zivko. He's managed to repossess a flat and have Ellen humiliated, what's he got to be upset with us about?"

"He hates you. He's said that to Michael. At least Michael had the sense not to ask questions — he really isn't as stupid as you think he is."

"I don't think he's stupid." That's not quite a fib. I'm looking into her tear-brimmed eyes. And I'm pleased to divert that strand of the conversation. I'm suddenly scared.

"Well, you think I am."

"That I absolutely deny." It's just not the word I would use. Anyway, I am feeling unsettled, putting it mildly — I need to get her out of here quietly and quickly, but she's emptied her glass and she's holding it out to me. *"I'm so glad I've told you, I felt sure I was just being silly, but now I can see you being so calm about it, I can begin to relax."* Thanks, poppet, I think. I'm giving a major acting performance here — calm is absolutely what I am not.

I'm not so generous with the wine. I don't want to seem to be rushing her, but I want to get to Refuge Conrad now. It takes another half an hour. It's nearly nine by the time I get to his place.

I'm extremely agitated by now — trying to seem calm for Merle has made it much worse for me. I am thrilled to see Boris when the door is opened. He smiles and holds out a hand. *"No bag?"* Oh, God, I'm struck that they've all jumped to that assumption.

"No, no, that was just one night," I say, just as Conrad appears in the hall. Now I feel terrible as well but he's smiling at me.

"I'd hoped you might make it. Have you eaten?" Just as calm and normal as you could wish for.

"No, no, I'd planned to, but we never got round to it."

"Wonderful, I'd hoped you hadn't, we've waited for you. I'm starving."

"I really, really have to talk to you."

The smile broadens, if anything. "Well, I'm thrilled about that but you're not going to persuade me that anything dire can happen before we finish dinner. It's pasta." Really? I think, but their logic is the same as mine, speedy prep. "Boris makes a wonderful sauce and it won't have spoiled for waiting an hour — but the smell has made me feel famished. Come on." He lays his arm gently along my shoulder, kisses my cheek gently and guides me back to where I ate yesterday.

The other three settle into this cosy domesticity far more easily than I do. Boris is acting as chef, Sandra is serving — even the wine, of which she pours little into her own glass. The talk is of food. Mostly it's Boris, and his descriptions of Romanian stews are probably funnier because of his near incomprehensibility — his feeble vocabulary has to be augmented by his physical indication of body parts, although I can't believe that testicles feature in so many recipes. It's Conrad, whose grandmother was Jewish, apparently, who expands our knowledge here. I didn't know about the family, but it's given him some odd dishes to describe, which he does with charm and humour. I'm relaxing, and it's not just the wine. The second bottle is still half full although the time has moved on. I'm quite surprised when Conrad is asking Boris if he can bring us some coffee. Desperate as I had been to disgorge my paranoia on to Conrad earlier, I'm now reluctant to leave the happy bonhomie of the table.

The atmosphere is different when Conrad and I sit in the front room. He listens calmly as I describe Merle's visit, but I can feel myself growing anxious again.

"I'm not doubting that Mr Zivko manages nefarious deeds, but I'd be very surprised if you, or anyone near us were a target. Still," he purses his lips and his head leans to one side, "in addition to execrable recipes — I may have omitted to mention that my grandmother's cooking tasted uniformly foul — she bestowed on me the gift of caution. You should hand on the name of man and company to your Henderson. We'll see what he can dig up."

"So, you do think there's a reason to be cautious."

"There's never a reason not to be."

"Will you check it out?"

He smiles. "Of course, to give you peace of mind, as much as anything. But I'll let you stay a tiny bit worried to encourage you to stay the night." I look at my watch. It's half eleven. I'm easily persuaded. "You won't be much pestered tonight. I have an early flight in the morning."

That's sweet, but it doesn't stop us. I tell myself it's only the security of sleeping in his arms that's deceiving me. But, when I wake to an empty half bed, I'm disappointed for a few reasons.

I wander down to the kitchen to make tea, in my knickers, but a shirt of Conrad's, and I find Boris inevitably busy.

"Are you back already?" I've assumed he's driven Conrad to the airport.

"No, Mr Conrad think you happier if I stay."

That's true, but it tells me he's more worried than he's let on. Yes, I feel safe with Boris — but I have my life to lead. "When's he back?"

"Tonight. Only Milan today."

I'm comforted by that. Now it's time to contact Henderson — and I have no idea what time zone he's in.

25

It was unusual for Peter to give her the grace of a work-free day on their travels, although dinner, with Wengwei and Mei, would be business. Claudia was feeling nervous about Wengwei's health — would he be able to last an evening, she wondered.

"The message I had was that he'd be fine for a couple of hours, but he wanted you to enjoy the city in the afternoon." They were unpacking in their suite. "For me that's either irony or something got lost in translation."

"Well, I'm already thrilled; you're just too travel-jaded. You know I've been dying to come here." Looking at photos, part of her habitual preparation ritual for new destinations, had not prepared her for Shanghai. She'd been glad of the sluggish journey from the airport to give her the best chance to appreciate the towering skyline unfolding as they approached the city centre. "But can we sit and have a coffee and look at the view before you get embroiled with Henderson? Oh, and thank you for not asking him here. I know we have the suite for meetings like that, but I'd rather avoid him. Will Mei meet him?"

"Of course. I mean, I don't expect him to work out here for Mei, but she should know more about how

328

these things operate in the West. We'll find out later if her father has something similar."

"He must do, mustn't he? I mean, from all you've picked up so far."

Peter seemed to be weighing up how much to say. "My impression is, he's been more, how can I put this, interventionist in the past, so he has at least a Henderson. But we all have skeletons."

It was the first time he'd openly said that to her about his own operations. She'd begun to assume that difficult issues had arisen sometimes but felt, encouraged by him, that ignorance gave her a level of deniability. There was no point in enquiring now.

"Are you going to bring Mei up here when you've had your joint session with Henderson, or will you call me down?" Peter looked ostentatiously out over the river, then through into the airy lounge with its equally compelling views, turned back to her and lifted his arms in a questioning shrug. She smiled. "I was going to suggest you do that anyway. I'm due back from my tour by three."

"I expect to be later than that. I have him on his own first, then she joins us at two." A bell rang. "Ah, there's the coffee."

***

She was back on time and the suite was empty. She felt exhilarated by the place, but slightly grimy from the bustle. There would have to be time for a shower and a change. It worked perfectly. She was ready and the tea had just arrived when Peter returned with Mei.

She greeted Mei warmly — and was pleasantly surprised by the response. Mei had always seemed austere and closed, but today there was a big smile and a hug. "Please, come and sit down. I've been walking around your wonderful city. It is your city, right? You just live in Hong Kong now."

Mei laughed lightly. "Ha, Alphonse says you always know everything. Yes, it is my city. I grew up here. My parents live here." Claudia could see Peter out of the corner of her eye, organising the waiter pouring tea. He'd not reacted, either to the mention of Alphonse, or of Mei's parents. Peter was adept at walking through minefields.

"Will you live here now?"

"I think I must. I will miss Hong Kong, but I expect I'll be there often enough." Claudia had heard that from Alphonse, who'd talked openly in their last phone call about the commitment Mei had asked from him — Claudia had surprised herself by responding calmly. But he was becoming more circumspect with her when he talked about Daiyu. She hadn't pushed him. She felt reluctant to discuss how much better things were now with Peter.

"And how did you get on with our Rod, may I ask?"

There were smirks between the ladies and Mei cast a glance to Peter, as if asking 'Will he mind?'

"Don't worry about him. He knows my views on Rod. I think I'm allowed to call him a necessary evil — but I do have one scurrilous question before we get down to business, did he ask you to dinner?"

Mei giggled, and then put on a haughty look. "Of course he did!" But then she laughed again.

"And?"

Mei turned to Peter again, as if to bring him into the conversation. "I'm seeing him tomorrow evening. If he wants to impress me some more about how his world works, then I'm very happy to listen." The ladies laughed again. Even Peter smiled. "But I have to say, I already learned a lot." Now she addressed Peter directly. "I can't thank you enough. I'm afraid it's an area that's very important. I'm already learning that from my father."

Peter was placing the cups in front of them. "It can't be helped, I'm afraid."

"Oh, even I've seen enough to appreciate that," said Claudia. "My one reservation is that Rod sometimes creates the problems he solves. I think he's like the fireman who starts the flames just to be the hero who puts them out."

"That's happened once," said Peter, with an edge of irritation.

"It's happened twice," said Claudia, with her own special memories, but with no wish to prompt a disagreement, "but there have been many areas where he's been invaluable."

"Oh, I've had to meet some of my father's old friends. They are fascinating old rogues. Completely outrageous still. One thought he could put his hand on my knee, even with my father in the room." She paused. "Of course, he doesn't know I'm Shen Wengwei's daughter, but he had been told I will be the chief executive."

"What did you do?"

"I slapped his hand, of course," she smiled, "very hard. My father looked quite proud of me. The other old boy laughed very loud."

"But you won't have to deal with them, will you?"

"My father says it will be a bad day if I need them. They are there like fire extinguishers. You want them to just stay on the wall forever."

"As long as one of them doesn't start a fire," said Claudia.

Peter drew breath sharply but seemed to think better of saying anything.

"The bigger problems will be the political connections." She hesitated. She seemed to have shocked herself. "I mean, it's just more important." But she scribbled on a pad 'bugged?'

"I've been cooped up all day; Claudia's had the walking tour. Would you mind if we sat on the balcony perhaps?"

Mei looked relieved as they moved outside and sat around the table. Peter leaned forward and spoke quietly, "I think we're safe. That's one of the areas that

Henderson checks for me and the Waldorf couldn't be caught permitting that — or even not detecting it, but you're very wise to be cautious, well done!" Mei sat up straighter, smiling, and looked pleased to have won a compliment. Peter brought them back to the topic. "It's an area we have little direct contact with in the West. Political parties just want our donations, they don't expect to interfere with our operations — but I had heard of the growing cadre of highly-qualified technocrats that fill the senior advisory posts in your government departments."

"Oh, tell me about it! Baba says I'm to leave everything to our liaison department, but I haven't been able to avoid meeting some of them. I have never met such arrogant people." Having finally said what she'd clearly wanted to say, she relaxed and laughed at herself. "Oh, thank you so much for being here. I couldn't possibly say that to anyone else. Even Alphonse would give me a lecture on tact and patience. He's been amazing. I've learned so much from him."

"Well, he speaks very highly of you," said Peter.

Mei smiled again. "Yes, it's his fault I'm here now."

They all laughed. Claudia worried for an instant that Peter might take the point too seriously. She needn't have.

"I think it's in your father's mind that you and I develop a similar relationship," said Peter hesitantly.

Mei reached out and touched his hand. "I would value that so much — but I'm very aware of how impractical that would be — but weekly telephone calls would be very helpful if you could manage that." She turned to Claudia. "And I do mean both of you. You seem to manage people better than I ever could. You're seeing Lou, tomorrow, aren't you?"

Peter chuckled. "I'm delighted to see your spy network's already in place."

"I wish. He rang me to tell me. He sounded quite smug, as if he was escaping from me and developing a special relationship. What have you got planned?" An edge had crept into her voice.

"Nothing yet," said Peter. "It's one of the reasons we're sitting here now. It seems to me he can be a permanent pain in the arse for you unless we can engage him constructively. Just letting him sit on the thirtieth floor, pretending to run a property division when you — I'm sorry, I don't know how to refer to your…"

"Fuqin — father. Wengwei is Baba, that's papa, or dad — but that's just between us, of course. And yes, I was thinking of sticking him there. What's your idea?"

"I'd like to see what he's like with money. If he can work with Tony and Henry on funds, he would be able to draw in a lot more business in this region, where we're weak, of course."

Mei's eyes narrowed. "But aren't you worried about a Dickinson dilution? That was why we had such problems funding the resort programme, I think."

Peter guffawed. Now he touched her hand. "I think I would have been disappointed if you hadn't, quite rightly, stabbed me with that."

Mei wasn't smiling. "But what would we do?"

Peter was instantly serious, but still relaxed and calm. "We'll have to review all those thresholds when we pin down the nature of the Senlin-Dickinson relationship, and for all that we use the brains of brilliant people." He smiled, "That's going, ultimately, to be you and I who do that. Sound OK?"

Now Mei relaxed. "Very OK with that."

"So, if he shows any talent…" Here he hesitated. "Look, I think we can agree that he's a shit, can't we?" Mei's laugh answered the question. "But I'm pretty sure he's bright and he maybe needs a mission. If he can prove to us in a year that he can make a contribution, I'm prepared to rename the fund business GKS and you and I will act as joint-chairmen." He paused again. "Or would you prefer I said chairpeople?"

"In the words of my favourite philosopher, I really couldn't give a fuck." They were laughing together again.

"Your favourite philosopher?"

"That would be Laotsi. I was just a bit free with the translation. But I like the idea about Lou. Would you train him in London and New York?"

"Your smile has a tease in it, madam, but yes, that would be the idea. We'd like to set up a Shanghai office anyway and locate your investment administrators in there. It will be a home and a head office for him to come back to."

"If he proves himself…"

"Of course, and you and I will decide that, with Tony and Henry."

"Four people make a decision?"

Peter looked at her for a while. She held her nerve. "Ultimately you and I have to agree — and we each have a veto — but he has to win their approval first." He waited.

She took a long time before she smiled again. "Of course."

They seemed to relax after that, but Mei's early deference had faded and, while she always addressed Peter respectfully, she seemed to become more and more of an equal. Claudia was impressed by how he almost seemed to encourage this in a way he never really seemed to with Alphonse, Henry or Tony. He did with Will and, in some areas, with her, but he was certainly allowing Mei to grow in a way that he did with almost no others.

At five, more or less on the dot, Mei looked up and said, "Quick change and then I pick up Baba. I must warn you, he looks different, even in these four weeks. We have a private room downstairs."

"Would you prefer we ate here?" Peter gestured to the suite's dining area. "It's like our home for four days — we might be more comfortable."

Mei thought for a second. "That's a lovely idea, thank you. I'll bring him at six."

"And we'll organise service. We'll see you in an hour."

There were still hugs before she left, even with the return planned early.

"Do you want to get changed? I can organise service."

"Wow!" said Claudia. "Thank you. But before I go shower, were you as impressed as I was?"

"Every bit, I think. This could work. Oh, before we do separate things for an hour, Rod had some stuff on Isobel's project — and he said she'd also turned up something interesting. They're meeting for dinner tonight. He'd asked her to detour here on her way back to Hong Kong."

"Well, that's one person who would easily handle him." But Claudia was concerned. "Is that issue threatening to get serious?"

Peter screwed his face a little. "I don't like how it sounds, but we'd best leave it to them."

"You mean it won't be our skeleton?"

"I hope not, but you might like to give her a call and invite her for a nightcap. Wengwei won't be staying late. Will you have the energy?"

"I'm the one who sleeps well on planes. I'm surprised you didn't notice. No, I'll call her. I don't think she'll need help getting rid of Rod, but we'd be a handy excuse."

He smiled. "You go shower, before we argue! I'll get dinner organised."

26

I was glad to get away. I needed a calm perspective on these things. I'd spent the weekend nights with Conrad. I wouldn't say I'd meant to, but I would have had to have deliberately avoided it — and I have a surprisingly open mind about his proposal. Surprising to me, anyway. And part of me kept saying I'd be leaving for four weeks — time and space to think about it then. And I sat on the fence with Sandra — it was only yesterday morning, before I left for the airport, that I took her in to the office and we talked through how she could help. Sandra, bless her, tried to be constructive — but Merle was a bitch. I didn't like leaving them to it, but...

Merle may be as stressed as I feel. Yes, Conrad tried to play it all down, but I have a suspicion he's following it up in his own way, trying not to worry me. Which worries me!

But I'm here now, Shanghai for the first time. Wow, it is spectacular, and I have a grand view of everything from my room, but I'll admit I'm preoccupied. This worry won't go away. I hope Rod has something for me this evening. Something to put my mind at rest.

But I feel safe enough here. Peter and Claudia are here. Mei's here. It feels more of a haven than Hong Kong will. I'll be seeing Alphonse on Friday, but I had the distinct impression he was changing other arrangements to accommodate me. Well, you know what I suspect. Then I get cross with myself as I'm in the shower. I was being very well cared for in London. I admit it's a problem for us control freaks — we do like to dictate everything.

And Conrad didn't let me do that. He even got quite toppy once or twice. I found it slightly amusing — but not unpleasant — and he carried it off with some conviction. He even insisted on having me on Monday morning before he left for his flight. It's not my favourite time of day but there was a certain novelty to it.

We'd eaten out the last three nights. I don't think he'd found a way of explaining to Boris that we didn't want to eat with them again. Twice was enough. I was just amused that he didn't just want to say — and the loving couple are off to bed early anyway.

But at least he'd come down from the celestial culinary heights of the Dorchester. I even got him to try shepherd's pie at a pub on the river.

He can do that too.

But now I'm nearly ready for Mr Henderson. That's Claudia! I'd easily switch to Rod, but she's planted this idea in my head.

I'll admit I'm intrigued — and, yes, I've made an effort this evening and the man, bless him, seems impressed when I arrive. I've been received by a flunkey. 'Mrs Allen?' — I won't think about how they guess, he must have been well-briefed, and well-tipped, no doubt — and I'm taken to meet this man at a table near the bar.

He stands, we shake hands and he tells me I look wonderful — that's inappropriate, this is serious business, but it's a nice start. I can handle it.

And he's presentable. I don't want to say more than that. His features are bland, but I suppose you could call them handsome. We go through the usual chit-chat about inbound journeys and body clocks but I'm in the middle of my day and not feeling too bad. He's come in from DC but seems bright and alert.

He's probably over sixty but doesn't look it. He's still very trim.

"I've booked us in Pelham's," he says. "It's discreet enough to let us chat but I do have a suite if the topic gets too sensitive for an open restaurant." I've had the story of him hitting on Claudia in a hotel suite, but that threat doesn't concern me. I am more worried still about the mysterious Serbian.

There's no need to rush into that, but I do need to register my escape clause — without looking like a girl — "That could be very useful, Rod, but I have said I'll call in on Peter and Claudia later."

"Of course," he says, cool enough to handle that. "We can cover our key points quickly, but I was looking forward to meeting you and I'd like to make the most of our evening."

I'm not going to jump in on key points. I let him speak. This man can tell me more about his world —

there must be similarities with some of Conrad's dark areas — I've been making him tell me about them over the weekend; there's a hinterland of swamps and dark forests that surround civilisation's smooth lawns and fine buildings. Of course I knew that, or I'd guessed at it, but it's become much more tangible now. But here's my martini.

He was good, I have to say. It felt a little like an interrogation for a while once he'd turned on me, but he'd reserved his curiosity about my social pastimes until after the main course, and he'd been frank with me when I'd asked about the role of parties in his work. I think, disappointingly, they're more for exploitation than enjoyment for him. That may be more American. I've never been really aware of it in London. Anyway, I'd quickly written him off as a potential play partner — not that the thought had ever really formed. I was more concerned by how often I found myself comparing him to Conrad. Anyway, when I got the 'Shall we have coffee in my suite to discuss Mr Zivko?' I wasn't feeling remotely threatened. I think he'd decided I wouldn't be his type anyway. I would guess he'd prefer demure. Right, that's not me.

But the Zivko story had me feeling colder. We'd settled with coffee and whisky — and another splendid view across the river into the city's exotic modernism. I love the challenges of modern buildings but, in my experience, the more dramatic they are, the more their architects feel that designers are an irrelevance — and that's so wrong! But I digress, these are thoughts running through my head as I stand in the window, awe-struck by the skyline.

He hands me the whisky. "Thinking of a business opportunity?"

"No, I'm already being drawn too much into management. That's not where the buzz is for me, though. I still want to think designs, so the business is as big as I want it to be. Where's the buzz for you?"

I appear to have caught him off guard. He doesn't have a quick answer. I can wait. I actually would like to know. I don't need his arm on my shoulder but I'm not going to be little-girlish about that. It can stay as long as it doesn't move. "I like organisations to work properly. It's where I started, and the other stuff grew out of that — making sure organisations have the right people in the right places and helping out when people get themselves into difficult situations. I also like fixing bad guys. I don't know where that comes from. I guess I've always fought bullies all my life."

I had the impression from Claudia that Rod might well be one himself, but I'm not — yet — so jaundiced. Nevertheless, I'm not really welcoming the arm on the shoulder. It's time to sit down. I move. I can have the skyline later. I won't sleep easily, I know, body clock — and yes, fuck it, anxiety!

"So, our Mr Zivko is a bully?"

"I think the real bully, as you already know..."

"Is Gerry Calvert."

He nods. He's sat opposite me now. He hadn't attempted to pursue me.

"Yes. He uses BPI to resolve some of the little conflicts in his business network. It's still the wild west in the Balkans but Zivko gets used well beyond those boundaries."

"Can I just be clear about this, does resolving little conflicts get physical?"

"Of course."

"I'm sorry to be so naïve, but…"

"Yes, there are hitmen involved but that happens in cowboy country. Calvert's Russian friends are far more dangerous than he is. But your friend Michael keeps them happy with the ways he moves their money around. Zivko is relatively small-time. But still dangerous enough."

"So, you offer me a little reassurance and then take it away."

"You'll be all right. Peter and I have come up with a plan."

"Peter's involved? When…" I'm flabbergasted.

"I spoke to him this afternoon. It's why I wanted to meet here."

"What…" Still flabbergasted.

"I want to be careful. We may be making two and two make twenty-two. Zivko could have been there for any sort of problem. If we jump to the wrong conclusion, we could be putting McKenzie in danger. These things can easily get too messy. You're in Hong Kong for four

weeks. Nothing's going to happen there. We'll work something out in the meantime."

"I suppose I'm supposed to feel reassured."

It's a kind of relaxed shrug I get from him. "We can already block off any danger. I'd just rather make a surgical incision. We want as little collateral damage as possible — and to make as few waves as possible. These things are best organised covertly — what we do shouldn't spill out." Now I get the stern headmaster look. "What that means, of course, is that you can mention this to absolutely no one except Peter — he may even not want to discuss it in front of Claudia." I nod. I understand, I think. "It means you don't talk to Mei, and you don't talk to Alphonse, OK?"

"OK," I nod — and it goes through my mind that he hasn't mentioned Conrad. Hmm, even at a moment like this, he's still in a corner of my mind. But then a mini-outrage takes over: Henderson knows about my arrangements with Mei and Alphonse. Get over it, Isobel — they weren't secrets, and someone's trying to protect you.

"Now, I need to do a little more work. You and I will be together again before you get on a plane to London." He's staring hard at me. "We are quite clear about that, aren't we?"

Have I been hesitating? "Oh, Christ, yes, of course. And thank you."

Now he leans back and smiles. "No, thank you. It's an interesting assignment" — I might be in somebody's gunsight and, for him, it's an interesting assignment — "and I'd heard so much about you. I was excited to meet you."

He gets a cold raised eyebrow.

But he pursues it. "Another place, another time maybe, after the project."

"I'd like that very much," I fib — come on, don't get all censorious with me, you'd have said the same! "I guess I should go see Peter."

He stands up, a gentleman to the end — except that, at the door, the kiss is too near the lips and then hand slides down from the waist a little. Oh, well, let them hope!

27

Claudia was glad she'd been warned. Wengwei did look frail. But he had a kind of glow as he came in on his daughter's arm. She looked more worried than he did.

His hand was a little shaky as he took Claudia's, but the smile was warm and long.

The handshake with Peter was accompanied by the shoulder clasp — the nearest either of them would come, she thought, to a man hug. "I've ordered the food for six thirty. I thought we should get as much business done as we could before we're distracted."

Wengwei sat on the sofa. Even that effort seemed to fatigue him, "You are kind, my friend. Before I get tired, you mean."

Peter managed to return the smile without looking awkward. Claudia felt less composed, but then spent a bewildered twenty minutes as the three of them agreed on an outline corporate structure with cross-shareholdings and co-chairmen. Wengwei was firm. "No, that is Meitang, not me. Maybe she not ready, but she get better. I already not able. And I only get worse," and, just as Claudia began to feel dreadful about that observation, Wengwei's face lit in a big smile, and he added, "or maybe not."

Peter laughed but Mei seemed to share Claudia's awkwardness.

"Look," he continued, "if get better, she still is head of Senlin and co-chair of Dickinson Senlin." There was another impish smile. "I say co-chair, Mr Giant, not co-chairman. You are dinosaur!" It was awkward laughter, but it was genuine laughter. "I be senior director, with Claudia."

Claudia was shaken. Had Peter proposed that separately? Wengwei was agreeing to proposals that Peter and Mei had finalised that afternoon in one of the most succinct papers she had ever read on a complex corporate organisation — they had taken all her points but produced a model of concision. At the time she had assumed it had been designed to be read quickly by the ailing man, but when she'd read it twice it struck her as a template for all such papers. And Wengwei had clearly quickly absorbed and agreed with it all during the hour his daughter had just spent with him — and she'd clearly also showered and changed in that time. Claudia was becoming ever more impressed.

"Good idea too with Lou. He is bright boy, but he is also, how do you say..." There was that big smile again. "A shit!" And now he laughed loudly, with Peter and Mei looking mildly embarrassed. "I know, I know." His laughter brought on a fit of coughing which disabled him temporarily, but he waved to show he was fine and expected to continue. "She tell me your view" — then he left a pause — "and then she tell me she agree." A little laugh again. "And I think you both right." Now he calmed down. "But your plan the only way for him. I tell him, last chance."

"Are you sure you should put it so finally?" Peter asked cautiously.

There was a flash of intemperance. "He my son, Mr Giant. He work, or he go property office and do nothing."

Claudia eyed Peter. He seemed to be expecting more.

Mei began to intervene. "Baba, I…"

She was silenced by him raising a hand, then he paused, he seemed to be thinking. "You both right, of course. I talk to him, but I tell him it's opportunity. I want he make it work."

Relief flooded into the room.

"So, you meet your special agent today, yes? Meitang tell me. Is good, is good. She meet my old special agents too." He began chuckling to himself. "Bao Li never have his hand slapped before. We all think it very funny. But we no use them any more. Just there in case of emergencies." Then he went still and quiet. "And she have to ask you, Mr Giant. Things in past I no want repeat, understand?" It wasn't clear who he was asking as he looked to both Peter and Mei.

"I understand," said Peter, and that seemed to satisfy everyone — except for Claudia herself.

Wengwei sighed and sat back. "There, maybe we eat now, I happy," he paused theatrically, "except for fucking cancer!" he exploded, and even Claudia couldn't help laughing with him.

He ate little, and Mei fussed over him — his attempts to deflect that betrayed by the smile he kept flashing her — and he was quick to agree with her when she suggested they leave as soon as the main course was finished. "OK to come back later?" asked Mei quietly as they stood saying goodbyes at the door.

"That would be lovely," said Claudia. "Isobel will be here later."

Mei's face brightened, then she looked puzzled. "Really?"

"Special agent stuff," said Claudia, but got a sharp glance from Peter.

"Oh, I won't come if it's inconvenient."

"Oh, no, please do. There's still plenty of stuff to cover — and what man could resist the chance to chat with his three favourite ladies? Your father would understand that."

Wengwei cackled a little, but the smile was wan.

***

"Should I not have said that?" Claudia asked when they'd gone. "You looked disapproving."

He put his arm around her. "It was unavoidable, my darling, we'd have to have said anyway. I'm afraid I'm just a bit priggish about it — uncomfortable with the joke. We'll play it down with Isobel, but there's a nasty little mess in there somewhere, according to Rod."

Claudia felt alarmed. "Is she actually in danger?"

"I personally doubt it — but we're not taking any chances and we have the makings of a plan. Do you want to know more?"

She snuggled into him. "Do you mind if I don't?"
"I'd rather you stayed judiciously incurious." He kissed her tenderly.

***

Mei was back before Isobel arrived. "He did enjoy that so much, thank you, he just gets tired very easily."

"Oh, I completely understand," said Peter. "I think he's doing amazingly well, and you seem to have sold all the points in the paper."

"I think it was pretty much what he wanted anyway. You two think amazingly alike."

Mei's eyes were a little red-rimmed, Claudia noticed, and it had taken her more than an hour to shepherd her father to his waiting car. She must have been to her room to compose herself again. Claudia was touched by that little vulnerability — if that's what it was, she thought. It was wrong to superimpose your own emotions on to other people's actions. But Mei did seem to care deeply — Wengwei seemed to be the father she'd been missing all her life. Peter had guided Mei to the sofas while Claudia's thoughts briefly detained her.

"So, why is Isobel here? You can't not tell me." She paused. "Or is this one of those 'better not to know' things?"

Peter smiled. "Well, it's certainly that, but I'm afraid I already know that will make you more curious."

Mei smiled back — and it struck Claudia, who saw Mei as normally so austere, that she had been spending the evening with the only two men who made her smile. "Of course you must tell me — but I will declare an interest. Isobel means a lot to me. I don't like to think of her as being in trouble."

"She'll be fine," said Peter, "but Claudia's already taken the position that she knows too much about the problem already." Mei looked disappointed and suggested, with a tilt of her head, that she wanted to know more. "But she knows more than you do anyway. So, I can give you some background and you can decide if you insist on knowing more."

"Thank you," said Mei, and settled back.

"Would you two like drinks?" asked Claudia.

"A small whisky, please," said Mei. Claudia got a small nod from Peter. He would have the same.

"A friend of Isobel's got into trouble in London, caused by a very unpleasant man. Isobel sorted the problem, but the man is still unhappy. We're worried there might be consequences for her. I don't personally think there will be, we're just being cautious."

"That's what Rod is working on?"

"It's one of the things. As you saw this afternoon, he does a lot more than that for me."

Now he got one of Mei's teasing smiles. "Including spying on Senlin?"

Peter chuckled. "Of course, just as your father had his spies on me — including government departments contacting the CIA and MI6. I know your father admires me and respects me but, let's be honest, he trusts me as much as I trust him."

Mei's face clouded. "As much as you trust me?"

Peter gave her a slow half-smile. "Shall we just say, we'll aim to trust each other in eighteen months as you trust Alphonse now."

She thought a moment. "I like that. Thank you. I'm learning."

"I'm also going to guess that Alphonse is the first person you've learned ever to trust in business. Am I right?"

Now her smile was the slow one. "Of course you're right, Mr Giant, you always are."

Peter laughed. "Now stop that. I think you're showing why women will rule the world within one generation. You just have more skills and more subtlety than we do." He held up a finger. "I admonish myself. I remain an enemy of generalisations. I apologise. I shall content myself with observing that you, Meitang, have completely outwitted me, Peter Dickinson, in this specific instance." He smiled and shrugged. "And I don't expect it to be the last time." The bell rang. Peter carried on seamlessly. "And talking of devils, that's probably Isobel."

28

It's turning out to be a very cosy evening, surrounded by my favourite people. One of them is still with me. Mei asked me back to her suite. I wavered. My life is more complicated than even I like it. So, she just came back to my room, ignoring my feeble protests. You see, a real top wouldn't have done that.

But I'm glad she's here. She's probably more subtle than I give her credit for.

"When you see Henderson tomorrow, all this is supposed to be secret. I haven't told you anything."

She looks mildly incredulous, and unimpressed. "But Peter told me. You hadn't said anything. I didn't even know why you'd had to fly back to London and miss Phuroc — just that you had a crisis." Then I get that wicked smile. "Still, you've had plenty time to regret that, haven't you? And it's Daiyu too, who'd have thought?"

She's being cheeky, and I'm feeling indignant. "Well, I would have thought, for a start. I encouraged her to spend time with him." And that's true, as you know.

"It's got a bit out of hand, though, hasn't it?"

I'm not really on edge. This is just making London seem more attractive — except for Serbian gangsters.

355

"I really am very relaxed about it. I'm even happy that you've reserved him once a month." I need to be careful here, this could stray into bitchiness, and she and I have far too much on our plates to lapse into that. But I have put her on edge now. "Look, my lover, we both have far too much going on at the moment. I am very happy we have found a night for each other."

"You didn't want to come to my room."

"You were topping me — and not in a good way."

Now she looks a little crushed. "I still need to learn, don't I?"

And I wrap my arms around my little bird. "I am here for you, you know, and I'm actually very glad you're here, so probably you were right. Now please, sit on the balcony with me for a while and tell me about your city."

It's sweet. Our chairs are side by side and we're holding hands. I don't get much history. It's a warm night, the view is amazing, and we're just relaxed together; now the little barbs have been pruned. She needs me, I know, and she'll need Alphonse. She's being very organised about that, very logical. I'm sure she'll move on — to what, heaven knows. I can see already how Peter is treating her as an equal — and how she's responding to that.

He seems very comfortable with Claudia now — and look how long that's taken him: three marriages; and three fortunes.

I don't suppose Mei's journey will be any easier. I look at her now. She's the one looking at the city — her city.

She's attractive — and in moments like this evening, with Peter and Claudia, she relaxes and she's even lovely, I would say. And she talks very tenderly about her father. But I suspect that, at other times, everyone else is confronted by the very capable super-bitch that I first saw in Alphonse's office.

She catches me looking at her. "What are you looking at?" she asks sharply.

I'm unfazed. "I'm just admiring you. I'm very impressed at how you're coping — and at how far you've come. I was remembering when we first met."

She softens now. "In Alphonse's office. I was in awe of you. I wanted to be so like you."

"Oh, my darling, you've outgrown me, I assure you."

"I don't know about that — but I do know I don't have as much fun."

I have to laugh — it may well be true, but fun's not a goal in life, it's an outcome. Not a topic for a conversation with Mei. I'm not even sure it's a topic for this story but there, you have it now. "Well, can we leave the serious stuff? I'd like mostly to relax tonight — but I will be happy with some fun as well. Shall we go to bed?"

And she stands up, and opens her arms to me.

***

She's gone when I wake. I'd expected that. But it was a lovely night. There have been very few girl-on-girl nights since our epic journey, nearly two years ago. I do enjoy it. Then I have a silly thought, wondering what Conrad would think of that.

We'd barely spoken during the night. Mei, I'm delighted to say, has been learning from Lily and, just with our natural resources — I have my box of tricks with me, but it stayed locked — we had a wonderful time. It was one of those experiences where you can't count, you just float on the waves — and Mei has learned to give, as well as take. Maybe she will find what she needs in a relationship but, in the meantime, with Alphonse and me — and Lily still, I assume — she at least can have some contentment, and she'll give enough to prevent her partner feel exploited.

You know what I'm going to say: she used to make love like a man in the early days.
There was a sheet of hotel notepaper on her pillow with a big lipstick kiss. And the lipstick kiss on the bathroom mirror? Come on, let's not grow old before our time. It was sweet. Cheesy, yes, but still sweet.

***

I hadn't booked a flight until the evening, I didn't know how the itinerary would pan out, but it gave me a day to walk around buildings and hotels and see for real what was being designed. I see the magazines, of course, but you need to insert yourself in spaces to see how they all work. And my, what a city! An overwhelming sense of dynamism. It does make the West feel so moribund.

29

Alphonse had always found it easy to deal with histrionics — male or female — he found it harder to deal with Daiyu's patient tolerance about changing their Friday arrangement. He would be travelling all week, including Friday in Shanghai, introducing the Langs to Peter, and was looking forward to the homecoming. But Peter had said that Isobel was dealing with a — 'difficult situation' had been his expression. Alphonse had needed no more information. He'd found Daiyu surprisingly understanding. Disappointingly understanding, when he thought about it after the phone call.

***

Can we order from the fourth floor again?

Had been the text from Isobel that he'd picked up as the taxi ferried him back from the airport. And, whatever the 'situation' was, that was a very welcome suggestion. He showered and changed before he texted back:

Ready now. Come whenever.

It was half an hour later when she arrived, probably the briefest interval she could have left without looking uncool. Or desperate.

It was a long hug at the door — longer than just missing him.

"Come on, let me look at you." She stood back, but didn't look back at him. "You look wonderful, but I thought this was just an 'at home, let's get a takeaway' sort of evening."

Now she did look up. She stroked his shirt. "Silk — for slumming at home?" One of her small smiles wrinkled her lips. "We don't let standards slip, do we?"

"No, we don't." He took her hand and led her to the sofa. "It's champagne, unless you fiercely protest."

She shook her head. "No protests."

He busied himself while she quietly took in the view — almost identical to her own. She would normally be talking, but he needed to let her decide what she wanted to say.

"Did you like Shanghai? Cheers, by the way." They clinked and sipped.

"Aren't you going to order?"

"If that helps you feel a little less agitated, I will."

And she faked a preoccupation with the view again. He phoned an order through to the concierge, then joined her on the sofa.

"I'll talk about the new place, if you like. Your designs look even more stunning than they do in Phoruc."

"You're pleased then," she said distractedly.

He put his glass down, took hers and did likewise, and eased her towards him as he leaned back,

He felt her resisting. "Your shirt!"

"I know that's not a ploy to get me naked in bed. Just don't worry about it." She would talk when it suited her, whether about her crisis or about her getting him to change his Friday for her, he didn't yet know. But this was an Isobel he'd not encountered before. But at least now she was leaning down on to him, her face placed carefully on the hand she'd put on his chest.

"I can think of a couple of things you might want to talk about, but I'm in absolutely no hurry. I don't even mind waiting until we're naked in bed." He thought that worth risking, and it did provoke a chuckle.

"Is that a promise?"

He hugged her. "Well, it wasn't meant to be a threat." She seemed to relax.

"There may be three things. And not one of them is Shanghai, but I did love it. Exhilarating!"

"I thought you'd see it that way. Are you going to do business there?"

She went silent again.

"Oh, does that have something to do with your secret topics? I retract the question, but I think you've given me an answer."

She sat up to look at him. Her eyes were teary. "You know, naked in bed is a good idea."

He smiled. "Yeah, fuck the food."

"Shit! Are you hungry?"

"Not enough to keep me away from your sweet naked body while I listen to your stories."

***

They soon lay, side by side, skin touching. He got the wicked smile from her as her hand went to his cock. "Stories!" he said.

"Yes, I was just checking in for later. At least he's half awake." But then their arms wrapped their bodies close together. They kissed tenderly. "Shall I start with the easy one?"

"Start somewhere, please. I've not seen you like this."

There was still a long silence. He stroked her skin and waited.

"Were you supposed to be seeing Daiyu this evening?" She seemed to tense as she asked the question.

"That was the original plan, yes."

"Why didn't you say?"

"Your needs seemed urgent." He paused. "Important, maybe."

"It's not that you're keeping secrets?"

"Well, as you've just seen, no, I've said I would have been seeing her. We see each other most weeks."

"Weekends?"

"We spend the odd weekend together, yes."

"You've never done that with me."

"Who knows what would have happened if you'd gone to Phoruc."

Not weekends, he didn't think — his relationship with Daiyu was becoming something different. But was it? She'd been quite calm about giving up their Friday evening. Maybe it wasn't so special for her.

"You're thinking," she said after a long pause.

"I'm waiting."

"You're lying." But that was said light-heartedly.

"I thought you were talking."

"I know. That's why I'm here, isn't it? I just had a guilty conscience about making you change your plans. I hadn't wanted to spoil an evening for you. Will you tell her about tonight?"

"Of course. Well, just a moment. I got the impression there are things you're reluctant to talk about. Like your London crisis, maybe?"

She tensed. "Who… Oh, shit, Peter of course. I'm supposed to say absolutely nothing to anyone."

"Well, I won't be telling Daiyu about that."

"Will you tell her you fucked me?"

"That depends."

"On what?"

"On whether I fuck you."

***

He didn't, in the end. Not even in the morning when they touched and teased each other's bodies. "Do you think we will again?" she asked as she held his almost-stiff cock.

"Oh, undoubtedly."

She looked away. "No, I don't necessarily believe that either."

"Are these relationships going to do that to us? Conrad and Daiyu?"

"I think we're going to find out, aren't we?"

"Yes, I suppose we are. But what do we do about Mei? You're under instructions as well, aren't you?"

"Oh, and I plan to obey. I'll even go along with a threesome again if madam orders it. It might be the only way I can still have you." They shared a melancholic little laugh. "I think you and I just mean a bit too much to each other, don't we?"

And that was right, he thought, after she'd left. He'd tidied away, the barely nibbled courses got disposed of first, before she was even awake. The coffee mugs were in the machine, the bed made, the strewn clothing in the basket. He smiled. All apart from the shirt. She'd brandished it as she left — having worn it while they'd drunk coffee. "It's all I get to keep," she'd said wistfully.

"Memories?" he responded.

She'd stepped back toward him and let herself be hugged. He could feel her wiping her eyes. She'd sniffed. "Before I get too soppy about this, I have to remember I have a fucking meeting with you on Monday morning." She'd leaned back and smiled at him.

"And we're with fucking Daiyu, too!" he'd said. They'd laughed, then hugged again.

It would be different, he was thinking, staring again at the view. Then, one day he would be back in the London apartment with its view of trees and buildings — 'no longer at ease in the old dispensation,' Peter would have quoted — so maybe he wouldn't. He reached for the phone to text Daiyu, feeling something perilously close to contentment.

30

I'd managed to put it to the back of my mind for two weeks. There's been plenty here to distract me, we're very busy. And it's been surprisingly easy to settle back in with Daiyu. Easier than it was before when we were like competing concubines. Now she can worry about whether Alphonse really needs to spend so much time in Shanghai at madam's behest. Still, on both of the last two Fridays he's been back early. I think they've spent the weekends together, but I don't want to appear nosey — although I am curious, of course.

It's made it easier for me that Conrad's rung a few times. He barely notices Sandra apparently but, according to Boris, she's keeping office hours. I should ring Merle, but I've been avoiding that. And Conrad never mentions the special topic.

But now Rod has rung. I suppose it's Friday evening for him but for me it's a rude Saturday morning awakening. He's here next week. I have to keep Wednesday afternoon free for him and no, he didn't want to discuss anything on the phone — and was I sure I'd spoken to no one.

Of course I hadn't.

Oh, Rod. Your business is lies. What did you really expect me to say?

Anyway, next Wednesday, and I'm not to worry. He has a plan.

Yeah, right.

***

I tell Conrad when I call him in the afternoon. He goes all pensive on me. He'll say what he wants to say eventually — he doesn't need prompts. Then suddenly it comes out. "Should I book a hotel next weekend, or could I stay with you?"

"You're here?" I splutter. "You have business here?"

"Sure, I have business there. Isobel Allen is my business. Look, I'll stay in a hotel if you want but I should see you about this thing of yours."

"You know something? No, wait, don't tell me, nothing you can discuss on the phone. Oh, but listen to me, going on about that. I'll be thrilled, and stay with me please, yes. But is it really that important?"

"No, not really, I just miss you. And I want to see your Asian world."

"Really? Well, whatever, I'll love having you here. I'll even meet you at the airport. But, oh, there are bits of your world I'm less curious about, in case you wanted to know."

"No, I'm not dragging you round Jeddah in a burqa. You can make your own choices about what you see. But I like Hong Kong. I'm excited."

368

About HK, or about me, I wonder. Aw, who gives a fuck! I am excited he's coming — and at least he made his 'reason' feel like just an excuse. But, when he's rung off, I do worry a bit. Then there's an interesting development. I call Alphonse.

"I'm sorry to disturb the two of you…" I leave a pause to let him contradict me. He doesn't. Gotcha! But that cheap little trick wasn't the purpose of my call, but it is good to know now. "I've just had a couple of phone calls and I could do with some company for an hour."

"Come down. We're here."

"Respectable?"

He laughs. "Of course." This is how it should be, easy access to friends.

I would say they're a little on edge when I get there. They're both looking far too smart for slumming at home — but that's how they are. I haven't given them time to change. The funny thing is, they both look good in shorts and tee shirts. That's what I'd be wearing. Anyway, I give them each a big hug after I've handed him a bottle with a 'don't worry, it's not for now, it's a thank you.'

After the hugs they're still looking puzzled. I sit down on an armchair — they can share the sofa. She gets water and glasses — you see, she does; it's his apartment but she's already playing hostess.

"How much have you told Daiyu about my London problem?"

She sits down beside him — not near him, oh, for Christ's sake, I shall have to say something soon. It's almost an insult that they pussyfoot around me.

"I've said there seem to be possible repercussions from your recent crisis, but that we're not really worried."

"That's the funny thing," I say. "I had managed to put it out of my head these past two weeks. But Rod," I look to Alphonse, he nods but, of course, Daiyu probably knows nothing about him. I turn to her. "He does special stuff for Peter Dickinson, security assessments, things like that." She nods, she doesn't need to know more. "Well, he called this morning. He still says there's nothing to worry about, but he's coming to see me next Wednesday — so, I'm sat here admitting to you that it's making me a little nervous again — and I needed company."

"Peter said you should be cautious, not nervous."

"Yes, my darling, that makes me feel vastly better." That was a bit sniffy of me, but he knows me well enough to laugh it off.

"Was your second phone call connected?"

"Well, in a way, it was. It was Conrad." Alphonse nods. "Have you told Daiyu about Conrad?" He nods again. I become theatrically exasperated. "If you both know I'm seeing Conrad why the fuck are you sat at opposite ends of the sofa looking like you're worried about catching plague? My God, I love you both and I'm thrilled you're together, please sit close and give me

*my cupid thrill. I put you together, for heaven's sake."
They smile and she slides up against him. "Of course,
you could have shown a more tasteful degree of
reluctance at the time." But they take the jibe, of course,
in the right spirit.*

"Anyway, Conrad's coming here next weekend."

*They both look appropriately awe-struck, "That's
wonderful — but what's the connection?"*

*"I don't know yet but," I hesitate, "what do you
know about Conrad's operations?"*

*Alphonse smiles. "Complex. I think it's partly oil,
but he seems to have a number of tie-ins — and some
property, too, that's where I see it directly. It's not unlike
Peter's set-up, but I think some of his operations are,
well," now he's worrying about offending me, "can I
say they're not as transparent as Peter's?"*

*"I think you've put that rather well. He says he'll
tell me all I want to know…"*

*"But he kind of suggests you might not want to
know too much?"*

That's Daiyu. She's nailed it. I nod.

*"Anyway, that means he can access some odd
channels of information and I think he's been worrying
about me. I know that because he's just spent fifteen
minutes telling me I shouldn't worry — and also trying
to persuade me that he's coming because he misses me."*

"That's so sweet," says Daiyu. "Will we meet him?"

*I'm taken aback. It seems a strange idea. But
Alphonse is squeezing her hand. "That's a wonderful*

idea. Is he staying with you? I'll book the Mandarin for Saturday..."

"Woah, woah, this is rushing away from me." But suddenly I'm struck that it is a lovely idea. Couples meet couples. Yes, we could see how that works. "OK, then, it's a deal. And thank you."

"So, are you going to tell us more about what this is all about, or did you just need to be with friends?"

She's a watcher, is Daiyu. I've learned that from working with her. She sees very quickly — and accurately, that's more important — into people; into me, especially. "You're right. I just felt the need to share it, even though I'm forbidden from saying a word, just in case you're asked." I look at Alphonse.

He seems surprised. "Peter, you mean?" I nod. "Oh, he absolutely wants me to keep an eye on you. He'll expect you to tell me all you want to."

I tease him a little now. "Will he know that Daiyu knows?"

Alphonse responds slowly. "He knows we're very close."

Ah, of course he does, I think to myself. Knowing that would help everybody — especially Peter and Claudia. Now I think that's sweet too.

I stand up. "Well, it has been a huge help, thank you for being here."

"Woah, woah, you're not going, for goodness' sake. Sit down at once!" He's doing mock stern and smiling.

She's smiling too. "I need to know more about Conrad. We can open that bottle now, can't we? We're just eating downstairs later, can you join us?"
And that seems like a wonderful plan.

***

Rod had booked himself into the Mandarin and allocated me his dinner slot. Yippee! Actually, I don't mind. My days are very busy and I'm not seeing him as threatening. My 'get to know him better' offer was made for after the assignment — and not meant to be taken seriously.

He'll be spending an hour with Alphonse. I got that from his email. It's not my business — well, if it is, Alphonse will tell me. They will meet in our office. I have to go to his suite. He probably knows I have the same harbour view as his hotel room — and I think he knows I'm not easily impressed — and certainly not easily seduced. I assume he takes me seriously.

It seems he does. Our greeting is pleasant and polite, nothing more. I'd seen him in the office, but I think the rules of his game are that we don't acknowledge each other in public. It was just as well. He couldn't interrupt me with Daiyu — and I had no wish to introduce him to her or to interrupt him with Alphonse.

"I've given us an hour before dinner," he says when I arrive. "That should be plenty of time."

373

"*This is going to be simple, isn't it? Safe and simple?*"

"*I'm pretty sure it will be.*"

"*I suppose I was hoping for something a little more comforting than that.*"

"*Well, we do know that Zivko is a very unpleasant fellow, but we can't pin anything on him in the UK.*"

"*Well, that's good, isn't it?*"

"*Not necessarily. He may just have been acting super covertly there. Through the Balkans, it helps him to have the reputation he's got. Fewer people mess with him that way.*"

"*Oh, thanks.*" *He was staying very factual and calm, underplaying the drama, if anything. I suppose it's how these people work.*

"*We have two things in our favour. One, we still think you're an unlikely target — but we have found Gerry Calvert guilty of wholly disproportionate revenge attacks — usually far from home, however. Second, Zivko knows his place in the pecking order. He's kind of a middle-level thug. The Russians don't use him much, only for little local squabbles.*"

I think I'm going to regret my question. "*Do people get hurt in these local squabbles?*"

"*People get killed in some local squabbles, but that's usually in the drug distribution network.*"

"*I'm not feeling better yet. You said we have a plan.*"

"*Yes, if you're up for it.*"

"*Tell me more.*"

"You go to see Gerry."

I'm surprised. "When do I do that?"

"On Monday week. We know he's in his office on the Monday and Tuesday. You'll ring him early afternoon and suggest an appointment."

"If he won't see me?"

"You tell him, or leave a message with his PA, that there are important loose ends to clear up on the Sandra affair — and it's very much in his interests to see you to make sure it's tidied up properly."

"Whatever are we doing that for?"

"We'll give you a script. You'll have to adapt it so it's your usual way of speaking to him, but there will be some key phrases you have to get across so that he knows that he and his henchman are being watched. And don't worry, it won't get traced back to the McKenzies."

I'm nodding, but my stomach feels empty.

"There is one thing that might make it easier for us. I don't like suggesting it but I've evidence that our confidentiality agreement, ma'am, has been breached." Now he's trying to make me feel like a naughty girl.

It doesn't work. "I'm going to admit that I've spoken to two people I trust absolutely — but I'm not the only channel of communication on this issue."

"But you have Conrad working on the project. You also have him here this coming weekend. There's no point in me expecting you to say nothing then, since it's clear you already have. It's too late to tell you that's dangerous, but he's a serious player anyway. Just not *serious enough to stop me finding out about where he's fishing — but if he's prepared to work together, that could help us."*

"You think he's left tracks?"

"Not really, but it wouldn't matter now if he had. Not if he's going to help. Anyway, I knew where to look for him. We've found out you two have been in cahoots for a while. He paid Sandra's Argosy bills, didn't he?"

"I'm finding this a bit chilling."

"Get over it. It's keeping you safe." There's no drama in how he says that. Yes, it's a bit arrogant, but it's surprisingly conversational.

"Do you come by all this information legally?" *"Of course." He's probably lying, but do I really want to know?*

***

'Chen Cars will pick you up an hour before my plane lands.' *is the text I got yesterday evening. He was due at two on Cathay, I knew. He thinks I don't work Friday afternoons? I wouldn't normally put up with that but, hey, he was coming around the world to see me. Exotically desirable as I undoubtedly am, I'm going to have to admit this is a first. And honestly, I had kept the diary clear. Equally honestly, I was strangely excited.*

And I haven't had an airport hug like that since... Well, since I met Will in Brussels. That's over five years ago and it was, until today, unique.

Now I feel peculiarly invaded! This is my space and now this other being is in it. Alphonse has stayed here, of course, as has Mei — but they both live here in the city, they have their own homes to go back to. But Conrad is here, actually staying for three nights — this is his home for that time. I've even had to clear wardrobe space — it didn't feel right to make him unpack in the guest room. Well, that's almost full already, amazing what you can accumulate in eighteen months — I'm no Imelda Marcos, but a girl needs space for shoes. And I didn't want to expose this foible to Conrad. Well, I'm not being fair to my gender to describe it as a foible. Everyone needs a shoe room.

Those are the trivialities that went through my head yesterday evening, getting the place ready. Now I've left him to fit himself into his allocated half of my dressing room. I've been thrilled to greet him — but we have to get this London Monday thing agreed before anything else can happen. I have warned him. I didn't want him thinking I was unenthusiastic about sex straight away. I mean, I was, but there is a very good reason for that. And he seemed to understand.

I have champagne waiting for him — I've put the bottle back in the fridge. I don't want to overwhelm the man, but this needs to be a proper welcome.

"Wow!" He's by the window, admiring the view. I nudge up close beside him, inviting him, I suppose, to put his arm around me. He doesn't disappoint.

"We'll walk later along the Kowloon waterfront. It's kind of a crappy walk this side, and the views are better over there. Plus, we get to travel on the Star Ferry. That's one of the boats just leaving now." I point down.

He hugs me. "I know what the Star Ferry is. And you're right about the walk, it's better over there — and I could use that before we eat."

"Are you hungry now? I should have asked."

"No, I'd rather get this other thing out of the way first. We have a plan, you say."

I guide him to the sofa, let him stretch out and I lean against him. "Yes, but first I have to say that our Rod knows you've been working on my case."

"I assumed it must be his man checking up on me."

So, there are men floating round in the middle of Europe working on some cloak and dagger assignment and I'm supposed to feel cautious, but not nervous. But I do feel a certain calm with his arm around me.

"His idea is that I get in front of Gerry on Monday week and make it plain that we know he has an unsavoury Serbian working on special projects for him. Rod thinks that would make him realise that he can't make any move, even supposing he's thinking of one, without it blowing up in his face."

"And where do I come in?"

"If I can imply that it's you who's fingered Zivko, then we don't expose the McKenzies to danger."

"So, we just put me in the firing line instead," he says, but he's chuckling. I'm not yet seeing the funny *side of it. "Seriously, are you worried? I don't want the McKenzies exposed, but you're becoming more important."*

"Nice to know," he says, almost flippantly, "but that fits with what I was thinking anyway. I had one of my local guys take me to Zivko's business in Belgrade, BPI. He wasn't there, and I didn't want to meet him anyway. I just left a card and a message that I wanted to talk to him about some local projects. It wasn't a very plausible story. I don't have a lot in the region now, and the old contacts work pretty autonomously. The important point was to let him know that someone was on his case. So that fits rather well. I assume Henderson just wants you to hint that I'm your source of information."

"Yes. It made sense to me. Would you mind?"

"No, of course not. I mean, I'd rather tackle Gerry myself, but I guess Rod wants to keep it personal."

"Yes, and I feel I should."

"OK, but how's he protecting you?"

"I hadn't thought about that. Do you think he will be?"

"Of course, until we have a clear indication from Gerry that there isn't an issue."

"Why might he do that? I'm just asking."

"Because part of Henderson's script for you will make it plain that Zivko's operations will be shut down if he doesn't, with all the consequences for Gerry's

operations. So, security. He's obviously told you nothing."

"No."

"I hope he's just trying to avoid worrying you. In fact, I'm sure that's it. He's getting you to go there on your first day back. That tells me he's minimising risks. Listen," and we're sitting up now, and I have these strange feelings of being very well protected — but seriously exposed, *"I'd like to contact him to check out what he's putting in place, but I'll actually offer to put my people on it, is that OK?"*

"Your people?" I'm feeling bewildered, but he's talking about this just as Rod did, with no drama whatsoever.

"It's an organisation I use to look after my more sensitive Arabs. I probably have a better London network than Henderson does." Now he puts an arm around me and kisses my forehead. *"And I'll feel better if I organise it."*

"And your people are very good?"

"Oh, yes, because some of my Arabs are justifiably nervous." He chuckles. *"Of course, the irony is they're being protected by what is an Israeli business. It doesn't matter. They never see any of it. Just as you won't. Is that settled then? I can call your Mr Henderson?"*

And that was it. It didn't get mentioned again the entire weekend — and we had a wonderful time: tourist trips; plenty of bedtime; and a boozy, fun evening with Alphonse and Daiyu. I even saw a more relaxed side of her — and she was even flirting with Conrad. I'll talk to the cow on Monday. Losing one man to her was unfortunate, losing two… I jest. It was a lovely evening; I've done nothing like it for years.

I left enough time on the Sunday for a proper playtime, which Conrad appreciated — and I thoroughly enjoyed. I think we were both happy to reassure ourselves that being a couple didn't mean abandoning fun. I even had to broach the subject of Mei and me. He didn't seem upset by that. I assume his offer to help wasn't meant seriously. I'm not sure I'd be very enthusiastic.

But I felt quite teary this morning when his car came.

"I'll see you Saturday, stupid woman," wasn't the most romantic parting — but he's been mostly very sweet all weekend, and there was a long hug and a kiss after that.

31

He met me at Heathrow! That was a surprise.

"I hope this is romance and not security," I said.

We'd already hugged and kissed. "This is romance," he said. "The tall young man with stubble by the pillar over there is security."

"Seriously?" I was shocked.

He laughed. "Don't be silly. Even I don't know which one is ours. Come on, car's this way."

We went via my place. It was just assumed I'd be staying with him. He trusted his driver absolutely, he told me on the way to the car, but we should discuss sensitive issues only when we were on our own. He did say he'd been talking to Henderson before we reached the car. 'It was good,' he'd said just before we came within earshot of the waiting driver.

It was Conrad's first visit to my house. "It's beautiful," he said as he came in.

"It's small," I said, defensively, "but I love it. Now I promise I won't be long. I'm only packing for three or four days, OK?"

"You can pack for as long as you want, as far as I'm concerned, but we should have our business tidied up by then. I'm due off on Friday, but I won't be going unless we're both comfortable — and Rod is too."

"He's Rod now?"

"We've had two long chats and exchanged emails. He's got contacts with a good operation, but we've agreed to use my set-up here."

"I don't know why, but I think I feel better about that. Please pour a drink or make yourself some tea or something."

I came down, I hadn't been long, to find him leafing through my show file.

He looked up. "I really am interested in a makeover, you know."

"So you should be. Refusal to renovate that house is a deal-breaker."

"We're still considering the deal, are we?"

"I think so." He stood up to hug me. "I want to get this week out of the way before I think too much of anything like that, though."

"I know, but you're worrying unnecessarily."

I got big hugs from Boris and Sandra when we got to Conrad's. They still seem harmoniously together, but I saw little of them over the weekend, although I did sit and talk work with Sandra for an hour before lunch on Sunday. Conrad seems to have allocated the front room to me. He spends most of his time in his office next door.

Sandra tries very hard to be polite about Merle, but I can tell the atmosphere's frosty. It sounds like she's finding useful things to do, however, and may even be enjoying some of it. She couldn't earn what she'd like to spend, but I think that's still a problem for another day.

Rod will be coming here Monday lunchtime, apparently. He'll listen in on my call and then go through my briefing. Needless to say, the prospect makes me very nervous, but Conrad seems calm the entire weekend, and he'll be hanging around on Monday. We're having dinner with Rod. "If Gerry follows up, it won't be a bad thing to all be seen together."

"Every casual observation you just toss out like that makes me feel about three times worse."

"You'd be worse still if I said nothing," *he says, casually again.*

I can only mutter, "You're probably right."

I'm nervous all Monday morning. Rod's due at twelve and the clock isn't moving. Conrad's asked at breakfast, "So, how would you approach this place? Or should I sell it and move somewhere else?"

"For God's sake, no!" *I'd said.* "It's a beautiful house — and a wonderful location." *He smiled at me across the table.* "You'd never have any intention of moving." *He nodded. He was just trying to distract me. It didn't really work. I've been fiddling with a few sketches — I did bring my pad — but they're all worthless, and the clock was still not moving.*

But then it did, and Rod was, of course, perfectly punctual, like those Germans who wait outside until the appointed time. There's huge bonhomie between the boys — for two men who've never met — and I'm almost ignored as we move through into my room and Conrad gives more of a briefing on how his security operation works. I could almost forget that they're there to protect me, it all seems so theoretical.

But then they turn on me, both looking inappropriately cheery. "Are you ready?" asks Rod.

"No," I say — they just laugh.

"Where's the phone with the earpiece?" asks Rod.

"In my study next door."

"Good." He turns to me. "We don't want you on speaker phone. I'll listen in while you're speaking. We'll try calling Conrad's mobile now, just to get you used to me sitting next to you. I'll stay out of your eyeline. The call will just be between you and Gerry, or his PA. My guess is he'll take the call himself when you use the script. OK?" He's looking at Conrad now. Conrad nods and we go through to the study.

I can't help thinking, when I enter the room, how much I'd like to change that dreary old dark wood men's club feel to the place — but then I remember why I'm there.

"Won't they trace the call?"

"Of course, we want them to. It's why I think you're in no danger. Calvert will know the firepower he's up against. Try calling Conrad now. Sit comfortably and face the way you want to. The window is usual."

Of course it is, and that's what I do. He pulls the visitor chair out of my view and sits on that, the earpiece to his head.

"Don't make eye contact with me at all. This is just between you and him — and you're in charge of that conversation, OK?"

The dummy call with Conrad is easy, although Rod tells me to keep talking for him to get his sound level right. Talking to order? It's not easy in my state, I end up saying 'la, la, la' for a while and then encourage Conrad to do the same — but he just tells one of his old jokes, and that gets Rod laughing. I shout 'Boys!' and Rod winces. That must have been loud, but we've proved the system.

And the call itself was easy. I was sweating on the PA's silence but the 'loose ends that badly need tying up' seemed to do it.

"Sadie, how lovely to hear from you. Where the hell are you?" He must know that.

"Back in London for two weeks."

"Wanting to talk about the projects, my dear, I'm afraid they're irrecoverable."

"No, Gerry, I'm picking up stories connected with other loose ends."

"Stories?" he asks after a pause. That has put him on the back foot.

"Yes, stories out of Belgrade." There's a long silence now. We'd expected that. "I'd like to come and talk to you about them. I can do four this afternoon."

It's quiet again, I assume he's talking to the PA. Then:

"Yes, I can do four. Will you come here?"

"Yes, I'll see you then." And I put the phone down.

"Brilliant!" says Rod.

Conrad echoes him. He's plainly been standing outside the door. He comes and hugs me.

"He's on the back foot. Meeting at his place shows confidence, I know you're worried about that, but it's a position of strength. He'll be running checks now on who's behind you and trying to find out who's been to Belgrade. He'll find that easily. We want him to. Are you feeling, OK?"

"Returning were as tedious as go o'er," I say, but why the fuck I'm quoting Shakespeare at this point, I have absolutely no idea. Now I need the toilet!

I have that feeling a few times before I arrive at Gerry's office. At five past four, as I'm instructed — 'just the right amount of tension being created — but then he'll make you wait ten minutes, probably.'

But he doesn't.

The PA takes me straight through.

And he does look nervous. But I probably do too.

"What's this about, Isobel?"

I get calm all of a sudden. "I'm not worried about the contracts, Gerry. I've enjoyed working on the places, but I don't think you and I are truly sympatico, so it's not a bad idea to accept the break. We're quite busy here anyway."

The last thing he wants is to listen to me talking interior design. He's looking even more agitated. Good.

"No, but as you know, you left me with a mess to sort out with a mutual friend — and got all threatening about another friend who I'd asked to help her."

"Conrad's heavy, you mean?"

"Yes, but he's not Conrad's only Serbian connection." I let that hang in the air, as I've been told to.

"You have Serbian connections too, don't you, Gerry?" His face doesn't move, but his fingers are twitching with a pen. "In Belgrade, I think."

"I'm sure I do," he says, not bringing off the nonchalance he intended.

"People, I think, who deal with difficult situations for you, with loose ends."

He's starting to look a little more relaxed. "And this is a concern of yours because?"

I have to remain completely unemotional here. "Because I don't want anything bad to happen to my two friends, or to me, for that matter."

"You think I'd really do that?" Why is he looking slowly more comfortable now?

"We know you're capable of some real shit, Gerry. Your Belgrade operation isn't that watertight and there's embarrassing information in circulation. Information that can be traced back."

Now he looks nervous again. It seems to be working.

"So, what do you want?"

"I want an absolute commitment from you that nothing happens to my people."

He seems to be weighing that up. "And I get what?"

"You'll get copies of the evidence I've got on some of your BPI operations."

"You have it with you?"

"No, Gerry, I want your commitment first."

"And you want guarantees you and your two won't be touched."

"That will do it."

"And you want the fucking flat back, I suppose." That's just street braggadocio, but he's obviously got a little bit comfortable. He's not really losing anything — we wouldn't put Sandra back where his heavies could reach her, he knows that.

"No, Gerry, just look me in the eye and tell me my people are safe."

It takes him a long while, but he seems very calm when he looks at me and says, "You and your people are completely safe, Isobel. I know you wouldn't trust my word, but you think you can read my face, don't you?"

I do, but I'm saying, "No, Gerry, I don't. I'm just relying on the risks for you being too big to go after my people."

"You're right, Isobel. They would have been. I think I'll be very grateful for your intervention. Is that it?"

"I think so." What else could I ask for? Nothing in writing would be given, or be worth anything if it were. We manage a handshake and I'm leaving within ten minutes of me arriving. I'm feeling empty, and pretty uncertain, but the S class smooths up in front of the

building as soon as I step outside. Both of the boys are in it. Conrad, on the back seat, gives me a silent hug when I climb in next to him. Rod turns around and shakes my hand. Conrad puts a finger to his lips — no word in front of the driver, but it's only a short trip to Conrad's — why would he leave the city? The location's wonderful. That's the trivia that my mind defaults to.

I go through it all once we're back at the house — not that there's much. But they're surprisingly interested in Gerry's demeanour and all my observations there. They want to know about hand gestures, and exact words. Fortunately, I have pretty good recall and I think I give it all back accurately.

Eventually Rod says, "That's superb. You could have a job doing this. Thank you. Are you happy you're safe?"

"I think so."

"We think you're safe," says Conrad. "Now I've booked the Dorchester again, are you going to complain?" I shake my head — I'm not at all hungry but the three of us should celebrate, even though it seems premature. But when would it not seem premature — we wait until nothing happens? I don't think so.

"OK, guys, I'll see you at the Dorchester then. It's good of you, Conrad."

He waves a hand. "Oh, I just fool her into thinking I'm a romantic, but my friends usually forget to send me a bill."

"You fucking cheapskate!" But we're all laughing, and somehow, that's got rid of a load of tension.

32

It will go down as my most memorable dinner ever, unfortunately.

We were on time, but Rod was at the bar, waiting. This time it's a hug and an acceptable kiss, no hand sliding down to my arse, either. And he and Conrad are long-lost buddies again — a big man-hug after... What, just two hours apart?

After the martinis, I'm even given time at the table to study the menu while they swap more war stories. Just as well, it's been changed since the last time. Conrad's wine choices are, I note, not as extravagant as last time. I appreciate that. I'm a working girl, deep down, and I do keep budgets.

That doesn't apply to shoes, of course. He's already noticed the increasing encroachment in his dressing room. He doesn't dare say a word, of course.

The meal was wonderful, and I suppose we were feeling jolly. I have to say that Rod, for an American, is quite quietly spoken. It's all the spook work, I suppose. The meal just flows, the service is completely unobtrusive and even Conrad is more of a conversationalist than I'd thought. I suppose he's a man's man. But he's been romantic enough these last two weeks.

Rod's talked to Peter, and he's happy, apparently. He's inclined to believe that Gerry, if he had any plans, had been contained.

It's one of those moments I'll remember very vividly. Rod had just said, 'I'll need to text my car' and then, calmly and unobtrusively, I have to say, he was in my eyeline as the waiter was topping up water, He began swiping his phone. He raised an eyebrow, nothing more, and showed the phone to Conrad. I was alert by then, and Conrad's cool shrug as he pulled out his own phone didn't fool me. He seemed to be pondering what to do.

"You'll have to show me," I said.

He pursed his lips and nodded and handed me the phone, saying, "Take your time…"

'Billionaire's Wife Found Dead After Sex Orgy' was the headline.

I froze. I found Conrad's hand on my arm, caressing me gently. "I just got the headline," he murmurs. "Do you want to check the full story on yours?"

Rod has been speedreading his. I hand Conrad's back to him and fumble for mine.

Conrad is just calling for the bill. That seems absurd in one way — but I understand he wants us to get away. "Will you come back with us?" he says to Rod. "We should check what we need to do, if anything. What alerted you?"

"A text from Peter. He wants us to call him. I will come back, thank you."

So, I'm back here now. I was delegated to tell Sandra and Boris. They weren't expecting to be disturbed, I don't think, but Conrad had obviously texted from the car that they should be ready to meet us.

Boris is there when we get dropped off. She's getting dressed, presumably. I'm in one of those going through the motions modes that seem to take over in disaster situations. I'm remembering my dad dying suddenly — and how detached and disconnected my mother had seemed when she'd told me; no wailing, no screaming, just a silence — numb, I'd always assumed, rather than stoical.

That's how I felt. There had been no details in the report. I guess the boys are discussing how they find out more. They're in Conrad's office. I'm in my room with Boris. She might be ages, so I'll tell him.

"Ellen Calvert's dead."

"Oh," he says. It's like I've told him there's no milk in the fridge. But then it seems to occur to him that we're all making a fuss about this.

"Bad?" And Sandra appears, more quickly than I expected.

"I've just told Boris that Ellen Calvert's dead."

"Oh, shit!" she says, and sits down unsteadily. "What happened?"

"We don't know. The news says she died of asphyxiation during an orgy, and she was well known for outlandish sexual behaviour."

"Sorry," says poor, sweet Boris. "As fix..."

"Strangled," says Sandra, and takes his hand as he stands beside her chair.

Boris just says, "Oh," and shrugs. Not much of an epitaph for poor Ellen.

"The thing is," and here I'm wavering a little, because I'm connecting some dots, "there was nobody else there. There had been a tip-off about loud noises from her apartment but when the police arrived there was just a dead naked body and scenes of an orgy. I think the men are trying to find out more."

"Oh." Sandra's looking very shocked — she may be making connections with her own historical vulnerabilities. "Poor Ellen."

And even I, who had no feeling of warmth for the woman, nor any reason to feel any, feel suddenly swamped with a mixture of grief and outrage.

I assume, when I see the boys in a moment, that they'll tell me what Zivko's mission was. Outrage? It happened this afternoon. I'm Gerry's fucking alibi!

33

Peter had said that Conrad would be away and asked her if she was free to visit Isobel. Isobel had seemed somehow disconnected, so Claudia found herself emphasising, 'So, I'll see you at Conrad's at seven-thirty on Friday' as she would to an elderly relative. But she'd got a snappy 'Yes, yes, I got it, seven-thirty Friday, here,' then, after a silence, a 'I'm sorry, Claudia, thank you very much, I'll need it.'

Claudia met the famous Boris, who opened the door and bowed awkwardly. "Isobel waiting," he said, but Isobel was coming out of the front room and wrapped her in a long embrace.

"You want I cook something, maybe?"

Claudia looked to Isobel, who moved swiftly from tear-fringed tragedy to an almost hysterical enervation. "We do a fabulous stew, don't we, Boris, and we use pork fillet if we can't find trotters. Can we do that?"

The poor man looked awkward. "I was just doing steak. You want?"

Isobel, still nowhere near normal, said, "That'll be fine. We'll eat with you and Sandra. Is that, OK?" That question was directed at Claudia.

"That's fine, really, whatever."

Boris seemed to relax. "Good, I tell her."

"What do I need to know about this situation here?" she asked when Isobel had led her into the front room. But the story was pretty much as Peter had told it. Isobel merely added that the relationship seemed to be growing — and that Sandra was making a fist of her job in the office — in spite of Merle's difficulties. Although Isobel expected these to diminish 'in the light of recent events.'

"And your relationship with Conrad? Am I allowed to ask?"

"Of course you are." Isobel seemed finally to be relaxing. "But can we deplete his red wine stocks before we get on to that? I will say, and maybe you can help me on this, that I was troubled by how they just seem to let the waves wash over it all. It's yesterday's news already, yet we have stuff on the hitman. Conrad won't do anything with it."

Claudia hugged her. "Peter won't either. I'm not sure I understand. Well, I fucking don't understand, period," she found herself saying with feeling, "however much they let us walk around in it, it still seems to be their jungle. Time to open your red?"